REDEEMED THROUGH LOVE

A Danjuma Story

UNOMA NWANKWOR

First printing October 2019

Printed in the United States of America

www.kevstel.com

*To my husband Kevin, and my kids—Fumnanya & Ugo.
Their support is immeasurable.*

Acknowledgments

To my Lord and Savior Jesus Christ. I thank you for paying the ultimate price that I may have life and for your grace which I do not deserve. Thank You for the gift of writing and I humbly pray I continue to be a vessel in this journey.

To my family, my husband Kevin who's my number one fan, cheering me along every step of the way. I love you and thank you. To my kids Fumnanya and Ugo, my gang, my pookies, my munchkins who keep me sane when insanity sometimes abound. I love you both more than words can express. I pray for God's continued protection over you.

A special shout out to Abigaelle Coly, my loyal reader. Thank you for pointing me in the right direction when I had questions about being a Muslim. The videos and books you recommended, were lifesavers.

To my parents and mother in-law, *Daalu.* Thank you for your constant prayers and speaking words of life, courage and hope upon me.

To my readers, author friends and sistah writers thank you, thank you. Sometimes support doesn't always come from the people or places you expect but trust in God and He will send the right people to you.

And we're back!

I never thought I'd type those words. When I ended Kammy's story in 2017, I did honestly think that was the END.

Ha! Jokes on me, right?

I love Halima but I wasn't sure I wanted to touch her in an independent story. Why? Uhmm…she's Muslim. I wasn't sure if I was brave enough to tell her story. I was honestly terrified to write this book. But I should have known. It's not by my power or my might. The Holy Spirit showed up and showed out for me and I'm so grateful I get to properly close out the Danjumas.

In Mark 16:15, Jesus said, *And he said unto them, Go ye into all the world, and preach the gospel to every creature.*

The keywords here are GO, OUT, INTO, THE WORLD, PREACH.

We aren't meant to hoard the gospel for ourselves, we're meant to witness to our fellow man. We can't make a difference sharing the gospel with the person that sits next to us in the church pew. However, for anyone to listen to what we have to say, they must know that we care about them, and not regard them as a task that needs to be checked off.

To be authentic to Halima, I did a lot of research into a religion I wasn't familiar with and learned a lot. Just because others don't believe what we do doesn't make them weird. As a Christian, our job is to persuade them to Jesus Christ. The only way to salvation.

I didn't put discussion questions at the back of the book because I really want you to be able to run free with it. However, if you have additional questions you can reach me at www.unomanwankwor.com

Also, for the first time, I've included the enunciation of the names of the key characters. And I have a glossary at the back of the book for Islamic terms and the Hausa & Igbo language used (although as usual, I infer the meaning in the text).

Be blessed and I hope you enjoy Halima & Ekene's story. This my dear reader is really, THE END.

Unoma

Praise for the Danjumas

All my books standalone, even if they are in a series. However, I'd be remiss if I didn't tell you that to enjoy the full essence of the Danjumas, you're highly encouraged to read from book One; A Scoop of Love.

"Whew! Unoma's characters were so real. They were honest, flawed, vulnerable, stubborn and saved by grace. I love when Unoma uses Africa as the backdrop for her romantic settings. Her spiritual message was clear: God's mercy and grace. Look out the Jamieson men, the Danjuma Brothers have arrived!!!" **~ Pat Simmons, Award-winning author of the Guilty Series.**

The following are reviews from Brenda Larnell of Romance In Color.

A Scoop of Love: Book 1

If you are looking for a sweet romance novel with a West African setting and a religious theme, then A SCOOP OF LOVE by Unoma Nwankwor is just the novel you seek. In this story, the reader is immersed in the West African culture of Nigeria through the heroine, Ibiso Jaja and her family, and the hero Rasheed Danjuma and his family. This story is book 1 in a series (The Sons of Ishmael) that focuses on the 3 Danjuma brothers, Rasheed being the first. The theme of forgiveness and letting go of the past in order to live in the present serves as the catalyst for Rasheed and Ibiso's story.

As mentioned, the setting for this story is Nigeria, specifically the capital city of Abuja. The bustling, energetic, northern city serves as the perfect backdrop for this story of the young restaurant/caterer entrepreneur, Ibiso and the established business consultant, Rasheed. As can be expected, the language and dialogue has an authentic foreign flavor that is sprinkled with African phrases and words throughout the novel. The family is a key element in this modern love story, and the author gives the reader insight into the strong family dynamic in the Nigerian culture. Rasheed is struggling to forgive his father who abandoned him, his mother and brothers. Not only does Unoma Nwankwor pen the West African culture in vivid details, but she also weaves the universal themes of love and forgiveness into a well written story.

Anchored By Love: Book 2

I loved this story, the 2nd book of the Sons of Ishmael series. Jabir and Damisi are star-struck lovers who stumble, fall get-up and eventually find their way to each other with God's guidance. I love how the author incorporated the African culture into this story. The importance of family was a key element in both their lives. Damisi found herself in a very vulnerable and real predicament that is very relatable today to a lot of young women. It is not until she was able to forgive herself that she was able to 'let go and let God". When he surrendered to God, Jabir realized his accomplishments were not due to his own efforts. ANCHORED BY LOVE is a great Christian love story. I highly recommend it.

Mended With Love: Book 3

Mended With Love by Unoma Nwankwor is now my

favorite story in the Sons of Ishmael Series. I loved Kamal and Ebele's story. This is a well-written story about forgiveness, maturing, unconditional love, and facing challenges. I also recommend the first two Books of the series that feature Kamal's brothers, Rasheed and Jabir. Mended With Love is a must read. Loved the Epilogue!

Enunciations of The Names of Key Characters

Halima (Ha -Lee -Ma)
   Danjuma (Dan - Ju- Ma)
   Ekene (A-Kay- Nay)
   Odili (Or - De- Li)
   Abubakar (Ah - Boo- Bah- Car)
   Chiaka (Chi - Ah-Car)
   Rayowa (Rah -Your -Wah)
   Tijani (Tea -Jah- Knee)
   Chibundu (Chi- Boon - Do)
   Kudirat (Coo - De-Rat) or Kudi (Coo- De)
   Danladi (Dan - La- De)
   Rasheed (Rah - She- Ed)
   Ibiso (E - Bee- So)
   Jabir (Jah - Bir)
   Damisi (Dah -Me - See) or Dami (Dah - Me)
   Kamal (Car - Mal)
   Ebele (A- Bae - Lay) or Ebi (E- Bee)
   Yohance (Yo - Hance)
   Umaru (U- Ma - Ru)
   Ekenedilichukwu (A- Kay - Nay- De- Lee - Chu- Coo).
This is Ekene's full name

With a slight turn in the front of the mirror, Halima Danjuma glanced once again at her appearance. The hugs her nieces had given her when they arrived at Gerald R. Ford International Airport some minutes earlier had her hijab twisted and loose. Her brother, Kamal, was getting married next month. Their family was growing as all her brothers were getting married and having children.

Damisi, her brother Jabir's wife, had purchased the dresses, she and Ibiso, her brother, Rasheed's wife, were supposed to wear for the wedding. It amazed her that she had gotten close to her brothers and their wives in the time since her father had died.

Since she was in Canada for business, Halima decided to make a quick trip to Detroit, pick up the dresses and then fly to South Africa from there to meet up with her mother. Satisfied that the head wear lay flat against the brown jumpsuit she had on, Halima rolled her luggage out of the women's restroom.

Announcements blared from the overhead speakers and the walkway between gates was filled with people moving to their destinations. She maneuvered her luggage to the right and left to avoid passengers who were more concerned with what was going on with their smartphones than where they were going. If there was one thing she hated, it was flying in Western airports. She had never felt any kind of anxiety until the last year. She'd heard horror stories of Islamic prejudice and discrimination and always prayed she never fell victim to it. So far, so good.

Through her peripheral vision, she saw the man who'd been following her for some time.

Maybe I spoke too soon.

He'd followed her when she went to get a coffee, then again when she went to the kiosk for a snack and now, he'd reappeared out of nowhere.

She quickened her steps. He quickened his.

I should have had Damisi mail me the dress. Five more gates, Halima, come on.

That was where Abubakar, her *mahram* and travel guard was. Abubakar had been assigned as her male guardian since she moved to Lagos some years ago. As a single Muslim woman, he served as her escort and protector. She never liked the idea of him following her around, so she'd asked him to stay put. "Three more gates to go," she coaxed herself.

The words hadn't left her mouth good when her arm was jerked. Her heart pounded as she tried to free herself from his grasp. His grip became stronger. She opened her mouth to yell, but shock muted any sound.

"Take this off when you people come here or stay where you belong." He punctuated his rant by wagging a finger in her face. "You cover because you don't want us to be able to identify you…"

In a flash, he lifted his other hand and tugged at her hijab. Adrenalin rushed to her heart when she realized nobody was going to help her. People kept on walking like no one could see him assaulting her. She pushed out of his reach and he stepped forward. He reached out to grab her again when he was shoved by a huge figure.

"Get your hands off her," the man said. He was now joined by a woman who stood by his side.

Her aggressor regained his balance and stepped forward. "Who are you? It's people like you that encourage them. I'm being a patriot!" Spit flew from his mouth.

The dark-skinned stranger who came to her rescue stepped in front of her. The woman with him helped Halima adjust her clothes as Abubakar came rushing over. Everything became a blur. Voices were raised as she was ushered toward her gate by the kind woman and Abubakar. The lady kept asking Halima if she was okay, but all she could do was nod. Her eyes watered. Not only was she attacked for no reason, but the accuser believed he was justified in his actions.

She plopped down in her seat and put her face in her hands. She shuddered as her aggressor's rage popped into her mind. She saw fear and the realization that she wore a physical representation of a religion he feared dawned on her.

In his eyes, she was the villain. In hers, she was the victim because she was no more to blame for terrorism than her brothers who were Christians were to blame for colonization.

Chapter 1

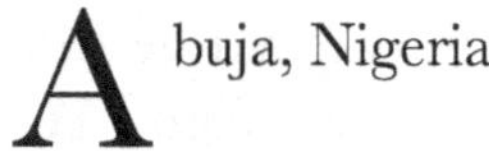buja, Nigeria

"I'VE BEEN MORE THAN GENEROUS. WHAT'S YOUR EXCUSE THIS time?"

Halima Danjuma looked up from the jewelry box she'd been rummaging through and made eye contact with the unwanted visitor. Danladi Usman, her betrothed, sat comfortably on the couch in her bedroom nook. For a few seconds, she tried to conjure up memories of a time she was attracted to him. Granted, he wasn't a bad looking man. Standing at a little over six feet, with caramel skin, low cut hair and alluring dark eyes, he was what she'd consider every woman's fantasy. Truthfully, at one point, he was her dream come true; a symbol of the security she was told she needed. But now things were different.

"Danladi, now isn't a good time to discuss this." She strode into her closet to get her red pumps to accompany the pink lace material her sisters-in-law had picked out for the day's occasion. She smiled, returning to her bedroom. Her brother,

5

Kamal, and his wife, Ebele's, six-month-old twins' christening ceremony was set to begin in about an hour. She sighed. Her mother knew this, but still let Danladi in when he came knocking a while ago.

"Halima, we have to discuss our *nikah*."

The word sent a shiver down Halima's back and not one of the feel-good kind. She sat on the bed to put on her shoes as he sauntered over to her. She looked up at him and his stare was just what she expected; cold. Danladi and her brothers never got along. Partly because he was just as bold, confident and sometimes as arrogant as they were.

He and Kamal's relationship was the worst. Thinking of her closest brother, she stood, picked up her overnight bag and placed it on the bed. When she got into Abuja from Lagos last night, Kamal had, in not so many words, threatened her for making him worry since she had to catch the last flight. He further went on to tell her he would be all up and down her case if she was late for the christening. If she kept up this conversation, she would be late.

"Danladi, we've been over this—"

"Halima, you were given to me as a wife and it's time you stepped into your role." He seethed. "You decided to do a second degree, then your father died, so you needed space to deal with that and your brothers, and now you live in Lagos running your father's company." He counted down with his fingers. "This was never the plan. But fine, you've sown enough wild oats. It's time for you to be the obedient Muslim wife you were trained to be."

Halima blinked several times. Then she lifted her left index finger to her ear. She couldn't have heard correctly but then again, the rage rising in her confirmed she did.

"Excuse me? What did you say to me?"

"I'm ready to get married," Danladi responded, ignoring her question.

Something in her snapped. "You are married!"

"Not to you," he seethed.

At that moment she could hear Kamal's voice asking her for the umpteenth time why she was still with Danladi. Halima placed her hand on her hip and shifted her weight to her left leg.

"So pursuing an education and having a career are now wild oats because I'm supposed to be a wife?"

"Stop twisting my words."

"I wasn't. They were clear to me."

"You're doing it again."

"What?"

"Trying to find a reason for us to disagree and drag this further." He shoved his hands into his pockets and slumped his shoulders.

"Danladi, look—"

Her words were cut off by his swift movement. He straightened his back and glided toward her. His hand moved to her cheek in a light caress. His eyes burrowed through her and a sinister grin spread across his face.

"Halima, I won't wait any longer. Before you leave Abuja this time, we must sort this out."

Danladi pushed past her and walked out the door without a backward glance.

———

An hour later, Halima sat in Overcomers Chapel. She'd been in this church a handful of times because of her older brother, Rasheed, and his wife, Ibiso. Halima looked around the newly renovated space. With each visit, she felt more welcomed. She had since stopped receiving fearful, penetrating stares. Now they were more inquisitive ones. Like, what's a Muslim doing in a church?

"I baptize you in the name of the Father, the Son, and the

Holy Spirit," the officiating Pastor said, jolting Halima out of her daze.

"Amen," the small congregation shouted.

Since it wasn't Sunday but Saturday, the guests were made up of friends and family of the Danjuma's. Halima looked down the pew and caught the eye of Ibiso who winked at her. She returned the gesture with a smile. Halima's eyes traveled down to her sister-in-law's fingers that were interlocked with her brother's. A sense of longing crept upon her as she looked at Damisi and Jabir, who had the same connection.

"Ladies and gentlemen…"

Halima turned back to face the altar.

"I present to you Nasir Steven Danjuma and Nafisah Ann Danjuma," the pastor said.

The twins were being held by Nse and Teja Lawson. The couple, who were Ebele and Kamal's best friends, flew into the country a few days ago from the United Kingdom. Kamal and Ebele stood behind them with the widest smiles Halima had ever seen. She was so proud of her brother. He'd come a long way from the bad boy soccer player star she'd known.

Everyone stood up and erupted into another round applause. The couples moved back to their seats and the ceremony continued for about twenty minutes. The crowd dispersed and several minutes later, the family congregated at Big Mummy, her stepmother's house.

"Why were you late?"

Halima looked up from Nasir who was in her arms to his father who stared at her like there was something he was searching for.

"He looks just like you," Halima said, ignoring his question.

Kamal's eyes softened with love and pride as they shifted to his son. "Yeah. I thought I knew what love was with E, but the twins are a totally different story."

"One day—" Her Smartphone rang. She handed Nasir

over to Kamal and reached for her purse. Halima looked at the number and her brows creased. *Why would Danjuma Head of Security be calling me, on a weekend?*

"This is Miss Danjuma," Halima answered. From the corner of her eye, she could see Kamal signal over her other brothers. If she wasn't preoccupied, she would have rolled her eyes. They were overprotective to the point of annoyance.

Halima listened in shock at what the person on the other end of the line was saying.

"Okay. I'll be there as soon as I can." She hung up and stared into three curious sets of eyes. She turned to the oldest of them all.

"There's been an accident with one of the drivers that was making a delivery to DeSab LLC. I have to get to Port Harcourt."

Rasheed blew out a breath. "I'm coming with you." He looked at his wife who was across the room and sighed. "Lemme tell SoSo that I have to move our plans back. "

Halima frowned. "You'll do no such thing. It's your anniversary and you've been planning this trip to Mauritius forever." She paused. "I can't have you dead. And that's exactly what you'll be if you cancel your sixth-year anniversary, especially since you guys have pushed this trip back for the last two years."

Rasheed sighed. "I should be there."

Halima touched his arm. "It happened under my division. I can handle it and you'll just be gone a couple of weeks. I'm sure nothing major will happen before you get back."

"Stone Cold, she got it," Jabir said, using his favorite nickname for Rasheed that was now actually a joke. It used to describe his strict demeanor, but he'd turned into a soft heart since he married Ibiso. "Besides we're here."

"Yeah, I agree," Kamal added. "We can't have you dead. Go on your trip. I'll go to Lagos if I need to."

"No!" All three of them shouted in unison.

Kamal stepped back and a crease took over his brow. "What y'all tryin' to say?"

"Nothing. Nothing at all." Rasheed said. "Jabir, I know you have that conference this week. I'll call Ekene to go with her instead."

Halima's heart raced at the mention of that name. "Didn't I just say I'll handle it?"

"And you will. Just not alone," Rasheed said.

"But I have Abubakar." Halima made one last attempt to get her brothers to see she did have someone with her. Her *mahram;* male guardian

"And what's he gonna do? Pray away anyone who tries to mess with you?" Kamal sneered. "Or lemme guess, chill on the side while you get attacked and—"

Halima shook her head. "That was three and a half years ago, and it was my fault. I told him to stay put."

"And he shouldn't have listened," Kamal countered.

They'd be here all day if she decided to argue with her brothers. "I give up. Let me go say my goodbyes and get to my mom's house."

Rasheed pulled out his phone. "Okay, I'll inform the pilot to prepare for takeoff."

"Tell him she'll have to stop at Lagos first,"Halima heard Jabir say as she strolled over to where Ebele, Damisi, and Ibiso stood.

Even after all these years, she still wasn't used to these three men trying to run her life. Good thing she only had to deal with it occasionally. Rasheed and Kamal lived in Abuja while Jabir, who wasn't so bad, lived in Lagos where she also lived. The thought made her think of Danladi. She wasn't going to be able to talk to him after all. He'd be upset, but she knew how to handle him. The man she wasn't sure how to handle was the one that she was going to see in a couple of hours – Ekene Odili.

Chapter 2

F*our Months later*

THE CHORDS TO "STRONG GIRL" BY VARIOUS AFRICAN artists started to play, alerting Halima Danjuma that someone was trying to get in contact with her. Now, the song of female empowerment sounded like the most annoying noise in the world. As much as she willed them to, her eyes refused to obey the command to open.

She turned over and fumbled through the covers of her queen-sized bed for the source of the irritating sound. Seconds later, she located it under one of her numerous pillows. With one eye peeled open, the name and time on the display screen of her iPhone X sent shock waves through her body. She'd been through so much the last several months, she couldn't deal with any more setbacks. At least not now.

"Why would they be calling me at this time?" she mumbled to herself. With hesitation and her heart beating rapidly against her rib cage, she accepted the call.

"This is Halima."

She listened attentively to the caller. The information relayed shot her body into a sitting position as her mouth dropped and her head spun in confusion.

"What do you mean he slipped into a coma? How? I just spoke to his family a few hours ago." She rattled the questions off to the caller.

Taking in a frustrated breath, she listened for a few more details before ending the call. She snatched her silk scarf off her head, flung the phone down and swung her legs over the bed. Before they hit the floor, she said the first of her five prayers, thanking Allah for waking her up from sleep.

Soon after, she made a beeline toward her bathroom, making sure to put her left leg first. She had to get to the hospital fast. As she turned on the shower and stepped in, she sighed at how everything had gone so wrong in such a short amount of time.

Halima thought to call her assistant, Chiaka and Abubakar. Her eyes darted to the electronic clock on the corner of her sink and she immediately nixed the idea. It was 5:15 am. No matter how many times she told all of them she was a grown woman, her overbearing brothers saw her as their little sister. With what she was about to do – drive herself to the hospital – she knew they'd have her head, after crucifying Abubakar, but she'd deal with them later. If what she was just told was true, life as she knew it was about to change for a while.

———

MOMENTS LATER, HALIMA HAD FINISHED GETTING DRESSED, tamed her auburn tresses into a bun and tied her hijab. Making her way downstairs, she called the driver's residence at the front gate. Taking her driver would lessen Kamal's wrath. A few moments later, she sat in the back of her white Lincoln Navigator with tinted windows as her driver navigated the streets of Lagos to Redstar Hospital. She laid her head back against the peanut butter colored leather seats and the events of the past few months flooded her mind.

Years ago, Mrs. Niyi retired as the Director of Logistics for Danjuma Group and Rasheed wasted no time —with the approval of the board —getting her to fill that position. Halima took pride in the work she'd done. She'd acquired a new storage warehouse for the cement-mixing facilities they owned across the country, and with updated technology, enhanced their own distribution channels and bought a few trucks to become carriers for others. She had successfully revamped the logistics department of the company.

Danjuma Group becoming carriers of cement for others was one of her biggest achievements. The initiative wasn't in the original business model and had increased revenue exponentially. Now she wasn't so sure the extra money was worth it. Everything was going well until recently. The money stream was now the source of her pain and numerous sleepless nights.

One of her drivers, Eric Okon, had taken a triple consecutive shift for two weeks in a row. This was against company policy since she ensured that all drivers rested properly from travel. He was able to get other lazy drivers to give him their shift because he needed money for the birth of his sixth child from his second wife. The thought alone made her cringe. How he thought he could afford two wives and six children on his salary was beyond her. However, that wasn't her business. Allah knew she had her own problems in that area. The headache came when he had an accident on the highway.

Not only was the Danjuma Group ordered by a Port Harcourt court to have the highway and bridge that was damaged repaired, they had also been in civil litigation with the shipper for breach of contract. Rasheed had been furious at the situation. He took the reputation of the company very personal. So, although he had reassured her a million times that he didn't think any less of her abilities to run the division, she still felt personally responsible. It was her department and she should've known or made sure she hired staff competent enough to know.

Within the hour, Halima gathered up her light sweater to shield herself from the cool June night and stepped out of her car. She scurried into the hospital and approached the receptionist's desk. As she opened her mouth to speak, the older lady that manned the desk raised her index finger at her, while she finished a conversation with another nurse who was filing her nails. Halima's face burned with anger, and she knew her fair skinned had turned red, when she realized the conversation was personal. Her characteristic demure demeanor had seriously eroded in the last couple of months, and this seemed to be the last straw.

She banged her hand on the desk. Excuse me! I need to see one of your patients," Halima said.

The women sized her up with their eyes, but she wasn't in the least bit worried. She had bigger problems.

"What's the patient's name and are you related to him?" the nurse asked. Reluctance laced her voice.

"I'm not related, but she," Halima pointed to the lady behind the computer. "Saw me here earlier today…or rather yesterday when I updated his account."

The woman rolled her eyes and peeled off a sticker to write her a visitor's pass. Just at that moment, one of Eric's wives came to the lobby area. Halima rushed over to her.

"Mrs. Okon, what happened?"

The woman's shoulders slumped in defeat. Her weary, tear-filled eyes gazed into Halima's. The sight somehow took Halima's mind to Big Mummy all those years ago, when she first met her brothers.

She was thirteen when she found out she had brothers who were birthed by another woman. One who, just like Mrs. Okon, was the first wife. But her stepmother thought she was the only wife. Halima remembered this same tired look when her brothers' mother had to look at her, her mother and dad as one happy family.

In many polygamous settings, the first wife was usually the one who had struggled with the man through thick and thin, before he decided to marry a second wife for one reason or the other. Such was the case with her brother's mother and now this woman who stood in front of her. Halima hadn't set eyes on the second wife since Eric was brought in last week from complications of that accident several months ago.

"Aunty Danjuma…"

"Please call me Halima."

A beat passed before the woman spoke again. "I don't know *o. After you commot yesterday morning, he been dey talk. E no too tey he begin cough. We go call doctor. Small time dey talk say him brain been dey swell. No do, no do he just sleep, no wake up again.*" The woman spoke in Pidgin English to describe how her husband had slipped into a coma unexpectedly the day before. She used the corner of her wrapper to wipe her eyes.

"Can I see him? Is the doctor here?" Halima asked.

"*No, the doctor just commot. He go come again tomorrow afternoon. My first pickin dey inside room. I wan go house check on the other smaller children.*"

In defeat, Halima hung her head and pulled her earlobe. She really wanted to hear from the doctor, but he wasn't there, and Eric's wife was leaving. She couldn't get any information without a family member. She prayed within for Allah to heal Eric as the Danjuma Group couldn't afford another death tied to its name. But bigger than that, he had six children and two women that needed a father and a husband.

———

Friday mid-morning, three days later, Halima inserted a flash drive into her computer to copy some files she had to share with Rasheed in a few hours. She'd already emailed the documents to him, but she wanted him to have backups.

"Hali, are you listening to me?" Kamal's aggravated voice came across the speaker of the phone.

"*Dan uwa na,* I've heard you." Halima stood and trudged over to the small fridge in the corner of her massive office. A grin spread across her face as she thought about how her sisters-in-law always teased her for calling Kamal "my brother" in Hausa while addressing Jabir and Rasheed by their names, as though they weren't her brothers. She and Kamal were the closest, and it just seemed to fit.

"But are you understanding me though, Lil Sis?"

"No, I'm dumb. Now can you get off the phone so I can finish up here? That way, I'll meet with you in exactly three hours as agreed." Halima shook her head.

Sometimes her brother thought he was her father. Even Rasheed didn't get on her like Kamal. She had come to get used to the bossy behavior he exhibited toward those he loved. He loved fiercely and she loved him right back, more than anything, but he was also a thorn in her side. The corner of her lips raised in a smirk as she thought how wrong she was to think that him being married would get his foot off her neck.

"Kill the attitude. You always say that, then I'll have to wait for you. How does that make sense?"

Halima chuckled because at this minute, one of his eyebrows would be raised and his head cocked to the side. She'd planned to visit her mother in Abuja with the three-day weekend ahead. Kamal was in Calabar giving a speech and instead of going directly to Abuja, once she told him her plans, he decided to stop in Lagos. She kicked herself for that slip because she knew telling him would result in him making a detour for her to fly with him. He flew into Lagos the previous night and was currently in Jabir's house in Ikeja.

"You do know that I am thirty-five years old and I can

take care of myself. I fly alone to Dubai, South Africa, Kenya, even the US and UK without you."

"I'm still older than you. So, your point? And second, you aren't alone. Abubakar is with you," Kamal said. She could tell he was distracted. Jabir's girls, Ana and Ina, who were now six, were probably running him ragged. All the Danjuma grandkids loved Uncle Kammy as much as his own kids adored him.

"Okay so you see, you didn't have to stop," Halima rationalized.

"Yeah, sure. Tell Abubakar I got something for him when I see him. I heard he let you drive by yourself some nights ago."

Damisi can't keep nothing to herself. Halima should have learned her lesson by now. Damisi was pretty good at keeping her secrets; one in particular. But anything she thought was putting Halima in danger, she'd rat her out immediately. Halima remembered when there was a kidnap attempt on her some years ago. Rasheed wanted her to move back to Abuja. Jabir was the one that she talked to about asking Rasheed to back off. He did, but only with her promise not to move around alone. She also had to move from her old house to one closer to Jabir and Damisi.

No surprise, Damisi probably told her husband who told Kamal about her hospital trip some nights ago. Jabir didn't really get on her like her other two brothers. However, she was still surprised he hadn't called to scold her. Sometimes she felt worse with him because his delivery was so unfazed, but stern at the same time.

"I'm not doing this with you. See you soon. Bye." Halima hung up before he could get another word out.

A few hours later, Chiaka, turned to leave as Halima had just finished giving her instructions on what to do in her absence. Eric Okon still hadn't woken up, but he was stable.

Abubakar advanced to where she was and picked up her briefcase.

Halima looked at her watch. She had just fifteen minutes to get to Kamal before he started blowing up her phone. If she was late, she wouldn't hear the last of it. She looked around one last time to make sure she wasn't forgetting anything. Ruckus from outside her door caused her brows to crease. Chiaka walked backward into the office while Abubakar stepped in front of Halima. She sidestepped him and watched in confusion as the receptionist, scampered in.

With both hands on her upper chest and a shaky voice, she said, "Madam, I tried to stop them."

"Officer, that's her. See how she's enjoying this big office." A woman Halima had never seen before spoke with disgust while waving her hand around the office. She placed her hands on her hips. "Enjoying this air-conditioned office and forcing my husband to drive all those long hours. If she had paid him properly, this wouldn't be happening." The woman had spit flying out of her mouth in anger.

"Madam, calm down," a police officer said.

"Who is she and what is she talking about?" Halima said. Her phone buzzed in her hand, she glanced at it. She quickly sent Kamal to voicemail.

"I'm Mrs. Okon and you killed my husband."

Halima's heart skipped a beat. "What is she talking about?" *This must be Eric's second wife.* Halima glanced over her. She looked more affluent than his first wife. She turned to who she assumed was a detective.

"Mrs. Danjuma…"

"Miss…"

"Miss Danjuma, I'm Detective Williams, and this is Officer Preye. We're from Ibeju Lekki station. Mrs. Okon here just lost her husband a few hours ago and she has named you as the responsible party. We need you to come with us, so we can ask you some questions," the detective explained.

"There must be a mistake." Halima stumbled back and leaned against her mahogany desk.

"That very well maybe, but we need you to come with us to the station."

"Station? Are you serious? Do you know who she is?" Chiaka shrieked.

"Detective, she'll come in for questioning, but not without her lawyer," Abubakar said. He was a burly man who stood at about six feet. His signature stance always had his hands clasped in front of him with his legs slightly apart. He feared no one, except Halima's brothers of course. Well, more like he respected them too much to ever counter anything they said.

As they all talked on her behalf, Halima felt her brain pounding against her skull. There was a full-blown argument between her assistant and Mrs. Okon, while Abubakar and the Detective went back and forth about her lawyer.

"Stop," Halima yelled. She'd had enough. She pulled out her phone and gave it to Chiaka. "Please call my brother."

"Which one?" Chiaka asked.

"It doesn't matter. Abubakar, let's go. Detective, lead the way."

Halima had no idea what lay ahead, but she was a Danjuma and wasn't about to crumble in front of anybody.

Chapter 3

"**P**apa *Ndewo*," Ekene Odili greeted his father, sashaying into his massive office located in the heart of Victoria Island.

His dad, who was on a call, smiled and gestured for him to have a seat. Instead, Ekene strolled over to the corner refrigerator. Bypassing the coffee and various tea selections, he took out a bottle of chilled water. The rain earlier left a chill in the air, but hot beverages were never his thing. Teas maybe, but that wasn't often. He made his way back to the massive black desk and sat in one of the chairs in front of it. He unscrewed the cap off of the bottle and brought it to his lips just as his dad got off the phone.

"How are you, my son?"

Ekene nodded his head as he swallowed. His dad still looked young for sixty-seven. The grays sprinkled all over his head gave him a more distinguished look. Strokes, however, didn't care about looks or age as his father suffered one a few years ago. The ordeal knocked the wind out of Ekene and in a way brought them closer together.

His father, Chief Frank Odili, was a prominent investment

banker in Lagos. Their relationship hadn't always been smooth, but that singular incident made their issues inconsequential. Ekene had to let go of past hurts and forgive his father. Especially when he saw what his friend, Rasheed Danjuma, went through losing his father.

"I'm fine. I stopped by to thank you for the referral. I was able to get Mr. Banjo and his company a huge settlement from those Chinese investors that swindled them." Ekene stretched out his legs and crossed them at the ankle.

His mother died of a brain aneurysm when Ekene was fifteen. He and his parents still lived in the United Kingdom at that time. Her sudden death was a devastating blow to the family, or so he thought. Imagine his dismay when his father was set to remarry less than a year later and relocate back to Nigeria. His father claimed that because of his education, Ekene should remain in the UK, but that didn't soften the blow of rejection he felt from his only living parent. Nothing he could say changed his father's mind though. Ekene remained in London with his mother's sister.

A month after the decision, his dad relocated back to Nigeria to be with his new wife. As the relationship between father and son became strained, his father began to blame the larger family, saying they pressured him to remarry so soon so he could have more than one child. Ekene didn't buy it. They remained estranged for many years. In the years he stayed in London completing his education up to college, his stepmother, Nkiru had a son and a daughter for his dad.

It wasn't until Ekene moved back to Nigeria and after his father's stroke some months later that he slowly allowed his father to repair their relationship. He was close to his siblings, but they were much younger, so they had very little in common.

"Good. Congratulations, my son. I'm so proud of you. How is the case going for your friend?"

Both men made an effort to have a standing lunch every other week and Ekene spent time in his dad's house with his siblings and wife. The gesture pleased his dad and made everyone more comfortable around each other, so he continued to do it when his schedule permitted.

"We closed the civil case two months ago. He had to pay some money, but not as much as it would've been." Ekene rubbed his chin thinking about the driver who he was told had to be readmitted into the hospital. His mind involuntarily wondered to Halima. He shook his head to clear the thought and immediately redirected it to the man in front of him.

"You should think about bringing that Midas touch of yours here to work for me," his father said, repeating the line like a broken record.

"I'm a lawyer, dad and I already work for you…as your lawyer."

"I mean with me. Here in the family business. I can teach you everything I know."

"How generous, but no thanks. Teach Emeka," Ekene said, referring to his half-brother.

"You know that boy wants to be a rapper. Trying to copy all these people like that yellow boy with hair hanging down his face and beards that reach his chest." His father's face scrunched up in disdain. He snapped his fingers. "And that other one who has hair in the front and long dreadlocks at the back."

Ekene laughed hard as his father described popular Nigerian rapper, Phyno and singer, Flavor.

"First of all, dad, those men you're referring to are very wealthy, so you should be courting them to invest their money. Both are Ibo like we are, so Emeka might be on to something. But then again, train Ego, to work with you. Who says women can't be CEOs?" Ekene asked, referring to his sister.

His father waved his hand, dismissing his suggestions. Ekene chuckled. He had said his piece. Whether his father took his words seriously or not was up to him. Ekene did know that his father better figure it out because there was no way he was giving up his lucrative law firm, Odili and Associates, to come work for him.

Ekene peeked at his Smartphone that chimed. He cleared the call and quickly sent a text to his assistant that he'd call back shortly. Looking back up to his father, Ekene asked. "How's your wife?"

His father rubbed his forehead in displeasure. Ekene wondered why he wasn't used to him calling her that after all these years. No matter how cordial they'd become, Nkiru would always be his father's wife and not his stepmom. After all, she didn't raise him. His aunt in London did.

"She's fine." Defeat laced his father's tone.

"Cool, tell her I'll probably be over this weekend."

"She'd like that."

Ekene stood and placed his hands in his pockets. "Okay old man, I was in the area and decided to stop by. Jide is in the country and I have to meet up with him."

His father paused, rested back in his oversized leather chair and lifted his index finger to his chin. Ekene knew exactly what he was about to say next.

"Will you be joining us in the village this year?"

Apart from investing, his father also ran a lucrative farm back in Enugu State where they were from. He loved to attend the annual New Yam Festival – a celebration by the Igbos to officially present the newly harvested yams to God and the ancestors of the land. It was a big celebration that brought in many tourists.

Ekene never felt that close to that side of his father's life. It was one he created with his new family, so since he'd been back in the country, he had never gone. If he had to admit it, the real reason was that the people, his father's family, all stood by and watched his father take another wife so soon after his mother died. These were the same people his mother had catered to whenever they all had visited home together or if they had shown up in London for one reason or the other. He knew he needed to let it go, but it was something he was still working on.

"I'll let you know, Dad."

"Good. At least you'll think about it. I'm being conferred with another chieftaincy title and I want my whole family there." His father sounded hopeful and Ekene didn't want to take that from him.

"Okay, old man. Got it. I have to go."

"Don't call me old until you give me grandchildren."

Ekene shook his head. On that note, he had to get out of there. Swaggering to the door he opened it and threw, "Bye Dad," over his shoulder.

———

Grandchildren.

His father's voice echoed in Ekene's ears. He shook his head to dismiss the thought. It wasn't that the thought repelled him; it was the opposite. His angst lay in how to get that to happen. It had to be her. He didn't set out for it to be that way, but that was the hand that he was dealt, and he had run out of ways to avoid playing it.

"Are you listening to me?"

Ekene glanced at Jide Adegoke, his childhood friend, while holding his hamburger inches away from his mouth. Jide was a top-notch accountant and was the only one out of the three friends- himself, Rasheed and Jide-that still lived in London with his family. He was visiting to break ground on the family home he wanted to build in Banana Island. It was his first step to relocating back to Nigeria in a couple of years. Ekene had been the first to relocate, followed by Rasheed a year or so later.

"What did you say?" He bit into the sandwich and relished the burst of flavor on his taste buds.

He smirked at the irritation that radiated from Jide's eyes. He put the burger back on his plate and chewed. He did hear the question. *Did he love her?* Looking at his childhood friend, he stretched his stiff neck. Did he? Heck, he wasn't sure of the answer himself some days.

"Come on, Kene. It doesn't take a native doctor to see it. I'm surprised Rasheed hasn't said anything about it." Jide tossed a fried shrimp into his mouth.

He grimaced. If he'd known lunch at the Hard Rock Café would turn into a mini counseling session, he would've passed.

"You sure you're in the right profession?" Ekene asked dryly.

"Huh?"

"I remember you being the same one that encouraged Rasheed to return home to SoSo some years ago?" He air quoted the word "encouraged."

Jide chuckled. "It worked out, didn't it? Two beautiful kids and I haven't seen that man so happy in all his grumpy life."

"Speaking of…when are you going to Abuja?"

"I see you're trying to avoid the question, but I'll be there sometime next week, unless Shade wants to go before," Jide answered referring to his wife of three years. "So?"

"So, what?"

"What's going on with you and Halima?" Jide took a sip of his Coca Cola.

"Nothing. I haven't seen or heard from her in about two months." Ekene shrugged.

"Really, I thought you two were working on that case together?"

"We were, but then at a point, Rasheed came back into the country…"

Jide's phone began to ring and he answered. Within the first few seconds, Ekene realized his friend was talking to his wife. When he told her where he was, from Jide's responses, she asked him to get something for her and the kids.

Ekene was happy for his friends. Who knew the most rebellious kids in their West London school would turn out the way they did? All successful with beautiful families. Except him. His heart twitched. Love was an emotion he had successfully eluded. In his opinion, the experience of the emotion wasn't worth the pain and scars the loss of it caused. The loss of his mother and subsequent abandonment of his father taught him that. For years, that had been his mantra.

His social life didn't suffer as he dated widely, but he'd never let his guard down enough for it to be anything more than a good time. All that changed that day several years ago when his best friend introduced him to his sister, Halima.

A handshake. A handshake that lasted only a few seconds when they were introduced packed so much intensity that he knew instantly, it could only mean trouble. Ekene knew he wasn't emotionally available so did the only sane thing he could. Avoid the auburn-haired beauty like a plague. But somehow his heart didn't get the message or realize that both of them together was an impossible and complicated situation. For years, he'd become an expert at overriding his heart's desire until that day four months ago with a phone call from Rasheed.

"Well, my two *kobos*, you can't help who you love." Jide's voice brought him back to the present.

"Who said anything about love?"

"Your body language."

"It's complicated."

"Then uncomplicate it. It's been several years. I know by now, even you know keeping your social life a revolving door is getting old."

After their initial meeting, Ekene got to know about Halima through Rasheed's spotty conversation. He felt anger at the injustice of her being forced to marry someone she barely knew – someone that had been chosen for her when she was in her early twenties. He desperately wanted to save her. It'd been years since he felt a semblance of connection to any woman. Anytime he thought of *her*, his heartbeat accelerated at a pace he couldn't get under control. Over the past couple of months, he had willed, begged, his heart to look for someone else. He had gone on numerous dates just to force his heart to conform. It was all fruitless.

"I neither admit nor deny, but Halima is different."

"Well, you better figure it out. I've listened to you talk about her for years as a friend. But now when you speak it's different." Jide mocked. "I'd hate to be you when she gets married and you have to still be her *friend*."

Ekene's chest grew tight at his cajole. Jide had correctly analyzed the situation, but Ekene wasn't willing to discuss it. Not now.

"Don't you have somewhere to be?" Ekene looked at his watch.

Jide chuckled and raised his hands in surrender. "Okay, I see those murderous eyes. Don't say I didn't call it. If I could figure it out, so can 'Sheed. You better tell him before he finds out himself."

"Didn't I just tell you that there's nothing to tell?" Ekene seethed. "Drop it."

His anger was misplaced. It was really at the fact that after forming a closer friendship in the last few months, Halima pulled a disappearing act on him. He must have read the signs wrong. No, he didn't. There was a deeper connection and now he was angry that he'd let his guard down because that feeling of loss was back and it was something he swore he wouldn't allow himself to ever feel again. But now it was too late. Halima Danjuma had his heart captive.

"A'ight, I'll drop it."

Ekene was about to apologize when he felt his phone

vibrate in his pocket. He reached in and took it out. *Speak of the devil.*

"Wassup 'Sheed," Ekene greeted Rasheed. The music in the background was loud, but it did nothing to hide the anger and agitation he quickly sensed in Rasheed's voice.

"Hold on, slow down. What do you mean by Kammy is about to commit murder?" Ekene listened some more. "Huh? How? Isn't he in Calabar and why is he at the police station?"

He stood, almost tipping the table over at the words Rasheed said next. "What do you mean Halima is in custody?" *Who dared?*

Out of the corner of his eye, he saw Jide stand, remove some bills from his pocket and place them on the table. Ekene pulled his jacket from the back of his chair and listened to the details from Rasheed as he scrambled to the door. Hanging up a few minutes later, he entered his car.

"What's going on?" Jide got in beside him.

"Man, I don't know. All I know is they got Red in the police station." He sighed. "I know a single hair better not be out of her hijab or I'm going to need to repent." Ekene put the car in reverse and sped out of the parking lot.

"Who is Red?"

Ekene heard the smirk in Jide's voice. He glanced over at him, but left his question unanswered. Ekene had given Halima that nickname soon after meeting her. Those bright auburn curls stirred something in his gut. He only called her that in private, though. His jaw clenched at the thought of *his* Red, sitting behind someone's counter or worse, in a cell.

"Yeah, you love her. Better talk to Rasheed quickly 'cause if he finds out, I'm not trying to be a referee."

Ekene didn't respond. It was true that Rasheed had gone from not caring about his baby sister to being the overprotective big brother. But that was the least of his concerns right now. He needed to get Red from where she was. Ekene brought his heartbeat back to some semblance of normal. In all of Jide's advice, he forgot one important fact. He and Halima didn't share the same faith. She was a Muslim.

Ekene sighed. He'd fought. But his heart didn't ask for the spiritual preference of the person it chose to love. His need to be in control had lost the battle to his growing desire for love and connection. He did have to figure it out. His sanity required it.

Chapter 4

"E, I'm good. Yeah, I'm coming home tonight. Love you, too. Kiss the kids for me. I'll see you soon."

Halima listened to her hard-headed brother end the call from the other side of the room. She rolled her eyes, chiding herself for not being more specific when she told her assistant to call her brother. Jabir would've been the better choice. Rasheed was in Abuja, which left Kamal. She knew he'd make matters worse, and he didn't disappoint.

When he arrived at the police station, Kamal demanded they let her go. Their refusal was not met well. Kamal was the sweetest human she knew until someone thought it was a good idea to mess with any member of his family. She rubbed her fingertips against her temples.

This can't be happening.

At least his wife had gotten Kamal to calm down. She was still the only one who could do the trick.

Halima wiped the sweat from her forehead with the back of her hand. She felt sticky and dirty. However, her present discomfort was nothing compared to the sorrow she felt for the Okon family. Eric Okon went into cardiac arrest and had died hours earlier. She'd been at the police station for close to two hours and was over everything.

Apparently, his second wife had an uncle who was the Commissioner of Police, hence the elaborate show, even though she hadn't done anything to contribute to Eric's death. The detective kept her seated behind a desk in an interrogation area while he asked her the same questions repeatedly. The only concession they gave was to allow her to talk to her other two brothers over the phone.

"And you, how you gonna stand there and let them take her anywhere?" Kamal addressed Abubakar.

"*Dan uwa na.* Stop! I agreed to come," she pleaded.

"Well, he shouldn't have let you. Period." Kamal placed his hands in his pockets.

Halima looked at Abubakar. Her eyes implored him to remain calm. She didn't need him responding and getting into a back and forth with Kamal.

"I agree. The minute they showed up in her office, I should've been called."

Her heart quickened when she heard the new voice that had entered the room.

He came.

That voice did something to her she would never dare tell anyone about. She felt so alive and guilty at the same time when he came around or she heard him speak. The raspy baritone sent shivers from the crown of her head to the sole of her feet. All the emotions Ekene Odili stirred up in her were so forbidden. It went against her *deen.* As a single Muslim woman, she wasn't to have relations before marriage. To make matters worse, Ekene, like her brothers, was a man of the Book.

The logical side of her brain knew all this, but her heart wasn't getting the message, as with a lot of things over the years. Ekene's presence or even the thought of him sent her heart into overdrive. Halima sucked in a breath and turned to face him. Her eyes met his, locked and immediately lowered. She turned back, but still felt him looking at her while he walked over to Kamal. In the short time, she'd taken in his grey pin-striped pantsuit that clung loosely to his thighs. The diamond stud he wore in one ear sparkled and it looked like he had recently shaped up his hair and beard which, he kept close to his face. He was unattainable forbidden perfection.

The police officer in charge stood and headed to the other side of the room at Ekene's beckoning. A few minutes and some words later, the officer cowered under Kamal's stare while Ekene paced the room barking orders to whoever was on the other end of the line. He exuded the same power her late father and brothers did. It also reminded her of two other men who were bent on making her life miserable, Danladi and her late father's brother, Uncle Musa.

Lost in her thoughts, she didn't hear when Ekene snuck up to her, but the tingling of her skin announced his presence. She turned to meet his gaze and lingered on his outstretched hand. Like so many times before, she wanted to feel his palm around her hand, but as was customary with her faith, she knew not to. He knew that too, but his clenched jaw and the unfamiliar look in his eyes dared her to leave him hanging. She'd seen his anger before and felt bad for the recipient. Now that was her. After a few seconds, she placed her hand in his. He pulled her up, gently dropping her hand after a tight squeeze.

"Are you all right?" His eyes suddenly softened with his voice.

Halima's eyebrows creased. "Is that all you're going to say?"

The only person acting normal was Kamal. At least she knew he'd act crazy. Rasheed was so calm with her on the phone. Jabir was angry and now Ekene was acting as if everything was okay. It was obvious none of them thought the situation was her fault. Her crime was she'd decided to handle it alone, and worst of all, going to the police station by herself.

"Yes…for now. We'll talk about why you didn't call me immediately they showed up, later." His dark eyes gave her a once over. "You must be hungry."

"Thanks, man. I got her." Kamal's words cut short her response.

Once he was close enough, Kamal drew her into his arms. She clung to her brother, resting her head against his chest. His cuddle provided the comfort she desperately wanted to prove she didn't need. A beat passed between them before he released her and lifted her head with his index finger. "Kene here did what he does best. We can leave now."

"No thanks needed." Ekene then stared down at her. "Next time, I should be your first call."

"Oh, there won't be a next time." Kamal raised a brow, waiting for her acknowledgement.

Halima nodded her throat raw with emotion. Tears stung her eyes, but she refused to let them fall. The ordeal was uncalled for. Eric had caused his problems starting with the accident the Danjuma Group got sued for. She'd personally gone over and above to get him and his family help, and now here she was, being interrogated for his death. The tension in her back began to dissolve as Kamal rubbed it.

"Let me get the driver to pull the car around. We'll get something to eat on the way to the airstrip." Kamal kissed her temple, dapped Ekene and headed to the door, but stopped short of exiting. "Hey Abubakar, walk with me. She's in good hands with him." Kamal winked at her as Abubakar dragged his feet behind him.

"Are you going to Abuja?" Ekene asked.

"Yes. I'll be back on Monday evening." She released a labored breath. "What happens now?"

"Now nothing. You go on your trip and rest."

"Don't patronize me."

Ekene studied her for a few seconds. "Highly unlikely, but worst case scenario, the family will file a civil suit, holding Danjuma Group liable for Eric's death."

Her eyes widened.

"Like I said, I highly doubt it, so for you, it's business as usual."

They stood in pregnant silence for a few seconds before she looked up at him. He stared at her so intensely, causing her to almost buckle at the knees. It reminded her of the reason she'd decided to avoid him over the past couple of months.

"Ummm, I should go. It's already late. We have to get to the airstrip and still sit through a forty-five-minute plane ride."

Ekene nodded and ushered her out of the station. They faced each other and the next thing she knew, a force was pushing her into his arms. The contact felt like home and her mind gave off warning signs her heart chose to ignore.

"Hey man, let my sister go. E's gonna kill me if I miss dinner." Kamal yelled as he held the back door of the car open for her to enter.

They jerked apart. Halima raised her palms to her cheeks, she was sure had turned tomato red. Ekene, on the other hand, smiled down at her, displaying the lone dimple on his left cheek.

Ekene lifted his eyes to the waiting car. "Kam, chill out. You're not in charge of anything over this way." The bass in his voice swelled her heart.

"Ha! Imma let you think that, so you can sleep well at night. Come on Hali."

"I'll call you tonight. Pick up. You've become pretty good at sending me to voicemail. Tonight, is not that night." His hypnotic stare kept her in place.

Halima blinked and rubbed her earlobe. How did she ever think he was clueless about her avoidance strategy?

"I will."

She walked to the car and got in. As the driver pulled off, she glanced back and saw Ekene still standing there, with his hands in his pockets. She kept her eyes on him until he was out of sight.

"Since when did you start hugging men who aren't family? What aren't you telling me, Hali? What about what's his face? You keeping secrets from me? Is that what we do?" Kamal rattled off questions her mind couldn't answer. At least not now.

"*Dan uwa na*, can we not do this now? I'll answer your questions later, I promise." Halima laid her head against the headrest. Seconds later, she felt her brother pulling her to his side. She placed her head on his massive shoulders and allowed sleep to take her away.

———

"Za, I'm fine. Now would you let me sleep?" Halima raked her fingers through her wet hair.

"But I don't get why you went with them," Zara Rice-Willis asked.

Three and a half years ago, Zara and her husband Terrance were the couple that came to her defense when she was attacked in the airport. Terrance, a pastor, had just finished a conference in Detroit, and they were on their way to Zara's grandfather's funeral in South Africa. When they boarded, their seats were next to each other, so they got acquainted on the seventeen-hour trip. During her stay in South Africa, they kept in touch and developed a friendship over the years.

"I was stupid. But I'm gonna hang up now. I know how you get, and it will be in the papers soon, so I wanted to give you a heads up."

"You better call me tomorrow. I know Mum will be calling me once she reads it and I need answers," Zara fussed.

"Goodnight. I promise." Halima massaged the back of her neck. Mrs. Rice, Zara's mom was a riot.

"Night, love you, sis."

Zara never ended a call without telling her that she loved her. It still sounded strange to her, but Halima had come to accept it. Her family expressed the sentiment all the time, but never had anyone else, especially of a different faith.

A couple of hours ago, Kamal had dropped her off to a quiet house. Without any details, she'd told her mother she'd be late and not to wait up. Halima was glad she listened because she needed the peace and quiet to gather her thoughts.

She walked up to the vanity and stared at her reflection. Although the wear of the day had been washed down the drain with a shower, her face still carried traces of strain. She unraveled the towel on her head and squeezed the excess water from her hair.

"Business as usual. Yeah, right," she muttered.

With the end of the year approaching, she had a lot to keep her occupied, like planning the annual staff conference and subsequent dinner. Both events, which her brother started once he took over the mantle of leadership, would be held in Lagos, as the Abuja office hosted the event the previous year.

Halima opened a drawer and retrieved a nightshirt. Minutes later, she was dressed and seated on the side of her bed. She closed her eyes and covered her face with her hands. She took in a deep breath and exhaled. When she opened her eyes, the corner of a bright orange paper was caught in her peripheral vision. She turned to her dresser and lifted it from under the stack of magazines. It was a pamphlet from Rasheed's church.

Being around her brothers for the past number of years, she'd become curious about the inner joy they now possessed, as opposed to when she first met them. Their love for her was unconditional, even though they didn't share the same faith.

They had an aura of peace, love, and freedom, making them seem lighter. The love they showed their wives was something she longed for but didn't dare to seek. That was until she stepped in Damisi and Jabir's church several months ago. Before, she didn't care about entering an arranged marriage to Danladi, but that had changed.

Jabir and Damisi were named "Couple of the Harvest" at their church. Damisi had talked about it for months. That day, their son, fell ill during the service. When Damisi called her to ask if she'd come get him, Halima obliged without hesitation. Her nephew was her little caramel and she loved spending time with him. Besides that, she knew how important what they were doing was to Damisi.

Upon arrival at the huge church, she called Damisi to tell her she was outside, but for some reason, her calls went straight to voicemail. Halima got out of the car and walked into the church hall where the ceremonial part of the day was being held. In trying to locate where her family was seated, Halima overheard their Pastor say something about the foolishness of a man called Nabal. What piqued her interest was the fact that he was mentioned in the context of an arranged marriage. She heard nothing else because, at that same moment, she saw Damisi approaching with her nephew.

The Quran taught that Allah created mates for them among themselves. But wasn't she supposed to be happy with the chosen mate? And hearing the reference that day in the church led her to Google, YouTube and lastly an online Bible. The Book, to her surprise, read like a history lesson instead of a set of instructions like she was used to in the Quran.

One of the preachers she came across on YouTube had a three-week series on the couple mentioned in the story. The man's wife was Abigail and they were in an arranged marriage. The online preacher described him as a "bad spouse." The preacher went on to say the lady, Abigail, got David who was a future king, thereby changing her status.

Halima's curiosity was not quenched so she went to the Bible to read the story. She wasn't impressed that Abigail was a third wife, but her wisdom and intelligence was something she admired. Halima scoffed at the memory because, in her sect, it was believed that when it came to matters of the heart, women didn't know what was right for them. Hence her father betrothed her to someone when she was twenty-five.

Halima shared that curiosity with Damisi, and that began her deeper interest in the religion her brothers practiced. That, and her genuine friendship with Zara. One day, Damisi invited her to a women's group where they read the Bible and fellowshipped. Halima still went occasionally but wasn't moved to abandon the faith she had been born and raised in – Islam. The one thing it did do was make her question some things, which led her to take an interest in the liberal/progressive Muslim movements.

Halima said her prayers and crawled into the cool sheets of her queen-sized bed. Moments later, as expected it would, Sade's "Sweetest Taboo" began to play. She picked up her phone, smiled and accepted the call.

"Hello." Her tone was low and tired.

"Hey yourself," he responded with a voice that prickled her skin every time. "How are you? No need to ask if you made it to Abuja okay since you were with Kam."

Halima let out a faint chuckle at the fight she had to put up to get Kamal to drop her off at her mother's home instead of making her stay overnight in his. He'd just got back from a trip and she had no desire to see him and his wife all over each other. Amongst all her brothers, that couple couldn't function without their hands or lips being on each other. For someone who'd been celibate for years, that wasn't where she needed to be.

"So, you just had to go and add another reason for me to be upset with you?" The normal softness of his voice when he spoke to her was absent.

"And what's the first?" She knew exactly what he was talking about, but she wouldn't be the one to admit it.

His grunt caused her to smile.

"You've been avoiding me. We're going to get to that, but first, why didn't you call me when those men came to your office?" He paused. "I was going crazy with worry."

"That wasn't my intention."

"Are we that bad? I mean you'd rather get in trouble than see me?"

"I didn't call anyone at the time. It wasn't personal." Halima rubbed her forehead. She didn't want him running with the wrong impression. Yes, she was avoiding him, but it was nothing he did. It was all her. Be that as it may, this wasn't the heavy conversation she wanted to have tonight. Besides, the phone worked both ways.

"Kene, you've always been good to me—"

"But?"

"But nothing. Can we not talk about this tonight?"

"No can do. Your brothers are like putty in your hands, but that's not me, Princess. I want to know why you would endanger yourself that way instead of calling me." His anger, laced with frustration, seeped through the phone.

Halima sat up against her headboard and creased her brows. She wished her brothers were putty in her hands.

"That's not true."

"You and I know it is. But that's not the point. We're talking about you deliberately putting yourself in danger. You weren't under arrest so why would you go with those people without your lawyer present?"

Two opposing emotions clashed within her. Aggravation and pleasure. The former at the fact that he was talking to her as though she were a child and he referred to himself as just her lawyer. He was acting just like her brothers. And the latter at the fact that he cared enough to be angry. She knew she sounded crazy, but there was nothing she could do about her truth. She imagined the six-foot four-inch, dark chocolate brown package pacing wherever he was with a scowl on his face.

"Ekene, I'm going to tell you like I tell my brothers, I'm a thirty-five-year-old woman perfectly capable of taking care of herself." She paused for his response and got none, so continued. "Abubakar was going to call you as my *lawyer*, but Chiaka got to Kammy first, then he Rasheed, and I'm sure that's who called you."

"If your little outburst and the use of my full name are supposed to dismiss me, it's cute, but not going to work," he said. "Considering I broke every traffic law to get you out of where you shouldn't have been in the first place, I want an explanation." His chuckle irked her.

She yawned. Hopefully, he'd get the message and get off the phone. She was done talking to him.

He took a breath. "Look, I admire the independent woman in you. I even get why you work so hard even when you don't have to. You're not fragile; your strength amazes me. But when you're in any kind of situation like you were in today, I draw the line at every feminist, independent bone in your body. You call me immediately."

Halima remained silent.

"Hello? Hali?"

"Yeah? Are you done?"

She heard him sigh.

"Promise me," he insisted.

"I'll call my lawyer next time detectives show up," she responded. As much as he knew her, she knew him and that hurt him as well.

"Don't make me catch a flight tonight." His voice vibrated with suppressed defeat. But her breath still managed to stall in her lungs at the thought.

It hadn't always been this way between them. She wouldn't lie to herself and say she didn't remember the electric current that passed between them when he shook her hand all those years ago. She knew then like she knew now that he was bad news in a good kind of way. That was the reason she stayed away from him. They couldn't help but see each other at her family's functions since he was her brother's closest friend, or with business when she acquired a new client and had to run the contracts through him. She was always intentional about making those meetings as brief as possible.

In the last couple of months, the dynamics of their relationship underwent a paradigm shift. She had no idea when it happened. Maybe their playful banter over food, and long hours working on the DeSab breach of contract case, put the chemistry they tried to deny all of these years front and center. Every moment she spent with him was so sweet, yet the moment they were apart, she felt like she'd committed a crime.

"Empty threats. Goodnight, Kene."

"Don't play with me. Goodnight, Red."

They ended the call. Halima was about to put the phone on the dresser when she decided to send a text.

I promise. It won't happen again.

Almost immediately the three dots signaling a response was on the way appeared.

Love casts out a multitude of sins, followed by a wink emoji, appeared on her screen.

Halima placed her phone to the side and turned over with a smile on her face. The more she got to know him, the more she understood exactly why he was one of Rasheed's best friends. Ekene was stoic, firm and handled her with care. He used the word love with her often. The depth of the word was something she didn't know, neither was she brave enough to find out. Now that she was home, she had a more pressing issue to address. It had taken her a while, but she was ready to face the three Amigos – her mother, Uncle Musa and Danladi.

Chapter 5

The next day, Ekene walked into the lobby of the high rise building off Adeniyi Jones. Acknowledging the receptionist with a head nod, he stepped into the elevator and hit the button to take him to his fifth-floor office. Every other Saturday, he opened his doors for his pro bono clients. With his paying clients increasing and normal workload being so heavy, he made sure to commit to only two non-paying clients a quarter.

When the elevator door opened, he stepped out turned left and headed toward his suite. Dressed down in blue khaki shorts with a white shirt and matching sneakers, he steadied his Powerade in one hand, opened the doors and powered off the alarm.

The front entrance of the suite consisted of double glass doors. Anytime he entered the office, he silently thanked God for the favor to have a space where his name adorned the walls. The lobby was decorated with a minimalistic theme in light brown colors, and on the walls hung rich paintings in contrast. It was a law office, but he never wanted anyone to feel like it was a place of doom. His office was located straight down the hall to the back. Along the way, there were offices for the few law clerks he brought on once a year. They used the work they did for his firm to attain academic credit. There were other offices for paralegals, law clerks, investigators and the two associates.

Ekene's desire to study law was born out of what he considered the injustice of his own life. His mother was the closest woman to him, and her death changed him forever. His father's abandonment made it more devastating. His willingness to let go the only person that tied him and her together—him— and start life with someone new without a blink was a huge injustice to him. And at that age, he didn't have a voice and couldn't do anything about it. The scar drove his love for law to provide justice and fairness.

His pro bono work, which was under The Chibundu Odili Foundation, named after his mother, was committed to giving women who had no voice one and shelter. The coincidence of the meaning of her name and his mission was uncanny as his mother's name meant God is My Shelter.

Ekene stepped into his office which was decorated in his favorite colors, black and gold, and set his drink on his glass tabletop. The modern look gave him a sense of peace in the office which was always busy. He got comfortable in his black, leather chair and powered on his laptop. He leaned deeper into his chair while the screen came alive. This place was his pride and joy.

Coming back from the United Kingdom, it was hard to fit into a profession where all the top-notch cliques had all been formed and snubbed their noses at any newcomers. One thing he never wanted was the clout of his father's name here in Lagos to get him any kind of special treatment. God placed him in a law firm that was more accommodating to his British accent and the fact that he had just taken the Nigerian Bar Examination. With something to prove, he worked an insane number of billable hours. After three years, that all went down the drain when he was passed up for partnership.

The betrayal of being passed up for partner propelled him to establish his own firm. That was the plan all along, but he needed to get his feet wet in a country he wasn't yet used to. Once he left his old firm, the clientele and goodwill he had developed followed him. With his savings, he was able to shape a firm that married the British and Nigerian ways of doing things. He valued his customers and made sure everyone affiliated with the firm did the same. He didn't care whether they came from wealth or not. Once they walked through the door, they were royalty. Years later he was one of the most expensive lawyers to retain, hence his pro-bono work and the requirement for those working for him to do the same.

———

A FEW HOURS LATER, EKENE WAS DEEPLY ENGROSSED IN THE papers in front of him when he heard a soft knock on his door. With a pen balanced behind his ear and one in his hand, he looked up to see one of the law clerks who had signed up to help this weekend, Rayowa Empiko. Ekene inwardly cringed, but his face held a smile. He didn't want to be alone with her today. And he wouldn't have been if Patrick, his assistant, hadn't called in an hour earlier due to a family emergency.

"Hello, Rayowa, how are you doing today?" Ekene asked.

He surveyed her attire which was inappropriate even for a casual Saturday. Like she always managed to do when she saw him, she lifted her hand and twirled one of the loose braids that had escaped the bun on her head.

Here we go.

"I'm doing fine, Sir. How are you? I'm here as promised to assist with the Tijjani case."

"I'm doing great, thanks for asking. And for sacrificing a few hours out of your Saturday to do this." Ekene stood. That was just the case he was working on, so it was perfect. But he was not about to sit with her in the close confines of his office and work on it with her alone. The office was expansive enough, but it was against his rule. Out of the corner of his eye, he saw her sit down and open the file she had in her hand.

"Let's move into the conference room. It's more spacious there. I can write on the board while you feed me the information on the Tijjani Estate.

"Oh, okay." Disappointment laced her voice.

The whisper of the Holy Spirit reminding him of that Proverbs 6:28 verse, asking him if he could walk on hot coals without his feet being scorched, made her feelings at that point irrelevant. His love life was a pseudo-nonexistent complicated mess, but he could manage that mess. Images from the movie, *Fatal Attraction*, set lightening under his feet as he headed out of his office to the biggest of the three conference rooms. He trusted himself wholeheartedly. It was the woman dressed in jeans that had too many rips in them and a flimsy blouse with a plunging neckline he didn't.

———

Two hours later, Ekene was ready to call it a day. What should have taken about four hours extended into seven, with Rayowa asking him questions he knew she probably knew the answers to. He stood and stretched his tired muscles.

"I think we're good for the day. First thing Monday morning, please get in contact with the IVF specialist and ask her if she would be willing to testify on the life span of frozen sperm. Prepare all the confidentiality papers just in case." He paused and rubbed his hand across his low beard.

"Yes, Sir." Rayowa stood and started gathering her notes. Once she had them in the folder, she began to stroll around the desk toward where he was. "Boss man, you didn't eat any lunch. I can order takeaway for you and I'll just wait until they get here, then leave."

Ekene shook his head slightly and declined. "Thank you. I have something at home. Besides I need to get going. I have a few stops to make."

"Are you sure?"

His stomach growled, betraying his confirmation. She giggled and flipped her hair back. Ekene clenched his jaw and slung his case bag over one shoulder. "I'll go pack up and we can leave." There was no need to keep indulging her. He returned to his office to grab his things. Minutes later, he made his way to his car after watching Rayowa leave. In that moment, he resolved to never be alone with her – unintentional or not.

Minutes later, Ekene reentered his car after picking up his order of *ayemase* and white rice from his favorite restaurant. He always told people that hadn't tried the dish that on a scale of one to ten, the spice was a twenty.

With the smooth melody of "Still the One" by Sauti Sol playing through his speakers, Ekene's mind went to his favorite attraction, Halima. Jide hit the mark when he said he no longer talked about her as a friend. They'd become very close during the time they worked on the DeSab case. They had traveled together for the initial mediation attempt. When that fell through, the actual court case spanned months. Rasheed was back by then, but the bond was already formed. During those months, they both realized they had a lot in common. Amazingly, chess and belonging to the same cycling club here in Lagos were among the few. In all of that, they still had never been on an official date.

Her physical beauty was like none he'd ever seen, but it was her insides that made him go crazy. She was kind, goofy, very charitable, demure, geekish and a homebody with a sense of style that would make top models bow. Ekene smiled remembering that time during Jabir's twins' birthday party that he saw her fiery side in action. Despite always being put together, she never let anyone intimidate her or walk all over her. Her brothers tried and she let them have their way most of the time, but when she put her foot down, they bowed to Hali's—as they called her—command.

They had debated faith a few times and she had asked him questions which he tried his best to answer. With their feelings growing for each other, he was very careful that he had the correct motive when it came to religion. He could see her curiosity for Christianity and sensed her battle to prove most of what he told her about Christ wrong. He wanted anything that would happen to be for the glory of God and not because she thought he would accept her more if she were Christian. He could now admit to himself he loved her, so her salvation meant more to him than his pleasure. However, he dared not get in the way of God's work.

Soon after, Ekene pulled into the entrance of his residence. With his initial thought of doing some woodwork shot, the only thing he wanted now was a meal, a shower and his bed.

Chapter 6

Halima threw her head back in laughter as Ekene told her about his day with Rayowa. Anytime she went to his office, the young lady always gave her the stink eye. She had told Ekene several times that she was out to get him for a husband, but he dismissed her.

"Red, it's not funny. That girl is just a baby and I'm tired of fighting off her not so subtle advances." Ekene's voice boomed through the phone's speakers.

"So, if she were of age, would that be okay?" Halima placed the device on the counter and took the broiled fish out of the oven.

Her mother had returned from the *nikah* of one of her friend's daughter with a headache and had gone to lay down while she prepared dinner. Halima knew that after the marriage ceremony, her mother would want to talk about how her own plans were coming along. Halima decided them talking over a quiet dinner would help the devastation of her decision.

"Ouch." Her finger accidentally brushed against the hot tray. She put it in her mouth.

"What's wrong?" he asked as his voice rumbled.

She ran her finger under cold water. "You…"

"Me? What did I do? I'm miles away from you."

"Your ridiculous story made me burn my hand." She chuckled.

"Sorry, Princess. You know if I was there, I'd kiss it and make it better."

"Hmmm, you see?"

"See what?

"Saying things like that is why people like Rayowa are after you." She laughed, poured the red stew sauce over the fish and placed it back in the oven.

"Ha ha. Quit it, that's not funny."

"Because she's a baby?"

"No, because she's not my type."

"What's your type?"

"Spoiled Princesses."

Halima stared at the phone. When he made declarations like that, he left her speechless. She dared not voice her thoughts. She was a coward, yes. So just like any other time, she changed the subject. "What does your faith say about marriage? Do you believe in soul mates?"

Halima heard Ekene's loud grunt. He knew she was betrothed to Danladi. He also knew she was having second thoughts. Like her brothers, he too had given up hope that she would stand up to Uncle Musa and her mother and tell them she didn't want to go through with the wedding. For that fact alone, he hated talking about marriage with her.

"Come ooooon, Kenny, answer me," she whined.

"Stop whining and don't call me that. I hate it when you do," he growled. "The last time I indulged you on this topic was… the last time. Unless you're telling me you're no longer being sold off," he snapped.

"Come on. Oh, and you do know I'm not scared of you."

"You might want to reconsider that stance, Princess. I keep telling you, don't make me act up. Kam has nothing on me."

Halima twisted her lips. That was kinda true, but Kamal still had him beat. She smiled as she recalled the Port Harcourt incident. They'd gone out to dinner after one of the mediation sessions. Ekene got a phone call, excused himself and at the same time, one random man thought it was a good idea to wander up to their table and try his hand. Ekene returned shortly after, his annoyance evident. It was when the man decided to grab her hand that she thought the vein in Ekene's neck would pop. Before she could form a complete thought, Ekene lifted the man straight off the floor. It was a move that had her pleading with him to let the man go while reminding him that he didn't want that kind of attention.

"Well…" his voice brought her out of her reverie.

"Jesus Christ gives us the perfect example of how a man and a woman should live as a couple. In sacrificial love, mirroring it to his sacrifice for the church. We believe marriage is a sacred covenant ordained by God. One man, one woman, as it was in the beginning." He hesitated, then continued. "Does that mean soul mate as we mean it today? The 'one'? I don't know. Even King Solomon that wrote the popular words, 'I have found the one my soul loves,' married other women. So obviously that lady wasn't 'the one.'"

"Hmmm." Halima's thoughts wandered off. This was one of the topics that looked fuzzy to her in her faith. Her number one problem was entering an arranged marriage. Christians did have arranged marriages, but something about being betrothed to a man who already had one wife no longer sat well with her.

"Talk to me. What's going on?"

"We'll talk when I get back. Meanwhile, tell me more about this man that froze his sperm, but his estranged wife is saying his current wife can't have it."

A few moments of silence passed before he started speaking. She knew he wanted to say more, but was thankful he didn't. Dipping her hands in the sink filled with soapy water, she listened as she washed dishes. There was no mistaking the passion in his voice as he proceeded to tell her about the Tijjani case.

The husband of his client knew he was dying of cancer, so he had his sperm frozen, with the intent that his wife could impregnate herself with it when she was ready and produce for him an heir. A short four weeks after his death, the clinic he used told her she needed to be ready in a month or they'd destroy or hand over the sperm to his childless, estranged wife.

Ekene explained that the woman was nowhere mentally, emotionally or professionally able to have a child and he was determined to ensure that her late husband's wishes were carried out.

Halima sucked her teeth. This was the kind of rubbish *wahala* polygamy caused. She had lived through it. Seen the toll it took on Eric's first wife and now this. Before now, she was ready to settle for the status quo in her life…but not anymore.

"So what if he didn't properly divorce the estranged wife? By society's standards, she was no longer his wife. The woman has even been living with another man. It should be the current wife's right to keep the sperm until she's ready, no matter how long that might be," he continued.

"I'm so proud of you. That woman would've been left out to dry because, more than likely, she has no one on her side," Halima said.

Her cheeks flushed as her mind wandered to how compassionate he was. It was one of the things that made him so sexy to her. She knew first-hand how much his retainer was, and he was doing all this without getting a kobo. As unprecedented as this case was, as soon as the first court date arrived, he'd also be the talk of the town.

"Thanks, Princess."

The doorbell rang and Halima trotted to the front of the house. She didn't bother with the peephole because if the person had passed the gate, they were good. She quickly wrapped a loose red scarf around her head and opened the door. The sight before her almost sent her into shock; Uncle Musa, and a few men she recognized as Danladi's uncles. Her eyes darted behind them to men, or rather teenagers, who carried gifts. For who? Certainly not her. She'd been prepared to break the news to her mother first and allow her to process it. Seeing this, she was going to look like the wayward daughter when she told all of them of her decision.

"Ermm, Kene, let me call you back."

"Is everything okay?"

"I'll let you know in an hour."

"Okay, one hour or I'm calling your brothers."

"One hour."

She ended the call and greeted. *"Assalamu Alaikum."*

———

"You cannot be serious!" Uncle Musa bellowed, pacing the room. "A'isha, I told you nothing good would come of any association with that Igbo woman and her bastard children."

Halima rolled her eyes at him referring to her brothers in a derogatory way. *Yeah, I wish you would call them that to their faces.*

Uncle Musa sounded all big and bad now but, he feared her brothers. Ever since Rasheed locked him out of the day-to-day knowledge of the company, his hate for them only grew. Halima had learned her lesson and stayed far away from him, only running into him on the rare occasion she visited Abuja. He was one of the reasons she made her mother visit her in Lagos instead.

Years ago, when it was only Rasheed in Nigeria, Uncle Musa continued and steadily increased his effort to discredit him. He spewed lies by way of media interviews to anyone that would listen. Rasheed being who he was, never let it bother him. All that stopped, however, the month Jabir and Kamal moved back home.

They didn't go looking for him, but the prime opportunity presented itself when they all, by sheer coincidence, met at the Sheraton hotel. Uncle Musa was there with some of his business associates while they were there for dinner. Halima recalled Kamal spotting him and immediately marching over. Naturally, Jabir and Rasheed followed. Although Halima couldn't hear what was being said, she enjoyed the squeamish look on Uncle Musa's face as Kamal took a seat and commandeered their uncle's friends who were enamored by the popular ex-soccer player. After several photos, he stood, towering over Uncle Musa who was still seated. Kamal smirked at him and bent to say something in his ear. From that day on, Uncle Musa was on mute when it came to her brothers. Unless like now, when they weren't around.

Her uncle's sandals clicked against the marble floor of her mother's spacious gold and white colored living room. He had been ranting like this for the last hour after she broke the news to him and Danladi's uncles that she was no longer interested in the union. As she expected, that didn't go over too well. They'd stormed out, warning her uncle to uphold the agreement his brother made to them years ago.

She had wanted to talk to her mother first. But as usual, Uncle Musa took it upon himself to bring the men to her mother's house without any kind of prior conversation. On second thought, she turned to her mother who was quiet on the sofa next to her and wondered if she was in cahoots with her uncle. Halima wouldn't put anything past her mother.

"They didn't put me up to anything. Instead, they've given me the strength to stand up for what I want. I want to be happy. I want to be courted." Halima was getting heated just thinking of the audacity of Danladi to be on holiday in Dubai with his first wife and their son while his uncles came to start the family introductions. The mere thought of it made her ashamed of herself. As did the fact that up until some months ago, she was willing to go along with it. Having a front-row seat to the way her brothers fought for what they loved and desired stirred something in her. Their willingness to go to the ends of the earth to please, protect, and provide anything that would put a smile on their wives' faces moved her. She wanted that. She needed it. She deserved it. And her brothers had made her see that.

"Halima, this was agreed upon by your father," her mother spoke.

"Father? A man I spent my whole life trying to please? Who made me feel grossly inadequate because he couldn't stand up for what he wanted?" Halima placed her feet on the floor, put her arms on her knees and turned in her mother's direction.

"Don't you dare speak about your father that way!" Uncle Musa thundered.

"I'll speak about him as I like. He was my father and I loved him dearly, but the truth is, your pressure and his weakness caused a lot of havoc. He didn't even deem it necessary to give me anything in his will."

"Is that what this is about?" her mother asked. "Is that why you don't want to obey his wishes?"

"Not the money, but the thought process behind it. Those same brothers you complain about have embraced me and would lay down their life for me in a minute. They have made me a very rich woman, but they've also taught me to never settle for less than I deserve."

"You are thirty-five Halima." Uncle Musa looked at her in disgust.

"And?"

"You need to get married. Danladi was chosen for you and you kept putting it off. Granted he was away for a while, but he's back, and he has been patient enough," her mother reasoned.

"I can't believe you, Mother. I thought you of all people would understand what I'm trying to say. Father was never truly happy with you. His heart belonged to another."

"Who does your heart belong to?" Uncle Musa asked.

Halima ignored him. No need aiding the heart attack she knew he would have if he could peek into her heart and see Ekene all over it.

"Mother, I'm not saying 'no' to marriage. I'm saying 'no' to an arranged one and to being second to any other woman."

"What do you mean? Our faith allows up to four wives. Your mother was a second wife…"

And we see how that turned out.

Her father still went back to beg for the forgiveness of his first wife and left the majority of everything he owned to the children they had together. Halima loved her brothers and although it took a while to get over the devastation of her father's actions, she had become wiser and gained so much more in her new family. Nevertheless, she wasn't ready to have her own children endure the same thing. Marrying Danladi would do that.

"I know what our faith allows, but it doesn't say it's required."

"Halima, you're not a young maiden. If you knew you no longer wanted Danladi, you should have spoken sooner. There are many other Muslim men out there. But who would want you now?" her mother's voice, though low, sent sharp darts into her heart.

Uncle Musa pulled off his cap and threw it on the couch in anger. "Aisha, *da gaske?*" He turned to her mother to ask of her seriousness in Hausa. "The way you're sounding, are you supporting her backing out of this arrangement."

Halima stood, having had enough. "Backing? Uncle, I have backed out. The only way I'm marrying Danladi is arms and legs bound and a cloth stuffed in my mouth."

"*Ban yi imani da wannan!* I don't believe this!"

"Uncle, *yi imani da shi.* Believe it." If it was something else her brothers taught her, it was to respect, but no longer fear their uncle.

Her uncle turned to her mother. If it weren't for the seriousness of the conversation, Halima would have chuckled at the shock that vibrated throughout his body at her defiance.

"Aisha, *ba za ku yi magana ba?* Won't you speak?"

"It's getting late. I'll talk to her."

Halima's eyes darted to the clock on the adjacent wall. It was almost ten p.m. She had to remind her mother, "Mother, please don't make any promises on my behalf. I know you think I'm washed up and can't attract anyone because of my age…"

"I didn't say can't attract…I mean—"

"What's all this attract business? You're only supposed to attract your husband." Uncle Musa paused. "That is why you wear the hijab, as a cover, a sign of modesty, not to attract the unwanted attention of other men."

"Uncle, that was what I was taught when I started wearing it when I was eleven. Then I had no say. Now I wear it as a political, social statement. Wearing it doesn't make me religious, it just makes me Muslim." The hijab to her was much more than her faith, it was her feminism and liberation from being judged according to her beauty or proportions of her body.

"*Wannan abin ba'a ne.* What? Oh, so living in Lagos and heading a division has made you bold. Don't forget, I still own shares in that company." He picked up his cap and rammed it on his head. He gave her and her mother an evil stare. "Be ready to marry Danladi in two months…" he walked to the door.

Halima stood with her weight on her left leg and arms folded across her chest, waiting for the conclusion of his threat. If she didn't know any better, she'd say he has a vested interest in her union with Danladi.

"Or else that clout and freedom you think you've gained will be a thing of the past." He opened the door, exited and slammed it so hard, a painting hanging on the wall rattled.

Halima took in a deep breath and turned to her mother. Her expression was blank. They'd always had a good relationship, but her mother was a traditionalist. And over time, their communication had been affected.

"*Yata, me ke gudana?*"

Halima had had enough for one night. So much was going on, but there was no point sharing tonight. That would be a battle for another day.

"Nothing's going on, Mother." A beat passed between them, the silence thick with tension. Halima needed to be surrounded by love. "I'll spend the night at my brother's house. I'll be back in the morning. We'll talk then."

Her mother sighed. "*Suna d'auke ku daga gare ni.*"

Halima trudged to where she sat and kissed her forehead. "No one is taking me away from you. You're pushing me away."

"How?"

"By once again, taking father's side over mine. Even in death, you can't disobey him to protect me?"

"Halima, *mahaifinka ya san abin da ya fi kyau.*"

"In my opinion, he never knew what was best for me. I'm just tired of keeping quiet about it. *Ina son ka uwa.*"

"*Ina son ku ma.* I love you, too."

Halima went up the stairs to pack an overnight bag. She dialed Ebele. It went straight to voicemail, so she tried Ibiso. She always asked her brother's wives before she came over. They were, after all, the real bosses of the house. On the third ring, Ibiso picked up.

"Hali baby, you forgot about me, *abi?*" Ibiso queried.

"Can I come over?" she asked in a near whisper.

"Of course. We're in Mama Danjuma's house now.

What's wrong? Hold on let me get Rasheed… hold on, okay." Halima sensed Ibiso's worry at her directness.

Seconds later, a deep voice took over the line, however, it wasn't Rasheed, but Kamal. "Lil sis, what's going on?"

"Please come get me." The tears she had been holding back threatened to overflow.

"Say no more." Kamal hung up.

Halima sat on her bed in defeat. She had to get her mind right. She'd also been having these dreams she'd told no one about. Everything was coming at once and she was about to lose her mind. At that moment, her phone started to ring. It was Ekene again and like the last five calls, she sent it to voicemail.

Chapter 7

Halima looked out the window with her mind in a riot as her brother drove down the streets of Abuja. It was late evening and the beauty of the city was illuminated by street-lights and the glow of the full moon. She missed the serenity of the city as it took a back seat to the bustle of Lagos. She felt her brother's stare but refused to look at him. Kamal had asked her if she wanted to talk and she'd declined. That's one of the things she loved about him. He loved having his way, but also knew when to back off. Once he made sure that she wasn't in any physical pain, he led her to the car and pulled out of her mother's driveway.

She thought about the events of the evening and was firm in her conviction that she had done the right thing. However, the pain in her mother's eyes didn't escape her. She had no idea if she was ready for the aftermath of what lay ahead.

When she decided to wear her hijab more liberally with some of her hair showing, she and her mother had gotten into an argument then. When she had questions about her faith compared to Christianity, she couldn't discuss it with her mom. She needed the advice of an older woman to help her sort out her thoughts. Big Mummy had always treated her like a daughter and although she never wanted to slight her mother by seeking outside advice, now she needed to for her sanity.

The ring of Kamal's phone brought her out of her reverie. She glanced over at him as he activated his Bluetooth.

"Hello," he answered.

He paused and turned to look at her. "Oh, hey Kene. Wassup man?"

Halima shook her head vigorously. She had a lot to sort through and talking to Ekene right now would complicate that. She'd apologize later, but now she couldn't talk to him.

"Yeah, she good. I think her mom pissed her off." He hesitated again. "I'll get her to call you tonight or tomorrow morning."

Halima couldn't make out what Ekene was saying, but from the contour of Kamal's brows, she knew that he was taking whatever Ekene was throwing at him because of her.

"Okay! I'll have her call you tonight. Now get off my phone." Kamal hung up the phone and let out an agitated breath. He glanced at her as they pulled up to his mother's house. Kamal put the car in park and turned to her.

"Hold on a second, Halima."

He had called her by her full name and that was never a good thing. She was in no mood to deal with the serious Kamal.

"Yes?"

"You have to give me something. I can't help or protect you if you don't tell me what's going on with you. Why did you leave your mom's house and why you got Kene breathing down my neck?"

Halima remained quiet. She rubbed on her earlobe and played with her fingers. How did she begin to articulate what she was unsure of?

"Come on. When have we never been able to talk to each other?"

"*Dan uwa na*…I'm not sure what's going on with me."

"Whatchu mean? Okay, just tell me why you had me come pick you up. Let's start from there."

"I was going to tell my mom that I was having second thoughts on marrying Danladi—"

"Second thoughts? I thought we agreed on the plane coming over you were going to tell her outright that you weren't going to marry him. Come on Hali, you've been feeling this way for at least four years. What's the problem?"

Tears rolled down her cheeks. Kamal lifted his hand and wiped them away. He drew her close for a hug. She held on to him tight. After a few seconds, she straightened her body and looked him in the eye.

"I mean I did tell them. But it's not as simple as you make it. I was born and raised Muslim. There are certain traditions that we have and are encouraged to keep. Our salvation depends on our good deeds outweighing our bad ones. Lately, I haven't been doing everything I should…"

"Does this have anything to do with Kene?"

"A little, I guess. Having you guys in my life these past years has opened my eyes up to things I wish I had known sooner. Before you all came back, it was just me. I did everything I was told, and I was content."

"Whatchu trying to say, Hali, that we corrupted you?" Kamal joked to lighten the mood.

"No, silly. The sense of family has given me new confidence to stand up for what I want. Not marrying Danladi, will bring shame to my mother. I'll be breaking Father's promise and Uncle Musa—"

"Uncle Musa? What does he have to do with this? Was he there with you tonight?"

Halima nodded and for the next several minutes, she told Kamal all that happened earlier. Every time she mentioned Uncle Musa's name, she could tell it bothered him.

"Why didn't you call me or Rasheed the minute they showed up at your doorstep?"

"Because I could handle it." Halima rolled her eyes.

"Okay, Miss Independent." Kamal raised his hands in mock surrender. "I don't know how many times I have to tell you that I really don't care how independent you want to be, I'm your big brother and will always be there to protect you. No matter what. Stop being so pig-headed."

Halima mushed his forehead and sniffed, drying her eyes. A beat of silence passed between them and he continued.

"Look Halima, I'll love you regardless of what you want to do. But I'm so proud of you for handling business tonight." He paused. "I won't pretend to know about your faith, but in mine, I have a God who loves me so much, He sent His Son to die for me. Man… that still gives me chills because, I won't even die for me." He placed his palm on his chest.

"My salvation doesn't depend on what I do. If that were the case, I'd come up short every single time. There's nothing, I repeat nothing, I can do in my own power to secure a place in heaven. Jesus' death is what reconciled me to the Father. All I have to do is confess that Jesus is Lord and trust Him with everything that concerns me."

"You see that's what I don't get. How could your Messiah be crucified? If He is anointed with the glory of God, how could He suffer? And die for three days." Halima shook her head.

Kamal laughed.

Halima frowned. This was why she hated asking Christians questions. They never took it seriously.

"Stop frowning. I laughed because I remember when I asked God to give me the wisdom to answer that question when someone asked it of me on one of my book tours."

Halima folded her arms waiting for a response.

"Look at it this way. If I take an empty jar and cover it, it has air inside. But the air is the shape of the inside of the container. Follow me. The air on the outside and the air on the inside are basically the same thing, just that the air inside has taken the shape of the jar. *Abi?*"

Halima bit her bottom lip and nodded.

Kamal continued, "If you smash the jar against the wall, the only thing damaged is the jar. The air would be untouched and just resume its shapeless nature."

"Okaaay…"

"When Jesus died on the cross, His body died, but the God in Him never died. He took the shape of a man, but was never only a man. He was also God. Remember, you told me that y'all go to Mecca and offer animals as a sacrifice, in remembrance of God rescuing the son of Abraham from death by offering a substitute? Well for us, Jesus is that Lamb of God who took our place. Why God did that, I don't know, but I'm so grateful."

Halima thought about it for a few seconds and what he said did make logical sense, but she still wasn't completely sold.

"Okay, I get it. Can we go in now?

"Not before you tell me if I have to have a talk with Kene." He stared at her.

Halima winked at him. "I don't know. Now let's—"

A knock on the window jolted her. She looked up to see Rasheed. His expression was a mix of worry and irritation and like a charm, her smile diffused it immediately. He pulled on the handle of the door and stretched out a hand to help her out.

"Good evening, brother."

"Are you okay?" he asked looking over her and ignoring her greeting.

"Yes, I'm fine."

"Okay, what took so long? The last time you and this one were gone this long, I had to call in our lawyer."

"That's your sister, the jailbird. That's a bad reflection on you, bro. For your baby sister to be in jail. Not a good look. You're slacking." Kamal teased as he locked the door and headed into the house.

With her mouth open, Halima watched Kamal swagger away like he just hadn't called her a jailbird. Rasheed took her bags from her and ushered her into the house.

"SoSo has been so worried. You coming with us or staying here?"

After talking to Kamal, she felt a little better, so she decided to go with her brother instead of staying with Big Mummy. "I'll go with you. Besides I want to spend some time with Yohance and Jumai before I leave," she replied, referring to Rasheed's kids

"Cool. We'll leave in a few." He opened the door. They strolled down the long foyer in silence and right before she got to the living room, Rasheed called her name. She turned to face him.

"Why is Kene calling me to ask if you are okay?"

Halima shrugged. "I don't know. Maybe he is worried about how the case is affecting me." She told him a lie that she was immediately ashamed of. Rasheed looked so much like their father and his cool, unfazed expression sometimes made her nervous. She had seen a side of him others rarely saw and that was when he was angry. However, nothing was going to make her share anything about Ekene with him. At least not now.

Rasheed grunted and his gaze penetrated her soul. "If you say so."

"I do."

———

"WE'RE ALREADY MID-YEAR. BEFORE YOU KNOW IT, THE END of the year will be knocking on our doors. Despite the excitement of the holiday season, there's still a group of us who have a hard time during the holidays. Others are feeling despondent at the close of another year without achieving what they set out to."

Halima cradled her eighteen-month-old niece as she sat in the pew of Overcomer's Chapel listening to their pastor. How she ended up here, she didn't have a good explanation. The morning had started with her niece's leg on her face and her nephew standing over her with a scowl on his. She'd gotten in the night before and after assuring Ibiso she was okay, she took a shower and was about to sleep when she heard her niece fussing. It was late and she wanted to give Ibiso and Rasheed some relief, so she offered to take her niece to her room. On seeing her, the little girl calmed down immediately and they fell asleep.

"Aunty Hali, why did you let only JuJu sleep with you?" her nephew questioned her without a greeting.

"Is that any way to greet?" Halima asked softly.

With the scowl still in place, five-year-old Yohance muttered good morning. He staked a serious claim over her. She had been around him all his life. Jabir's kids were born and partially raised in the United States, while Kamal and Ebele spent extra time in the UK before coming back with their twins.

"Come here, 'Hance." Halima beckoned. Her nephew grudgingly came to her and she hugged him tightly. "Remember I told you, you are the big man around here. JuJu is a baby. Besides I came in last night and you were asleep."

"Will you spend the whole day with us?"

Halima had really wanted to rest a little and go to her house to speak to her mother. She felt guilty about the way she'd left. The excitement in his eyes hypnotized her into agreeing. She didn't know then that it would start with church.

Shouts of "Yes, Lord" and "Speak it Pastor" brought Halima's wandering mind back to the present.

"Today I want to talk to the hurting and despondent

group. You might be feeling like life is hard, you've lost that enthusiasm or you're not moving ahead. Notice I used the word feeling because it's a sensation your mind entertains when it no longer has the will to do what it needs to do to overcome," the pastor continued.

Halima looked over to Ibiso and Rasheed. Their hands were intertwined as they listened attentively. Yohance, who pleaded, with his father to excuse him from children's church, sat to her left. The pastor strode to the middle of the church with his iPad in his hand. Halima shifted uncomfortably as he approached. She didn't wear her hijab, but she had her hair tied in an Ankara, red and brown print that matched her wrap-around dress of the same material.

Why was he coming next to her? Did he know she didn't belong here? He stopped just to the left of her, but looked around.

"So, did the man at the pool *feel*. Turn to John 5 and go to verses one to nine." He swiped the screen of his iPad. After a few moments, the pastor started to read about a man who had a condition and was stuck at the side of a healing pool for thirty-eight years. Until who they referred to as the Son of God, but she knew as a great prophet, approached him and asked if he wanted to be healed.

"Do you want to be healed?" the pastor asked.

There was murmuring in the church. Halima noticed a lot of people nodded their heads in assent.

"Come on church, we can do better than that. Do you want to be healed?"

This time there was a thundering yes.

Healed from what? Aren't they already healed to be in a church?

"To be healed, we have to regain our confidence in an unchanging God. Jesus already knew what the man wanted, but desired to work with him in partnership."

Halima pondered his statement. She wasn't paying full attention in the beginning, but now he had her attention. With the fact that the man had had his ailment for several years and she had been complacent in her life for almost as long, it seemed like the sermon was directed at her. At this late stage of her life, she was desperate to break out of the life that was laid out for her.

She was the Chief of Operations of a company that was worth millions. In the last seven years, she'd traveled far and wide, doing things she'd never imagined. Still the looming or formerly impending marriage to a stranger left her feeling unfulfilled. She was wise enough to know that Danladi and his family, and even hers, wouldn't roll over and accept her decision, but the sense of satisfaction she thought she'd feel breaking the news to them wasn't there.

"The man needed help. Jesus knew this, but he wanted to meet the man in his mind. He had to have the desire to be healed. He had to have the willingness to pick himself up. Once he acknowledged it, Jesus told him to pick up his mat and walk." The pastor paused for a few minutes. Halima assumed he wanted his authoritative point to sink in.

"My brothers and sisters, walking with Jesus doesn't make your problems disappear overnight. It does, however, give you the authority to fight. Because we know He is with us." The man paused. "Mathew 11:28-30 says, *'Come to me all you who are weary and heavy laden, and I'll give you rest.'* Find rest in Jesus today. He is our Salvation and the Truth. The only…only way to God our Father."

Halima felt a chill at those final words. That wasn't what she was taught. But it sure did sound good. And despite her desperation to deny it, she needed someone to cast all her burdens on. She was indeed weary.

Chapter 8

A few days later, Ekene was still seething. He tossed the phone on his desk and ran his fingers across his head. He stood, shoved his hands in his pockets and stomped to the windows in his office with a tense look on his face. Stopping short of being a stalker and flying to Abuja, he had done everything to get in contact with Halima, but he got her voicemail every time. She promised to call him back immediately after, but not only had she failed to do so, he knew she was aware that he was trying to contact her. There was no way that Rasheed or Kamal hadn't questioned her about him calling them.

The sun was setting over the city and the hues of orange and red showcased the magnificence of God's creation. Across the horizon stood buildings of varying heights and designs. On the ground, blaring of horns from the different modes of transportation signaling the chaos of rush hour. The city was in constant motion. Although he had relocated from London, which was equally as busy, Lagos took a lot of getting used to. One could easily get lost in the crazy momentum.

Crazy.

That word fit his past few days. For his heart at least. He

should have kept himself in self-preservation mode as he had since he first met Halima. He was doing good. Loving her from afar kept his head on straight. He was sure that if he couldn't be with the one he loved, he would find one to love. But life wasn't working out that way for him.

He returned to his desk, sighed deeply and began to pack up his laptop. He was no longer any good for work and there was no need staying at the office longer than necessary. He wondered how long he would be able to keep away from her. His initial anger kept him from going to Abuja, but as the days passed, the fire turned into a painful ache in his heart. The familiar pain was one he'd never wanted to experience again. The last time, he almost didn't survive.

A few hours later, Ekene found himself navigating his car down a road he'd told himself he never would. He was listening to a leadership podcast and the host, who was a Christian, happened to be talking about pride and leadership. The guy was teaching that their entanglement with ego can lead to arrogance. The man used the story of Dinah, Jacob's daughter. He said that just like a good team can be destroyed by the pride of its leader, the actions of Jacob's sons destroyed something good.

The podcast made Ekene think of how a forbidden romance could be destroyed. He wasn't even thinking about her brothers, but his own pride. That led him to turn his car around and drive to Halima's house. He knew she was back from Abuja. Although it pained him to do, he was waiting for her to come to him or at least reach out. The time he'd given her had just run out.

———

"What do you mean you've been attending church?" Kudirat shrieked.

Halima adjusted the volume on her ear pods, unlocked the

front door of her house and entered. She kicked off her shoes and sunk her feet into the deep, cream carpet.

Kudirat Bashir, her closest childhood friend, had just returned from completing her master's program in Business in Aberdeen. Kudi, as she called her, was from a more modest background and was rooted in their faith. They met in secondary school. Unlike other girls who shied away from Halima because of her background, but preferred to tease her instead, Kudirat embraced her. They gravitated toward each other when Kudirat inserted herself in the middle of a fight she was having with another girl in their boarding school. She got right in the middle of them and put a good old-fashioned beating on the biggest one of them all. Although she and Halima had ended up with one week of kitchen duty, no one ever messed with Halima again and their friendship grew.

Kudirat was married to a fine Muslim man, Ibrahim. Her family had arranged the marriage for her. Lucky for her though, she was his first and only wife. And although they weren't affectionate in public, Halima saw true love glow between them. The success of her marital arrangement made Kudirat an even greater believer in the process. So much so that she had opened an Islamic Marriage Bureau in Kaduna. Her company, named Amongst Ourselves, was dedicated to helping Muslim families find mates for their loved ones.

At first, Halima thought the idea was ridiculous, but she was the most sought-after matchmaker in the country within the Islamic community.

"You missed the word 'sometimes'?" Halima responded.

"Who cares about that word? What carried you there in the first place? What happened to Danladi? Are your brothers forcing you to change your faith? *Haba* Halima!" Kudirat's voice dripped with agitation and fear.

Halima dropped her bag on the couch and walked into the kitchen. Her flight touched down in Lagos earlier today and she headed straight to her office. She had several meetings and things to catch up on after staying in Abuja for four extra days. Part of the reason she waited was to talk to her friend. However, she'd moved her flight and Halima had to return home. Hearing her almost having a conniption over the phone made her glad they weren't having this conversation in person.

"You know, more than anybody, how my brothers are. So leave them out of this." Halima opened the fridge and stared into the half-empty appliance. Staying with Ibiso was a setup. She'd eaten an assortment of delicacies at any time of the day, giving her the illusion of a five-star hotel. Halima loved to cook, but rarely had time for it. She regretted her decision of not stopping to get dinner. Now she would have to go back out.

"I know, I know. I'm just trying to make sense of it all," Kudirat said.

"There's nothing to make sense of. That's why I haven't said anything to you. I knew you would jump to trying to fix me instead of listening to what is going on."

A beat of silence passed between them while Halima took the stairs and headed to her bedroom to change out of her red pantsuit. There was a Rice Palace nearby. The eatery was new, and she loved it. The chef prepared a wide variety of rice dishes. Any combination you wanted, they had it. Her mouth salivated at the thought of native palm oil rice, loaded with dry fish and assorted meats.

"Okay, I'm sorry. I'm just shocked. I thought you and Danladi were okay..."

"How can you think that? You were the one I complained to that he rarely comes to see me. Sometimes I think I'm supposed to be getting married to his assistant or driver."

"But—"

"But nothing. We're not all as lucky as you are Kudi." Halima looked into her closet and brought out grey leggings and a knee-length, button-down, baby blue shirt.

"Hali, but what changed? He's been that way for years and you were going ahead with the *nikah*?"

"I went along with it because, on some level, I didn't think I deserved better."

"Okay, I get that...a little. Do you want me to put you in my database and see if we get a match?" Kudirat asked. The hesitation in her voice indicated she wasn't done with her thought. "It's the church part I don't understand."

*There it is...*Halima laughed. "No, I do not want to be one of your lab rats..."

"My clients aren't experiments," Kudirat snapped.

Halima laughed again. "Okay, if you say so."

"I do."

"Okaaay. *Yi hakuri*. I'm sorry." Halima changed. She looked at herself in the mirror and frowned at how awful her red hajib clashed with her clothes. She removed it and replaced it with a black scarf. Satisfied, she hurried back down the stairs. Her stomach growled. It was time to wrap up this conversation.

"Remember I told you when I went to pick up my nephew from church a while ago?"

"Yeah."

"Well, I heard something that day and became curious. So, I researched, and my curiosity as they say, killed the cat. I became enthralled with the Book. Especially that Old Testament. It makes the drama we had in boarding school look like a child's play," Halima chuckled.

"It's not funny, Hali—"

"Calm down. You act like I just told you I was converting. Being around my brothers and their wives has opened my eyes. I do want the kind of love they have. Danladi is not that for me."

"I will pray to Allah especially for you because you're scaring me. I like your brothers, but I was so afraid something like this would happen, especially when you said you were becoming a liberal progressive."

Halima paused in thought. "Speaking of sects. Do you know that they have only one way to God…their God?" Her mind went back to the message she heard on Sunday. "It's so different from us who have different sects as a result of the confusion of who succeeded Prophet Muhammed."

"*Haba*, Halima. How deep are you?"

Halima giggled because her friend was in full throttle panic mode. When she discovered Ekene, there was no telling how she would react. Her chest tightened at the thought of him.

Avoiding him this past week hurt, but it was necessary. She knew he was pissed and worried, but she needed a clear head to figure out a way forward. Her life was complicated, and she had to detangle it before contacting him. Communicating with him amid what she went through these past couple of days was bound to cloud her thinking. It was the key reason she avoided him for two months prior. With a clearer head, she was now ready to face him. She would have called, but she wanted to see every reaction that crossed his face as she talked to him. The cycling club would be the perfect place Saturday morning.

"Halima Danjuma?" Kudirat snapped.

"Huh? Why are you calling my full name?"

"Because I've been asking you a question, but you wandered off. Hmmm. Is it another man?"

Halima rolled her eyes and shook her head. "Why does it have to be a man? Maybe I'm bored with this your talk."

"Well, until I get my answers you're stuck. Hang up and I'll call you back or better yet, pop up in Lagos." Kudirat sucked her teeth. "Now answer me."

"What was the question?"

"I said, how deep are you?"

"Huh?"

"Why do you know that the prophet Jesus is the only way to God? I hear them say that, but why are you even comparing it to our sects?"

Halima shrugged. "I mean… we have many sects? Why?"

"They have many types of churches, don't they?"

"Yes, they have many denominations, but all their denominations believe the same thing. Jesus is the only way to God."

"The question would be, why is it that their God will have only one way to get to Him?" Kudirat sassed. "There are different types of people; color, race, class…why would He give only one way to get to Him?"

"When I asked my sister-in-law, Damisi that same question, she answered me with a question—"

"Hmm." She scoffed. "What did she say?"

"If you let me finish… She answered by asking me how a God Who is so holy gives us anyway to have a relationship with Him at all." Halima remembered asking the question some months ago on their way back from the women's group she frequented. The glee on Damisi's face was contagious as she described how loving and kind God was.

"*Haba* Halima. *Ina tsoro.*"

"Why are you afraid?"

"Are you listening to yourself? You are using words like us and we."

Halima was about to reassure her friend that she wasn't leaving Islam any time soon. Just as that thought crossed her mind, a chilling breeze swept over her and she heard the words "*Do you want to be healed?*"

She closed her eyes and shook her head to make sure she wasn't hearing things. Before she could convince herself, she wasn't hallucinating, her doorbell rang.

"Who is that? Isn't it late?" Kudirat asked.

The question caused Halima to look at the time. It was a little after eight in the evening. That meant she'd been subjected to Kudirat's interrogation for over an hour.

"It is late, Mother." Sarcasm dripped from Halima's voice as she approached the door. Kudirat was one month older than her, but the way she acted one would think her seniority was by several years. Halima checked the peephole and her breath caught in her chest, causing her to gasp.

"Who is that?"

"Ermm…Kudi…let me… call you back."

"Since when did you start stuttering? Halima, who's that?"

"Halima." Ekene's voice thundered through the door. "I know you're in there. You got two minutes to open the door."

He had called her actual name. *Yep, he's angry and this time, he's justified.*

She needed to dismiss her nosy friend. "My regards to Ibrahim—"

"Nope, this isn't happening. I'm going to search for some suitors for you in my database tonight. You will not bring shame to your family's name with whoever is visiting you at this time in Lagos."

"Kudi, goodnight. *Ina son ku.*" Halima ignored her friend's rant as she prepared mentally for what awaited her on the other side of her door. She hung up and took in a deep breath.

"Halima!"

Halima opened the door. Ekene's face was smoldered underneath his stony expression, his rage evident. She was tempted to close the door in his face when she inhaled the aroma of native palm oil rice. Mentally weighing her options, Halima decided he could say what was on his mind as long as she was eating when he did.

Chapter 9

Ekene, not trusting himself to speak, stepped into Halima's home and closed the door behind him. This was his second time in her house, but the first time alone. As he remembered, the fragrance of what he now knew was lavender potpourri permeated his nostrils. The sweet aroma that calmed him the first time did nothing for his current mood.

He moved toward her and she took a step back. *She's cautious…good.*

He would never hurt her, but right now, he needed her to know without him saying a word that freezing him out was no longer acceptable. And he dared anyone, even her, to challenge him. Playtime was over; now he was fighting for keeps. As his car ate up the road on his way here, the stronger he became in his conviction to make her a permanent part of his life.

In tension-filled silence, he stared at her. She bit her lip and slanted her head to the side. The way her smooth, fair-skinned complexion glowed, and her smoky eyes returned his gaze angered him. How dare she be so calm, and he was losing his mind? The things she did to him with her eyes should be outlawed. He was mad and there was no pretending about it, but he knew he had to handle Halima with care. He'd be delusional to claim to understand all that was at stake for her. But still, he needed answers.

"Really?" he asked her, walking toward the kitchen.

Her light footsteps followed behind. If he wasn't so upset, he'd laugh at how easy and well-controlled her strides were. But he knew better. She wasn't about to play him like her brothers.

"I'm sorry?" she asked.

Not looking her way, he responded. "Not good enough. Explain." He placed the bags of food on the marble covered island in the middle of her kitchen and began opening cabinets. "Plates?"

"Top right."

He brought out two plates and rinsed them off in the sink. Drying them, he dished their food, but noticed she was still silent.

Ekene placed both hands on the island and stared into her face. She lowered her head, a motion he knew wasn't out of shyness, rather based on how she grew up. It was a sign of respect for the male. He hated it. He needed his woman to look him in the eye.

His woman. *Boy, she got me twisted.* He understood it, but now wasn't the time. He used his index finger to lift her head. Normally, he wouldn't touch her. It took the strength of a thousand men and the fact that she belonged to another to hold him back every time he was near her. Now, until she told him otherwise, all subtleness was out the window.

"Halima now is not the time to go mute on me. Why haven't I heard from you in a week, despite my numerous calls? You had to know...no, you did know I was worried about you. Why did you treat me with no regard? Do I mean so little to you?" He threw out question after question. They had floated in his head for a week. Now he needed them in hers and answered.

"Kenny, just give me a minute—"

"No, you don't get to use a nickname I despise at a time I'm liable to break something."

She stared at him wide eyed. "I've never seen you like this before."

"Get used to it if you don't give me the answers I seek."

Halima remained silent. Ekene stood with his arms across his chest and waited. He looked at her and the food he had just dished. It was going to get cold, but there was always the microwave.

"Okay, I know you have every right to be upset. I'm sincerely sorry. I just needed time."

"Why?"

"Things are fuzzy for me right now."

"How?"

She remained silent. A beat passed between them.

"How?" Ekene repeated, his posture never changing.

She tugged on her earlobe through her scarf.

Gosh, she's beautiful, he thought. But he quickly got himself together. "Halima…"

"Okay, okay…"

"You, us, Danladi, Islam, Christianity, what the future holds, my place in it…"

Ekene saw the tears glazing over her eyes. She did possess the Danjuma stubborn streak and knew she wouldn't allow them to fall. He was torn between grabbing her in his arms and allowing her to put her emotions in words. What she had just said was a mouthful of information that he wasn't sure how to unpack. Neither did he want to interfere in the expansion of her thoughts.

"Tell me." Ekene turned back to the food and put the plates one by one into the microwave. His heart rate doubled at the mention of him and her use of the term "us" but when Danladi entered the mix, the plummet felt real and painful.

Over the next couple of minutes, as they ate, Halima proceeded to summarize her conversation with her uncle and her mother over her now invalid arranged marriage. The joy he felt, he couldn't physically express because he heard the conflict in her voice. Just like Jide had said and he also noticed, he had observed changes in her. So, her refusing to marry the Danladi fellow was no surprise. However, he also knew how important her mother and her faith were to her. Her family's name. The only difference now was that she was struggling to reconcile her happiness and freedom with living up to an expectation that had been laid out for her over decades.

"All my life, I spent living up to an unrealistic expectation. I tried so hard to please my father. The need grew when I found out that I had brothers at thirteen. When I was young, I saw the way his eyes would grow weary every time he talked to Big Mummy, trying to get my brothers to talk to him, but they would all refuse." Halima propped her elbow up on the table and rested her chin in her palm. "So much of the hatred I had for Rasheed was misdirected. In my mind, every time he frustrated or made Father so mad, I'd go out of my way to do something to try and make it better. Try to get him to see that I was still his child. The betrothal, the wearing of the hijab. I wasn't ready for any of it, but I went along with everything."

"You can't blame yourself for the past. You can only correct the future," Ekene encouraged.

"And that's what I'm trying to do. All my efforts in trying to please Father proved futile, even in death. This might sound extremely bad, but his death gave me the best gift I could ask for. My brothers. Getting to really know and love them has been the best thing for me. But still, I feel so guilty…dirty for trying to live for me."

Ekene desired nothing more than to wrap her in his arms and make it all better. But he still had to make one thing clear.

"Red," he called to her softly. "I hear you and, believe it or not, I understand. However, shutting me out is unacceptable. You have to promise me you won't do that anymore."

She nodded her head.

"No, baby girl, I need you to say the words. I don't care if you don't want to talk, but you can't shut me out. Not anymore. You're allowed to be mad, angry, even frustrated, but I need to know that. I was kept in the dark and it nearly drove me insane."

"I promise and I did say I was sorry." She twirled her food around with her fork. "Every man in my life seems to be angry with me."

"I'm glad I'm one of the men in your life." He smirked. "However, let's clarify. I'm the most important one."

"Please don't let my brothers or worse, Yohance, hear you say that." She giggled.

Ekene grunted. "I can handle your brothers. And I'll just buy 'Hance a new game. He'll be cool."

"Handle my brothers, huh? Ooh, that would be interesting."

For the next few minutes, they ate their food in a mixture of comfortable silence and idle talk.

"Finished?" Ekene asked, reaching for her plate.

Halima nodded. He took their plates to the sink and discarded their scraps while she packed up the rest of the food into smaller plastic containers. He stood at the sink with hands under the running water while his thoughts were on a race of their own.

Her words had sunk in. Although Rasheed was his best friend and he got along well with the twins, he also knew how protective they were of her. He also knew their feelings about Danladi. Ekene had only seen the man in passing once, but knew Kamal couldn't stand his guts.

Would 'Sheed think I'm not good enough for his sister? Nah.

Kamal would be a tossup. He didn't only dislike Danladi because Halima would've been a second wife, but because he was marrying his sister period. Jabir, he couldn't read yet. However, he would face them head-on. As he fought the imaginary battles with his hands covered in soap suds, he smiled.

He had temporarily forgotten that although she had left Danladi, she was still a Muslim who didn't believe in the Lord. He loved her but wondered if it was smart to have a relationship with her since he wouldn't have the option to do life with her. He could if he wanted to, but what type of home would he have? Christian and Muslim? What about their kids?

Ekene glanced over his shoulder and saw Halima deeply engrossed in a book. She was forever reading. Her introversion was characteristic of someone who grew up in seclusion for most of her life. He dried his hands and stared at her a little longer. She lifted a cup of tea to her lips and took a sip. She loved teas and coffees. He'd dare say she was addicted.

"What are you reading over there?"

She looked up and her dark, smoky eyes caused his heart to skip a beat. *Seeking Allah, Finding Jesus* by..." She turned the cover of the book, "By Nabeel Qureshi."

His eyes bugged. So many questions flooded his mind, but his mouth felt as though it held a ball of cotton.

"Good read?" Was all that spluttered out of him.

She shrugged.

He'd never heard of the book. Ekene sauntered over to her and kissed her on her forehead lightly. It wasn't where he wanted to place his lips, but patience was a virtue. "Come walk me out."

"You're leaving already?"

"Yeah, just came over to feed you and set you straight." He winked at her. She chuckled but he was serious. Grabbing his keys and jacket, he headed to the door with her at his side.

"Lock up and…" he motioned his head toward the book in her hand. "Let me know if you have any questions?"

Ekene started the car and "Nara" by Tim Geoffrey and Travis Scott began to play. As he backed out, he nodded to the beginning lines of the song and gave a silent praise. Despite the unspoken acknowledgement of their feelings, Ekene was bent on not pressuring her about her faith. He prayed for God to work that out if it was in His will. However, there was nothing in his prayer that said he wouldn't help her "find Jesus" if she needed him to. He made a mental note to look up and order the book when he got home. If she was rolling, he was riding. At the end of the day, Jesus would prevail.

Chapter 10

"I see you've been doing a lot of practicing." Out of breath, Halima alighted from her Schwinn Gold Cruiser Bike.

While they worked on the DeSab LLC case, before her two-month disappearing act, Ekene had introduced her to the sport of cycling. He loved the pastime, and on his desk stood miniature black and white bicycles. His key chain was also a bicycle. The cycling club was based in Ikeja and they rode specified routes every Saturday. She too had come to enjoy it. It was very diverse, with many expatriates, and included people from all walks of life.

Ekene laughed as he got off his bike. "You would've known that if you weren't running from me." He wiped his face with his hand towel and tossed a cold bottle of water her way.

Halima caught it, twisted off the cap and raised it to her lips. Before he popped up two days ago, she'd already decided to stop running. She tugged on her suit. The new grey Nike hijab sportswear was cute when she put it on in the morning, but now, she needed it off. The Lagos heat was no joke.

Ekene rolled their bicycles to the corner of the clubhouse where the club held its meetings and leaned them against the wall. She walked ahead of him as he opened the door to the air-conditioned space.

"I didn't run," she whispered.

"Race, sprint, dash, scuttle, scamper…whatever you want to call it. That's what you did, Princess."

"You do know I can't stand you sometimes." Halima sat in the chair he pulled up.

"That's what you like to think." He sat next to her and she was about to respond when the gavel starting the meeting sounded. She was getting better with her comebacks, thanks to Kamal, but with Ekene there was never any winning.

"Whew, that was a good work out this morning," the president of the club said.

Everyone cheered. Halima glanced at Ekene and saw his dimple on display. Of the things he loved, this was where she saw him happiest. She'd longed to know the story behind it but never asked.

"We are already in the summer season and a lot of our sponsors will be leaving the country on holidays. We need to get the logistics tight for our charity event," the president said.

"I thought we agreed on Kit Collection," one man asked.

"Kit *ke*? What will people do with kits nowadays?" A woman asked. "People will prefer stuff that is tangible for everyday life. That should be where we focus our energy."

"I agree," said another woman. "We're approaching the second week in July, so we should plan fast, so we'll have things set before kids return to school in September."

Halima nodded her head.

"Are you going anywhere this summer?" Ekene whispered to her as the others went back and forth.

"No, not this year." August every year, she and her mom left for South Africa where her dad left her a house. They holidayed there until mid-September. It was her time to get away from work and just relax. They'd start in South Africa, but end up in Europe before coming back home.

"Why? What's up."

"I'll be with my brothers at their mother's."

"For real?"

"Yes, this year, Big Mummy's church is giving her an honor called *Ezi*... I forgot the name," Halima said, in a hushed tone.

Ekene smiled. "*Ezinne* of the Catholic Women's Organization."

"Yep, that's it. That's where I'll be. What is it? Kammy was about to explain one day, but got sidetracked as usual."

"Yes! Yes! That's a very good idea. I know vendors will jump at the chance," a man across the room said.

The rest of the club members clapped and Halima and Ekene looked at each other puzzled.

"You always distract me," Ekene whispered close to her ear.

Halima giggled.

"When I lived in Atlanta, there was this family that did it every year during Christmas and Thanksgiving," one of the members said. "We can use the same concept, but do it as a back-to-school drive. Since we're a small club, we can't do it on a large scale, but we can ask for sponsors. Every little bit counts." His eyes beamed with pride.

"I agree. So, all in favor of getting a venue where we'll provide medical checkups, dental care, makeovers and a lunch for two homeless shelters, say aye," the president said.

"Aye," the club members thundered.

"Okay, good. We'll have a signup sheet for those who want to join the planning subcommittee."

Ekene lifted his brow.

She shook her head. "I can't be part of a subcommittee, but I'll do what I can. Remember, I have to plan the Danjuma Group Employee Conference/Dinner. This year I'm hosting it here in Lagos."

Ekene nudged her with his shoulder. "Check you out."

Minutes later, the meeting adjourned and some of the members filed out of the building while others hung around to talk. Halima and Ekene stopped to acknowledge a few people before they left the clubhouse. They both took their bicycles from against the wall and wheeled them to where their cars were parked.

Ekene had put on his Ray Ban shades and she followed suit with her dark sunshades. They got to his car first and he put his bicycle in the trunk. Seconds later, he took her bicycle from her and wheeled it to her car. She popped the trunk and he put it in.

"No Abubakar?" He asked.

"He really isn't supposed to follow me everywhere, mostly travel. Besides, I knew you'd be here."

Ekene escorted her to the front of the car and opened the door. She sat with her legs on the side steps of her vehicle while he leaned on the open door.

"So, you got a date for the dinner?"

"I'll be working. I don't need a date," Halima responded.

"Are your brothers bringing their wives?"

"Err yes…"

"Did what's-his-name escort you last year?"

"Ha! Petty much? Yes, Danladi went with me."

"So again, I ask, who are you going with?"

Halima removed her shades. She intended to see his eyes, but he still had his glasses on. Halima stood and raised her hand to remove his glasses. She tried to read his expression, but it was blank. It was the same look on Rasheed that irritated and intimidated her sometimes. So just like she did with her brother, she decided to have fun.

"Um, I have this—"

"Who? Are you still in contact with Danladi?"

"Danladi is not the only man on the planet. You do know that, right?"

"Yes, I do, but you haven't answered my question. Has he

contacted you?" Ekene was staring at her like he knew the answer.

But he couldn't know that since she got back from Abuja, Danladi had called her several times, at first asking for an explanation, then pleading before finally resulting to threats and rage. No, he couldn't know that. Nobody did.

"Halima?"

"Yes, Ekene?" She raised her brow.

"Tell me."

"Whether I'm going with anyone or whether Danladi has contacted me?"

"Both and stop playing with me."

He was getting way more serious than she wanted. She looked beyond him to the parking lot. Their cars were the only ones left.

"Would you go with me?" She teased him, blinking her eyes rapidly.

"Nice try. Now answer my question. Has he contacted you?"

Halima nodded. Ekene's jaw clenched and his eyes turned into slits. "Calm down, Danladi is harmless. I was going to marry him a few short weeks ago."

"I don't care if you were going to marry him yesterday. If he contacts you again, let me know. You were betrothed to him for too long for him to just walk away. A man in his position would go to any lengths to make sure you uphold your end of the arrangement."

"*Haba*! Not you, too. What happened to me being able to take care of myself?" She placed her hands on her hips.

"I know you heard when I said that, if you're in danger, all that 'I can take care of myself' talk goes out the window." His brows furrowed.

Halima rolled her eyes and turned around to get back into the car. He had just taken a playful moment and turned it into something else.

"You're a brat. You know that, right?" He smiled and brushed the tip of her nose with his index finger.

"I'm not. Can I go now?" she asked.

"Yep. Wind the window down first."

Halima did as she was told. He put her seat belt on, closed the car door and leaned against the door frame. Halima feigned annoyance and struggled to keep herself from looking at him.

"I like your bratty ways, so it's all good." He paused and Halima turned to him. "Does your faith allow dating?"

She hesitated. The Sunni sect her father raised her in didn't forbid dating, although there were parameters. With a non-Muslim, it wasn't advised. But she'd been doing a lot of things that weren't advised recently. Which was one of the reasons, she was considering taking off the hijab. She felt she was disrespecting what it stood for. It was more than a sign of modesty; it was a commitment. One she found herself breaking mentally as each day passed. She never wanted to disrespect it, but she wanted to experience and go on new adventures. She'd been struggling with the decision.

"Yes, but within limits," she answered.

"Well, so does mine. So, will you go on a date with me Princess?"

"Depends."

"On what?"

"If you apologize for calling me a brat." Halima pouted.

Ekene laughed and stood to his full height. "Not a chance. I'll pick you up at seven."

Halima narrowed her eyes at him.

"Is that supposed to scare me? I see I have my work cut out for me." He shoved his hands in the pockets of his track pants. His muscled shirt had wet patches from sweat and the water he poured over his head earlier.

Halima grunted and started her car. She wasn't going to get a different response from him, and she needed a shower.

He stepped back and she pulled off. Inwardly, her heart leaped for joy. They were going on their first official date.

———

Halima stared at her reflection in the mirror, something she'd been doing for the last several minutes. Compunction and assurance played a game of tug of war in her head. She'd gotten home earlier after leaving Ekene. Not wanting to make a second trip out, she stopped at the market to stock her fridge back up. Still floating on clouds, she cooked and cleaned while talking to Damisi on the phone. She loved all her sisters-in-law, but she and Damisi were the closest. The fact they both lived in Lagos played a huge part in their dynamic.

Damisi had been on her way to interview a woman who was convicted of killing her twin boys in a suicide attempt for her *Woman at the Well* show. She needed some advice on trying to stay as neutral as possible. Even though she had a full-scale team, Damisi always ran the questions by Halima, especially in difficult cases. After reassuring her she'd be okay, Halima took a nap and an hour later, with India Arie's "He Heals Me" playing in the background, she soaked in a coconut milk bath, and then took a quick shower afterward.

The song, despite her initial internal battle, now had a dual meaning for her. The question *"Do you want to be healed?"* had been reoccurring in her dreams. The song was no longer reserved for Ekene but made her think of the claim of the unconditional love of their Christ. That was what prompted her to buy the book she was currently reading. She wanted to see how the people of the Book were able to convert the author of the book, who was formerly Muslim. Did he ever feel what she'd begun to feel?

Despite her confidence a while ago about life and the decisions she was making, as she stared at her freshly curled hair, made up face and peach flirty jumpsuit, her poise began to dwindle. Her inward tussle was in huge contrast to her outward appearance.

Her mother's disapproving face flashed before her. Halima glanced at the clock on her dresser. Ekene would probably be on his way. She could pretend to be sick. Or just not answer when he pressed the doorbell. She contemplated taking off her strappy sandals.

It's only a date. I'm not marrying the man. She chided herself. She let out a deep breath. As far as she knew, she wasn't marrying anybody any time soon.

She shook her head to dismiss her doubts. One by one, she put on the African-themed wristlets and rings she always wore on her fingers. Every finger got one. She was obsessed with rings. Indecision continued to sour her mood. She would be judged by her bad deeds versus her good deeds. How many good deeds had she done lately?

Do you want to be healed? Free from the yoke of slavery? She heard again, but never had the question come with that last part. She furrowed her brows as she looked around the room.

Her doorbell rang. A decision had to be made. She'd longed for this for years, but never saw it as possible. Now that it was, she was no longer sure she should go on the adventure. It would be one of a lifetime, but was it worth her soul?

The doorbell rang again. On autopilot Halima stood, wrapped her hair in a bun and put on her head covering. She picked up her light cover and went downstairs. She'd already agreed to go out, so quickly decided to keep her word. She placed her hands on the doorknob, sucked in a deep breath and exhaled a labored one.

The masculine, sandy scent of his cologne hit her immediately she laid eyes on him. For the seconds that followed her breath was caught as she took him in. Ekene had on a grey, casual linen suit with a white tee. On his feet were white Air Jordans, while his wrist and ear were adorned in his usual jewelry; a watch and a diamond stud. From the look on his face, he appreciated her style.

Halima was brought out of her gaze when she felt his hand caress her face. She moved to the side and he stepped into the house.

"You wore it different. Why?" Ekene questioned, referring to her head covering. She could sense the concern in his voice.

It wasn't as tight and showed more of her hair than normal. Halima rubbed her earlobe and lowered her head. "It had nothing to do with you. Everything to do with me."

He lifted her chin and stared into her eyes. "Okay, I'll take that…for now." His eyes raked over her. She felt the temperature in the room rise. "You do know that I'd never want you to change anything about you for me."

"I know," she said lowly.

"Good. You look amazing. You ready to have some fun?"

She lifted one brow at him. "People that don't drink tea or coffee cannot be trusted, so I don't know your definition of fun yet." She grinned.

Ekene chuckled and ushered her out of the house. He locked the door and returned the key to her. "You don't trust me, huh?"

"Not with fun, but I like you, so let's go."

"You like me. Let's explore that." He opened the car door and she got in.

"I put my foot in my mouth with that one."

"Sure did, Princess. Now we're gonna talk about it…all the way to the theatre." He closed her door and trotted to the driver's side.

Halima looked on the dash and saw tickets to the musical *Moremi*. This man knew her so well. She loved Nigerian history about strong women warriors. She lived vicariously through them because, until recently, she dared not be like them.

"So, about that liking me thing…tell me." Ekene smirked as he clasped his seat belt.

Halima rolled her eyes at him. "These tickets say eight o'clock. Drive."

He glanced over at her before pulling off. She knew him well enough for her to know that a reprieve now didn't mean he wasn't getting his answers later.

—————————————

Chapter 11

—————————————

Ekene had to keep reminding himself their safety was paramount because he kept stealing glances at her instead of focusing on the road. He knew she hadn't meant for him to see it, the uncertainty in her eyes, but he had. His heart longed for this, but now, he couldn't help but wonder if it was a good idea. The loss of his mother taught him to love hard and cherish the moments that he got. He probably misread the signs, but he now wasn't sure she was ready for them to get close.

For the last two days, they'd communicated daily for almost hours at a time. Or briefly between meetings. He'd concluded that she had the ability to make him lose focus. The feelings he had reminded him of why he stayed away so long. Now they were going on their first date and the doubt he saw in her eyes had him worried.

She looked beautiful. Her jumpsuit showed her perfectly shaped curves. Her well-manicured toes colored in light pink sent a tingling sensation up his spine. Her face wore light makeup and her lips called his name. She made him aware of things he'd deliberately ignored because of his faith over the years. Everything he had told himself about handling her with care almost flew out the window until he noticed her hair covering was different. He never wanted her to change for him. Her response to him was fine, but he felt something deeper was to blame.

"So, you love musicals or are you just going here for me?" her silky voice drew him out of his daze.

"You know I enjoy art, but tonight is all about you, Princess." Ekene pulled up to the valet section of the Terra Kulture theatre. He got around the car fast enough to open the door for Halima. Helping her out, he tossed his keys to the attendant and thanked him. They were greeted by an usher to whom he presented their tickets. And soon after, they were escorted to the VIP section.

Within minutes, the show started. *Queen Moremi The Musical* was a real African superhero story. It was brought to life through several colorful costume changes, recited words, music and dance, displaying the rich ancestry of the Yoruba people. The Queen was the daughter to one of Ife's (an ancient Yoruba city in the south-west) bravest warrior/hunters and another princess. The Queen, as a child, was raised to question injustice and stand up for the oppressed, no matter who or where they came from. In the end, the Queen answered the call of love, but with it came a price. Queen Moremi was pivotal in liberating the Yoruba race, but at the expense of her husband, son and the risk of her own death.

Ekene's initial desire was to ensure Halima had a good time. One of her hobbies was collecting these artifacts of ancient royalty. Pictures of them adorned her foyer. In watching the play, he related to the Queen's passion also. Ekene glanced over at Halima. She had a lone tear running down her cheek.

The curtain closed and they both rose with the rest of the audience to give a standing ovation. A few seconds later, in a move he didn't expect but welcomed, Halima intertwined her hand in his and placed her head on his shoulder.

"You okay?" Ekene asked when she tightened her fingers around his.

"Yes," she whispered, as they headed to the door. "It was just a lot to process."

"I brought you here to enjoy yourself, not be sad." He handed his ticket to the valet.

"I'm not sad. Just reflective." Her stomach growled.

He smiled down at her. "Okay, let's get some food in you and if you want to talk about it, I'm all ears."

As they drove to the restaurant where he'd made reservations, Halima leaned her head to the side, taking in the sights of the Lagos nightlife. He also noticed when she turned to look at him, although he didn't meet her stare. He had tried to talk to her, but had gotten single word answers, so decided to settle for comfortable silence.

"I must be a boring date." Her voice was low.

His eyebrows creased. "Why would you say that?"

"You've been trying to talk to me, and I'm so wrapped up in my head."

Ekene glanced at her and returned his eyes to the road. She must not know how deep his feelings ran for her. Well, she couldn't because he'd never told her. "Some hearts understand each other, even in silence…"

The smile he longed to see returned.

She replied. "And I love talking to you even when I have nothing to say."

The familiar thump in his heart reappeared. He reached for her hand and squeezed. Whatever was bothering her, he'd know by the end of the night.

———

"You're not a coward and I still don't know why you'd refer to yourself as such." Ekene picked up the glass of water in front of him and drank. "I wish, you could see yourself through my eyes."

His irritation over another choice of less than flattering words she was using to berate herself grew. Especially over things that were in the past.

"But you don't understand. I'll be thirty-six soon and—"

Ekene reached across the table and took her hand in his. "And nothing, God still has a plan for your life. And here's a little secret – you're not powerful enough to have blown it."

The waiter interrupted them by asking if they wanted dessert. Halima ordered a coffee and a slice of apple pie with vanilla ice cream.

"It's just that looking at Queen Moremi…she was courageous, fearless and sought what was right, no matter the cost. I love my mother, but I've always despised the weakness in her. I know it has a lot to do with our faith and culture, but I do not think submission should make you weak—"

"And it shouldn't. Following someone's lead isn't a sign of weakness. It just means that everyone has a role to play. Society has dirtied the word to suit our own needs, but biblically, women are told to submit to their husbands and their husbands to love their wives. It doesn't mean that the woman doesn't have the right to question and has to follow blindly. In another passage, husbands and wives are told to submit to one another. For us, the command is a mirror image of Christ's relationship with the church. Submission isn't a mere agreement at the final point of decision."

"Well, that's how it was in my house. What my father said was law. And for all these years, I've been the very thing I despised the most. I'm so angry with myself."

"Let me know when the pity party is over."

"I'm not having a pity party. Why would you say that? I'm telling you how I feel" Halima's voice rose an octave.

"I know that, but we've dwelled on it too long. What are

you going to do about it? You can talk about it all day. Is that what you want? Or do you want to move ahead?"

The waitress brought out Halima's dessert and he smiled as she ignored him while she prepared her coffee. The moan she let out after a spoonful of her dessert stirred his loins. He desperately wished she wouldn't do it again. In silence, she handed him an extra spoon and pushed the dessert to the middle of the table. He took it from her, and they ate the decadent treat without another word.

"I want to move forward."

"You talking to me now?" He raised his eyebrows.

"I really don't like you sometimes."

"Yeah, and we've established the reason why."

She gave him a hard stare.

He laughed. "I told you before, you don't scare me with those."

She groaned and scooped another spoonful of her dessert. He watched as she brought it to his lips instead of hers. He opened his mouth to take the treat with his eyes never leaving hers. After swallowing, he stared at her. He wanted a taste of his own kind of dessert – her lips.

"You better stop doing that."

"Why? You don't like me feeding you?" she asked with a twinkle in her eyes.

"On the contrary, but I might end up liking it too much," Ekene confessed.

Halima shrugged. "I might like it, too."

Moments of silence passed between them. Certain they were thinking about very different things, he silently asked the Holy Spirit for control as his eyes roamed her outfit and imagined the possibilities. He blinked and reverted his mind to their prior conversation.

"We both can relate to this; life is like a game of chess. Sometimes you make wrong moves, realize them, and reroute yourself. I told you the story of my upbringing. What I didn't tell you was how I found the church and was able to forgive my father."

"Tell me." She smiled, mocking the way he spoke.

"Quit it. You can't do a me on me."

"Yes, I can. Spill."

"I saw how your father's actions and death almost took 'Sheed on a path of no return. I was on a mission to be a top shot lawyer, so I'd be able to fight for injustice for women who didn't have a voice…like my mom. I couldn't let bitterness and unforgiveness keep me locked down. Rasheed was rising to the top, but he was stuck in a rut. I didn't want that." He took a breath. "I don't want that for you. I know you think it's too late to find whatever it is that you're looking for. You can, but you got to move, Princess."

"I have so much guilt about disappointing my mom, but I want to be happy."

"Then be happy. You've decided."

"So how did you lose your demons? The rage of losing your mom, your father's actions and all the other emotions?"

Ekene summoned the waiter and minutes later their check was paid. Ekene stood, "Your demons never go away. I now have the power to live above them."

"How?"

"Jesus, Princess. Jesus." He took her hand. "Come on let me get you home."

———

On the drive, Halima controlled the music and he found himself nodding his head to the melody of what she had introduced as "There's Hope" by India Arie. This was what he loved about her. She was complex, yet so simple. She was an intellectual, but goofy at the same time.

"Has a nice melody to it," he said.

"I love her. Her songs always have meaning. Who do you like?"

"Everything Kirk Franklin, Eben, Adekunle Gold and Phyno. And I'm sure some others."

"Oh, speaking of Adekunle Gold, I love Simi. And Yemi Alade."

"Why does Adekunle remind you of Simi?"

"Please don't tell me you didn't know they were dating and had a secret wedding this year."

"And why would I know that?" His own pseudo-love life was complicated enough.

"I forgot you're getting up there in age. Do you even have any social media accounts?"

Ekene let out a boisterous chuckle. "Get a little sugar in you and suddenly you're a comedian. To answer your question, no, I don't but someone runs an account for my firm." Being a year younger than her older brother, he expected the age cracks.

"Whew! I need to get you updated. Even if it's just one. For your age, maybe, Twitter." She laughed like she had said the funniest thing in the world.

"Which one are you on?"

"IG, I love pictures. But since you like all those quotes and talking about law stuff, Twitter should be good for you."

Ekene snickered again. "You'll pay for this."

"Are you threatening me?"

"Now you know better than that, Princess. It's a guarantee." He glanced over and winked before coming to a stop in front of her house.

Ekene got out of the car and walked around to help her out. Side by side, they strolled to her door. He took the keys from her and unlocked it.

"Thank you, Kene. I had a great time tonight. Also, I apologize and thank you for not letting me ruin the perfect evening with self-pity."

"It was my pleasure. I'm always available to set you straight."

They stood staring at each other. Ekene knew that was his cue to leave, but his legs refused to obey the command. He inched closer to her and she began to rub her earlobe.

"Are you nervous, Princess?" he asked, in a low tone.

"Err…"

"You know you're always safe with me." He leaned his forehead against hers. To his satisfaction, she didn't move away. Instead, she straightened her body, so he didn't have to bend much. Their foreheads stayed connected for several minutes as they took in each other's breath.

"At first, you made me feel nervous. Now you make me feel safe," Halima whispered.

"Good." He kissed her forehead and turned to leave. "Goodnight, Princess. Lock up."

Ekene walked the short distance to his car and got in the driver's seat. He looked back at her house. "Almighty Father, You're a miracle worker. Please bless me with the one my soul yearns for," He prayed, then started his car and headed home.

Chapter 12

Halima looked down at her crimson-stained hands. No matter how many pieces of clothing she ripped to cover the wound in her chest, the blood kept flowing. She dragged herself to her bed and fumbled around for her phone. Once she got it, she dialed Abubakar, then remembered he had been placed on a leave that Kamal had imposed. She felt her breath leaving her body. She dialed his replacement, Umaru.

"Yes, Ms. Danjuma," the man answered the phone on the second ring.

"I…need…you to come to the main house. I've been…" Halima felt herself going in and out of consciousness.

Moments later, her front door was forced open. She heard loud footsteps up the stairs and then Umaru and the gateman entered. Confusion and fear etched their faces.

She pointed to her chest weakly and they both tried to remove the dagger in it. It felt stuck. As they twisted, she yelled in pain. After a few more tries, they were successful. It surprised her that she was still conscious, but she was.

"Please take me to my brother's hospital. He'll know what to do." Jabir was the best heart surgeon there was.

Sometime later, she was being rushed to the operating table. Relief washed over her although her pain was still present, and the blood hadn't stopped flowing. As the anesthesiologist prepped to put her under, she noticed Jabir wasn't in the room.

"Wait, where is my brother?" Her voice was but a faint whisper.

"*Do you want to be healed?*" A hushed voice floated through the air.

She looked around. No one in the room seemed to notice that someone or something was talking. And still, no one had answered her question.

"*Do you want to be healed?*"

Halima heard that whisper again. She began to sob harder. "What kind of question is that? I'm dying here. Where is Jabir?"

"*Do you want to be healed?*"

Halima ignored the question. "Please, just get my brother."

Halima continued to sob as she slowly felt herself drifting. She didn't understand why Jabir didn't come to save her. The weaker she got, the more she realized all the plans she'd made for her life had been an exercise in futility. She'd wasted her time wrapped in the cocoon of fear and timidity.

"Aaaah" Halima yelled, waking up in a cold sweat. She placed her hand on her heart, checking for blood stains. She stretched out her hands and wiggled her toes. *I'm still here.* Her heart raced and pulse pounded. Sitting up with her back against the headboard, she leaned over and dragged the extra blanket at the foot of the bed around her shoulders.

"Allah, what kind of torture is this? It's getting worse," she muttered to herself. She'd been having these dreams for a while, since she'd left Abuja several weeks ago. But it never got to the part where she had to go to the hospital or even died. The voice that was now a thorn in her side, kept asking if she wanted to be healed. Healed from what? She was in great physical shape. The more she tried to ignore the dreams, the more vivid they became.

In the book she was reading by the Muslim turned Christian, he wrote about having visions and dreams. *Are these just dreams or is the God of the Book trying to tell me something?* Unlike the author of that book, she wasn't on a quest to prove anything, but that seemed to be the path on which she was headed.

Too afraid to go back to sleep, she went in search of her iPad. She had no idea where to search in her Quran for answers. And she didn't own a Bible, so YouTube was her next best option. She didn't want to wake Ekene or Damisi, so this was something she had to do for herself. The dream this time was too real to ignore.

After two cups of tea and about three hours on the internet. Halima felt better, but her mind was still jumbled. She had typed in dreams, visions and God and saw a talk by a Dr. Tony Evans. It was titled, "When God Talks." She intently listened to the message, trying to find answers to what she was experiencing. She ended up binge watching several of his videos and subscribing to his podcast.

"Legend has it that an angel would come down and stir the water and at that very moment, most of the people that needed healing rushed into the pool." Another preacher's voice came through her ear pods as Halima stared into her closet for something to wear. Although Dr. Evans had sort of cleared up the visions, dreams and the why God uses them mystery, Halima needed to delve deeper into what she now knew was John 5:1-5 of the Bible. That whisper kept bothering her and she had to know more. With her iPad slanted up against her vanity, she pulled out a gold and black print skirt with its matching long-sleeved black blouse.

"When Jesus approached, he asked this man do you want to be healed. I would suggest that Jesus asked because he needed to confirm that the man was willing to participate in his own healing. But like we all tend to do, the man blamed his continued disabled condition on the fact that there was no one to help him. Meaning he probably believed this myth too. But Jesus, who was never One for the theatrics, swept away the magic water theory by simply telling the man to get up."

Halima stood in front of her full-length mirror and held the attire up to her chin. Satisfied, she dressed up and wrapped her hair before covering it with a gold hijab. As she put on her jewelry, her thoughts honed in on the words the preacher said next.

"In faith, the man picked up his mat and walked. But hear me now, not everyone would be happy with the decisions you make because even though the healing of the man was a good thing, the Jewish leaders still found something to criticize. Their reaction shows that no matter how much proof God provides, there will be people that refuse to see the truth."

Halima sat on the bed and put on her shoes. Was this her? Was she blind to the truth? She was beginning to believe the author of the book she was reading and some of the holes he pointed out about her faith. But what did he know? He might have just been another confused soul. She had weird dreams, but that was about it.

Halima closed her iPad and placed it in her bag. She picked up her briefcase and headed down the stairs. As she relaxed in the back of her car, she pulled out some contracts and schedules. With what had happened to Eric Okon, she double checked everything.

Her lips turned up in a smile as she remembered Ekene said he'd drop by her office later. They hadn't seen each other in a couple of days because of an unexpected development in the pro bono case he was working on. But over the last three weeks, they'd spent every free moment they could together. Mid-day lunch dates, art gallery visits, wine tasting, and painting or simply playing chess at either of their houses after dinner.

She'd gotten closer to him, but her dream earlier had confirmed that things were too smooth to be good. Her mother acted like she was still betrothed to Danladi. Danladi, on the other hand, kept calling her and Uncle Musa hadn't said another word. Apart from Danladi's calls, the level of chaos she expected wasn't there. Yes, it was too smooth. There was a storm ahead.

———

HALIMA WASHED HER HANDS AND OPENED THE DOOR TO EXIT the adjoining restroom in her office. She stretched her body and strode over to the window. Taking her shoes off, she sunk her feet into the plush carpet. Using her phone, she scrolled through her social media feed, giving her mind a much-needed break. Usually, she'd marvel at the breathtaking view of the Lagos Island skyline, but currently, it was a haze as the past eight hours scrambled her thoughts. She'd spent the day either in back-to-back meetings or troubleshooting something she shouldn't have had to. She'd sent her assistant home about an hour ago since her mother suddenly became ill. Halima strolled back to her desk. Her phone buzzed.

Are you still in the office?

With a smile on her face, she texted back. **Yes**

On my way.

Everything okay? Her brows came together. She had to cancel their lunch date and he was okay with that as he, too, had an emergency come up.

See you soon, Princess.

Halima grinned.

"I hope the person you're grinning with has nothing to do with you calling off our wedding?"

Halima looked up at the sound of that familiar voice.

Danladi stood at the entrance of her office with his hands in the pockets of his traditional Hausa attire.

"Danladi…" she clutched her phone.

He stalked closer to her, causing her to take a step back. She'd never known him to be violent, but with the tone of his recent messages, she couldn't be too sure.

"Is that anyway to greet your future husband?"

Halima ignored his question and asked hers. "What are you doing here?"

"Am I not welcomed to my future wife's office?"

Halima tugged on her ear lobe. He let out a light laugh. It sounded sinister. He came to see her once in a while so no one from security would have alerted her, but there was no reason why he should be here now.

"I thought we said all we had to say over the phone," Halima said.

"How silly of you to think that. I told you that you can't wake up and decide you don't want to get married."

"I didn't just wake up—"

"Really? What would you call it? Up until six weeks ago we were too be married and now we're not." He paused and pointed to her. "…well according to you."

"Look, I'm sorry for springing it on you." She wrung her fingers. "I just couldn't go ahead with it. I couldn't be a second wife and moreover, I don't love you."

Danladi shot forward and Halima backed up. "Love?"

He kept strolling toward her until she was trapped between him and the wall. He was breathing so hard that the flare of his nostrils frightened her.

"When was love ever an issue? Our fathers agreed a while ago—"

"Without my consent. And that notwithstanding, you went ahead and got married."

"So, I can have as many wives as I want. Besides, you

weren't ready when I was. So, I married someone else to allow you to go for your further studies."

"Allow?"

"Yes, allow. And you took my kindness for granted. I should've been stricter with you."

"You do know I'm not your child?"

"Then act like it," Danladi barked.

At that point, Halima had had it. She tried to walk past him, but he held on to her arm. She tried to tug herself free from his grasp, but it became tighter.

Danladi stared down at her. Without her shoes on, he was considerably taller than her. "Listen to me…"

"No, you listen to me. You've got exactly one second to let her go or you won't like the consequences."

Danladi turned around to the source of the angry voice and Halima stared into the eyes of the man who was in complete possession of her heart.

"And who are you supposed to be?" Danladi asked, letting her arm go.

Not taking his eyes off her, Ekene replied, "Your worst nightmare if you ever talk to, come close to, or put your hands on her again."

He stretched out his arms and she ran into them. Burying her head in his chest.

"Halima, you will disgrace your family like this? Is this why you're throwing this tantrum?" Danladi asked.

"Last time I checked, I was the head of her family and if she says she's done, then she is done."

Halima heard her brother, Rasheed's, voice and contemplated whether to lift her head from Ekene's chest. She didn't want her brothers to find out about whatever they had going on like this. She was going to talk to them this weekend. Ekene was her brother's friend and she didn't want any bad blood between them.

"Rasheed, you know the custom," Danladi said.

Halima raised her head and watched her brother approach Danladi. Rasheed wasn't Kamal or she'd be very worried, but one thing plagued her mind. Why was he here?

"I know the custom. Which is why I respected her wishes to go ahead with the marriage although I was always against it. However, my sister is no longer interested, so I suggest you leave."

"But Uncle Musa…" Danladi started.

Rasheed chuckled. "Musa nothing. Danladi, I've never had any problems with you. Please don't let that man get you into trouble that you can't get out of."

"Are you threatening me? I'm not afraid of you."

Rasheed laughed. "I'm not the one you should be afraid of."

Halima watched him glance over to Ekene but wondered if he was talking about him or Kamal.

"This is not over." Danladi walked toward the door and Ekene moved her securely behind him.

"For your sake, I hope you just take the loss and move on," Rasheed warned.

Danladi paused at the door. Then he turned around. His eyes found hers. They were dark and menacing. "Be prepared for the *nikah* or lose everything you think you have here."

Ekene started toward him. "Didn't I tell you not to talk to her again?"

Halima held on to him, but he seemed to be dragging her along as he moved closer to the door.

"Kene, we got bigger issues and you can't handle them from a jail cell," Rasheed said and Ekene stopped moving.

Danladi smirked and left.

The room was filled with thick tension. Halima turned and so did Ekene. Rasheed was leaned against her desk with his arms folded across his chest.

"Man, if I didn't know any better, I'd think you're feeling my sister." Rasheed's jaw clenched with a smile that didn't reach his eyes. He shook his head. "Nope, it can't be. It must be some big brother/protector stuff going on."

Halima looked down for a few seconds then raised her head to look at both men. Ekene took determined strides toward Rasheed.

"I'm not her brother, 'Sheed," he said.

"Then what exactly are you?" Rasheed asked with a raised brow.

Chapter 13

Ekene returned his friend's hard glare. He toyed with whether to get into it with Rasheed now or spin it, so they wouldn't be sidetracked, considering the reason they were here in the first place. Whatever he decided, the heat from Rasheed's gaze warned him that he had to tread lightly. He wasn't a punk, but he had Halima's feelings to consider. The standoff lasted for a couple of moments before he heard the voice that always soothed his spirit.

"Rasheed—"

"Stay out of it, Hali. I'm guessing my *friend* and I need to have a chat." Rasheed's stern tone sent Ekene into defense mode. He knew Rasheed would never do anything to hurt Halima, but he wouldn't let anyone talk to her like they had no sense, not even her brother.

"Easy, 'Sheed,' Ekene warned.

Rasheed cocked his head to the side and frowned. "You monitoring how I talk to my own sister? Me?"

"Stop it, both of you," Halima said.

This wasn't how he wanted the conversation to go with his friend. Halima loved her brothers dearly and although she was grown, he knew their opinion of her mattered more than anything. He also knew that arguing with them wouldn't be a good thing for his case. Despite that knowledge, Rasheed's stance right now was a bit of a shock. He thought if there was anyone, he'd have to argue with, it'd be Kamal, not his best friend. He needed to take another approach.

Ekene looked down at Halima. "Red, we're good. Can you give your brother and me a minute?"

Her face creased in a frown. Her stubborn streak was about to rear its head, but he silently prayed she'd read his pleading eyes and listen.

"You do know that this is *my* office."

"That's not in question, but I really need to talk to your brother."

Rasheed maintained his stance and remained silent. His shock was evident, and Ekene knew him well enough to deduce his patience was waning.

Halima eyed both men. She walked over to Rasheed who softened his glare. "You weren't supposed to be here until next week. Is everyone okay?"

"Yes. I came to talk to you about something, but that can wait because I need to talk to Ekene now."

Halima sighed knowing, just like he did, that she was fighting a losing battle. "I'm tired and ready to go home. I'm going to the breakroom for some tea so you can have your *chat.*" She walked to the door then paused. "When I come back, please be done. And if one chair is out of place, I'm calling SoSo."

The mention of his wife's name brought a smile to Rasheed's face. "I'm shaking."

"Ha! Okay, we'll see." She smirked, opened the door and left.

The tension in the room returned and Ekene decided to break it. "Man, you've known me almost all my life. I mean your sister no harm."

"I'm not so sure about that," Rasheed said pointedly.

"Are you kidding me?" Disbelief wasn't the word to describe his feeling as they both stood facing each other, daring the other to make a move. Several beats passed between them with Rasheed ignoring his question, but following up with one of his own.

"You haven't answered my question. What are you to my sister?"

"Look, your sister is beautiful and she's good company. We've been spending time together getting to know each other."

"Well, stop it. I don't even want to know when it started. End it." Rasheed seethed.

"What do you mean stop? You're not her father and I don't need your permission to spend time with Halima," Ekene fired back. "I'd love your support, but don't need your permission."

"You don't have my support," Rasheed growled. He sauntered to the center of the room. "I entrusted my sister to you. Here I am thinking you're on business and you're trying to push up on her?"

"What? Push up? How old are you and who uses that phrase anymore?"

"You know what I mean…"

"I'm not pushing up on anybody. But are you saying I'm not good enough for your sister?"

"What exactly are you doing with her?"

"I've told you what I'm doing."

"To what end?"

Ekene thought about it. He'd been so caught up in the euphoria of their budding situation, that he forbade himself from thinking that far ahead. His pause must have taken too long because Rasheed spoke again.

"Yeah, that's what I thought." Rasheed paced and Ekene stared at him. He wondered what his deal was.

"Are you now a Muslim?" Rasheed asked.

The question caught him by surprise. "Huh? No!"

"Did Halima convert, and I didn't know?"

"You know she didn't."

"So, leave my sister alone," Rasheed barked. "Nothing good will come of whatever this is."

"I can't believe you think so little of me…"

"This is not about you. It's about her. I don't believe in her faith or its rules, but as long as she has chosen to remain a Muslim, I will not allow her to be disgraced."

"I'd never do that to her. I care about her deeply."

"The fact that you don't get the bigger picture angers me. Come on man, you're my friend. How deep is this thing?"

"Deep, but really…what's your deal?" Ekene was perplexed.

"My *deal* is that she's going to get hurt and disgraced in her faith. And I will not allow that."

"With all due respect man, I love you like a brother, but in case you haven't noticed, I don't care what you will or will not allow." Ekene ran his hand down his face. "For years, I've done everything in my power to stay away. But I can't help who my heart is fond of. Halima is smart, stubborn, annoyingly opinionated, and insanely beautiful and sexy."

"Man, I don't want to hear all that," Rasheed roared.

"But it's true."

"That notwithstanding, I know you're not dating just because and as long as she's Muslim, she can't marry you. So, tell me when you're done with spending time and her feelings are deeper, what happens?"

"How are you planning a wedding when we've just been getting acquainted for some weeks?"

"What I saw just now wasn't just *getting acquainted*. Like you said, I've known you a long time. Your feelings are deep and so are hers. I need you to end it before she ends up hurt." Rasheed's nose flared.

Ekene's anger rose. His rage wasn't directed towards his

friend but the potential of the truth in his words and frustration with the situation. Both men stayed in silence for a few moments before Ekene brought his gaze directly to Rasheed's eyes. He took a deep breath.

"I'll never hurt Halima. We both have feelings for each other and are enjoying getting to know one another."

"Have you not been listening to me?" Rasheed asked.

"I have and now I want you to listen to me." He paused. "I don't know what this is or where it would lead, all I know is that my heart ceases to beat without her."

"You of all people know I can't sit back and let my sister—"

"Although I respect your protectiveness, contrary to the opinion of you and your brothers, your sister is grown and can make her own decisions." Ekene's chest rose. "Do you think I didn't try to fight this? Do you think I don't know the impossibility of the situation or the huge mountains we must climb? I begged God to give me my heart back. But she got it, man. Halima got my heart and I don't even want it back anymore."

Rasheed growled. "I really want to kick your—"

"Well, get in line because I want to do it too, but it is what it is and I'm not complaining. I ask that you give us the space to explore our feelings."

Rasheed turned his back to him and moved forward. Ekene could tell his friend was deep in thought. They had been through so much together over the years and although the situation was what it was, Ekene knew that nothing Rasheed had said tonight was personal.

Moments later, Rasheed turned and walked toward him, not stopping until he invaded his personal space. He looked him straight in his eyes. "I hope to God you know what you're doing. Because, if you hurt her, you'll have me to deal with. Friend or not, you don't want those problems."

With the same intensity, Ekene responded. "I'll never

intentionally hurt Halima. If I do, whatever you bring, I'm taking."

Rasheed cracked a smile. "You're better than the clown that just left so…" He shrugged.

"Oh wow! Thanks for the compliment." Ekene shook his head. "Does this mean we're good now?"

"No, I'm just backing off…for now. That's my sister," Rasheed responded incredulously.

"I guess I'll take it."

Rasheed shook his head and slipped his hands in his pockets, his stance more relaxed. "Be ready. Because when Kammy hears this—"

"Kammy hears what?" Halima asked.

Ekene's heart did its usual flip at the sound of her voice. They hadn't heard her come in. He stretched his hand toward her, and she took it. When she got close, he kissed her forehead and was pleased with the smile that adorned her face.

"I can't believe this." Rasheed turned away from them, making his way to one of the chairs in front of Halima's desk.

Halima gave him an uneasy look.

Ekene whispered in her ear. "He's okay, just in shock." He followed it by a wink and led her to where Rasheed was.

"Don't be trying to hide behind Kene. We're still going to talk," Rasheed said to her.

Halima nodded. "First, are you going to tell me why you're in Lagos?"

Rasheed looked at him. "I was going to, but I'm going to let Prince Charming here do the honors."

Punk.

Ekene had called Rasheed immediately he got the delivery to his office this morning. He wanted him to be present when he gave Halima the news. One, because he was the CEO of Danjuma Group and two, because he was her brother. Never did he think they'd get sidetracked by him needing to defend his feelings for Halima. Now Rasheed was leaving him to put a frown on her face.

You're scaring me. What's wrong?" Halima sat in her oversized leather chair.

"Nothing to be scared of, Princess," Ekene responded.

"Red? Princess? What the…?" Rasheed asked.

Halima's face flushed in embarrassment.

Ekene cut his eye at him. "Not now, 'Sheed."

He turned back to Halima. "Earlier today I got a visit from the law firm the second Mrs. Okon retained. Danjuma Group is being sued for being liable in the death of Eric Okon." Ekene studied her. Her expression was stoic. "Halima, you're being named personally in the suit as being responsible for Eric's schedule that led up to his accident."

"What!?" She shot up from her chair.

"Calm down, Sis. We both know that won't hold in court. The bigger problem is the board and that's what I want to make sure you are prepared for."

"I don't understand…"

"Your uncle is up to some mischief. I haven't fully confirmed yet, but I think he's been rallying some gullible members of the board since the DeSab case." Rasheed paused for a minute. "Since that case, our investors have been antsy that we were getting careless in our dealings. But that's all they were, worried. Nobody acted upon anything since they all still trusted us. However, Eric's death has been in the news. Despite the statement we gave, the guy's family has been on the news any chance they got. The board has gotten more nervous.

When it comes to their money, people want an established, comfortable and controlled company where they feel secure. So, their nervousness puts pressure on the board."

Halima let out a deep, angry sigh, frustrated with the whole thing.

"We also have to be prepared for the press," Ekene said.

He hated what he had to say next, but he needed her to be prepared and was committed to protecting her with his life. "Because of the case a few years back with the plant at Lokoja, the press might connect the two to drag your name through the mud."

The tension was back. The lone tear that glided down her cheek shot Ekene to his feet. He pulled her into his embrace and allowed her to sob. She was one of the strongest people he knew and to see her break down tugged at his heartstrings. He was no longer just her lawyer to make sure that her company was okay. She was his woman. Even if she didn't know it yet, she was his and no one would mess with what was his.

Chapter 14

Halima jumped when the alarm sounded on the oven. She had gotten lost in the news headline that seemed to run around the clock. The news anchors did exactly what Ekene said they would. They linked her to both incidents, questioning whether she was competent enough to run the logistics department of Danjuma Group. They claimed she had the job just because she was the late Zayd Danjuma's daughter.

What hurt most was that with her being in the news, they found a way to drag her brothers and their wives into the news as well. Damisi and Kamal suffered from the unfavorable press the most. It bothered neither of them since they were used to the spotlight, but Halima was so sad that it was even happening.

It had been a week and a half, and she thought that by now, some other news event would've pushed hers to the back. Ekene, as promised, submitted their response to the courts and they were now in wait mode. Halima groaned, threw her legs over the sofa and strolled into the kitchen. She encased her hands in an oven mitt and opened the oven door. She retrieved the tray of lemon cupcakes and placed them on the island. Baking was her stress reliever. She broke off a piece of the confection and blew on it before popping it into her mouth. She moaned as the sweet, tart taste took over her taste buds. Baking was one of the first things she and Ibiso had bonded over.

Thinking of Ibiso, she and the rest of the family would be arriving the next day. She wouldn't be able to dodge them or Ekene any longer. The first couple of days, her family smothered her to the point of frustration. It was as though none of them understood that she was a big girl and wouldn't break. That was one of the things she hated about being the baby of the family. It was so bad that her brothers now had their wives handling her with kid gloves. It was also the reason she currently needed space from them all. And Ekene.

After the shock of the news had wound down, it occurred to her that he had called Rasheed to fly from Abuja to break the news. She was at the center of it and didn't need Rasheed's hand holding. She kept telling him that, but he was insistent on handling her. The same patriarchy she was trying to escape from with Islam was exactly what Ekene did. He assumed he knew what was best for her without consulting her. Truthfully, his action came from an entirely different place, but in that moment, it didn't matter. Despite what his words said, his actions differed.

She sang the lyrics to "Dreamer Girl" by Asa playing in the background, and moved to the sink. Filling the kettle with water, she placed it on the stove to boil. Minutes later, she left the kitchen with a cup of raspberry herbal tea in one hand and a cupcake in the other. The week had been exhausting and she was glad to have this time to herself. The sudden ring of her phone told her that alone time might not be in the cards for her tonight. Setting her stuff down, she took out the phone from her pocket. She glanced at the screen and contemplated answering her mother.

When the news first broke, her mother was supportive.

She even came down to Lagos to stay with her for two days. However, with each passing day, her tone changed. She was still supportive, but insinuated that her life was being disrupted because Allah wasn't happy with her. Like this was punishment she deserved. Halima was going through enough, so instead of arguing with her mom, she avoided her. The ringing stopped. As she was about to let out a sigh, it began again.

"Hello, Mother," Halima answered.

"*Haba* Halima! You had me worried…"

Halima waited. She sat on the stairs.

"Why haven't you been answering my calls?"

"I've been busy. How are you?"

"I am fine. When are you coming home? I want you away from that place."

"Mother, I'm fine. I can't just up and leave. I have obligations. Remember the dinner…" Halima's voice trailed as she remembered she hadn't had the time to tell her mother she would be in Enugu for the summer.

"*Yata* I'm worried about you," her mother said.

"Don't be worried. I'm fine. The company lawyer is handling it. They have no case because I didn't do anything wrong. If I did, I'd take responsibility."

Her mother was eerily quiet. That couldn't be good, but Halima had no energy to argue. They had been doing a lot of that lately.

"Danladi came to see me," her mother said.

Halima didn't respond, but bit into her cupcake.

"He told me what happened in Lagos and asked that I plead with you."

"To do what? I already told you that I'm not marrying Danladi. We've gone over this. I don't love him."

"He said something about your brother's friend. Are you having a relationship with a non-believer, Halima?"

Her life was already crumbling into pieces. What was one

or two more secrets exposed? Now she was going for broke. "Mother, his name is Ekene. He's a Christian, but we're just very close friends."

"That's not how Danladi described it."

"Why ask me since Danladi has all the facts?"

"You know I don't mean it like that. It's just that in the past year and a half, you've not been acting like the daughter I raised."

"Why, Mother? Because some things no longer make sense to me. I'm trying to get answers, because I know I deserve more."

"What is it that you're searching for?" her mother asked. "You have always been able to find instruction from the Quran. When last did you go to Jumu'ah?"

Halima didn't know if this was a good time to tell her mother she hadn't been going, opting to visit church instead. She didn't attend Jabir's church, but instead found a small church near her house. Anonymity was important to her as all she had been taught was beginning to slip through her fingers. With no fuss, she prayed her answers might come. The week of her vivid vision of the dagger in her chest was the last week she'd entered a mosque. She wasn't ready to leave Islam over a dream, but was now waiting in her prayer for God to give her a sign of some kind.

"Mother, I've been meaning to tell you something. But if you can't even support me on not wanting to become a second wife, I shudder at what you would think."

"When have you not been able to talk to me?"

"You really have to ask?"

"What is it, my daughter? Believe it or not, I want the best for you," her mother said.

Halima closed her eyes and from within, gathered the strength she knew she'd need. "I'm questioning which God we've…I mean I've been serving."

"What is that supposed to mean? You're serving Allah!"

"I know that, but is He the God of the Bible? The One whose only Son is Jesus the Christ and not a mere prophet?"

"Oh, Allah have mercy on you. Those brothers of yours have finally gotten their claws into you." Her mother sobbed.

"Calm down, Mother. No need to talk about my brothers like that. Remember they are the ones funding your lifestyle," Halima cautioned.

Despite the will, Rasheed gave her mother a generous allowance and had opened two boutiques for her. Damisi gave her the necessary press to popularize her businesses. Jabir made sure she saw the best doctor annually and Ibiso catered all her store openings at a huge discount.

"You raised me to be strong and gave me a solid education. Why are you now so against me using that same knowledge?"

"Things of a spiritual nature do not need your white man's knowledge."

"True, but I no longer want to be a blind follower, especially if I see and feel differently. I searched for the truth. The People of the Book say that Jesus is The Truth. So, it's only right I find out if that's true."

Halima's mind drifted to the book she was still reading. In the past several days of turmoil, she searched the Quran for comfort, but couldn't find any. Instead, like the author of the book she was reading, all she saw was a God of conditional concern. One who wouldn't love her if she didn't do the utmost to please him. She was flawed like all other humans. How could she survive with a God who loved her conditionally? That already made her feel worse and condemned?

"Are you no longer Muslim?" her mother asked in a hushed whisper. Apprehension laced her tone.

Halima sighed. "I am, but I've decided to take off the hijab."

Her mother gasped. "Why Halima?"

"The hijab doesn't make me religious, it just makes me

Muslim. Sadly, we've made it a measure of how religious a person is and that is like putting a Band-Aid over a bleeding wound."

"But it is a sign of modesty. Are you trying to show off your physical assets? It will attract the wrong kind of man."

Halima chuckled. If only her mother knew that even with the hijab, she had men pursuing her. "Mother, that's another thing. Does it really deter men or make them more curious so they are tempted to see? And my hair is not my assets."

Halima waited as her mother got a few more sniffs, grunts and begging of Allah out of the way.

"The cloth on my head doesn't make me an angel walking on earth. I have my own demons and struggles to fight every day. Nevertheless, it is more than a covering of the head; it has significance, I agree. With all these thoughts going on in my mind, I feel I'm disrespecting it by keeping it on. And that is something I do not want to do."

"Your father would be so disappointed and quite frankly so am I. You're my only child and you have decided to bring shame to my doorstep," her mother hissed

"Mother, that's not my intent, but I also want to be happy. Marrying Danladi won't do that. Also not getting the answers I seek won't do that either."

She only had herself to blame for this pain. If she had been woman enough to speak her mind years ago, things would have at least been better than they were now. What she did know was that no longer was she willing to sacrifice her happiness or inner peace for others.

"Instead of fighting me, why not pray that I get the clarity I seek, get over this lawsuit, and survive the Board."

"I will because this madness is getting out of hand. If I had known this would be the turn of events, I would've insisted that you get married to Danladi years ago. All your so-called confusion wouldn't be there now."

It hurt Halima to know that in all she said, her mother

wasn't really concerned about her peace of mind, but was stuck on saving face by her marrying Danladi.

"Okay, Mother. I'll be going with my brothers to their village for summer—"

"What? Since when do you miss our summer holidays?"

"It's just this year. If I can, I will come down afterwards. Big Mummy is being conferred a title and she invited me to go."

"I said it! They're taking you from me—"

"I'm a whole person. Nobody can take me where I don't want to go. I love you."

Her mother sucked her teeth and hung up the phone. Halima stared at the device and exhaled a long-labored breath.

Dear God of the Bible, this is a lot to bear. Please show me that I'm on the right track. That your Son is the way to that track and the Holy Spirit will comfort me through all of this. Halima found herself praying.

Halima stared at her now cold tea and half-eaten cupcake. Dragging her feet to the kitchen, she discarded both and went upstairs.

Several moments later, with her nightly routine completed, Halima slipped between the purple satin sheets that covered her bed. Her phone buzzed. She rolled her eyes because she wasn't in the mood to talk anymore tonight. She stretched to the foot of the bed and got her phone. There were two texts – one from Kudirat and one from Ekene, both in direct conflict with each other.

Kudi Bestie: I finally found a match for you. He's my cousin. He'll be in Lagos this weekend and I told him you needed a date for your company thingy. His name is Tanimu. And you're welcome bestie!

Kene: You've been running…again. Time's up Princess. See you this weekend.

She responded to neither. Her mother was still heavy on her mind. She really wanted to be happy. She deserved the joy she heard the Pastor preach about, but at what cost would it come to her. Her friends? Her mother? Her peace?

Chapter 15

"Yes! A weekend without the kids," Ibiso screamed and lifted her flute of sparkling cider.

"Thank you, Jesus." Damisi and Ebele followed suit, lifting their flutes as well.

Halima shook her head and laughed. "I'm telling my nieces and nephews."

"Don't be a snitch, Hali baby." Ibiso winked at her.

Halima smiled. Her sisters-in-laws had landed the previous night for the party that was later in the evening. After breakfast with her brothers earlier, they ditched the men and came to Platinum Hands for a few hours of pampering. Being Danjumas, they were immediately shown the VIP section of the exclusive spa. Dressed in plush white robes, they were currently getting pedicures and manicures. Later, they'd be treated to full-body massages and facials.

Ibiso and Ebele's kids were with Big Mummy while Damisi's kids left with the nanny earlier in the morning to Abuja. For now, the plan was for them all to attend the company function and head straight to Enugu where Big Mummy and the kids would be waiting.

"We love those little buggers, but sometimes they gotta go. Mummy needs alone time too," Damisi sipped from her flute.

"Me, I need extra alone time because Kammy is about to make me injure him," Ebele sighed. "I love that man down to his dirty underwear, but sometimes he irks my soul."

"Leave *dan uwa na* alone." Halima giggled.

"Okay, I'll remember that when you call me fussing that he's trying to regulate your life. *Shebi* he fired Abubakar without a second glance."

"True, I still don't know how you tamed him. I remember when he used to visit Jabir and I in Detroit when we were in school. The things that came out of his mouth were out of this world." Damisi laughed.

"I remember when he came back for the reading of his father's will. The day I met his brother…"

Halima watched a wide smile spread across Ibiso's face as she reminisced over the time she met Rasheed. To see them all in love made her think about Ekene. It had been two days since she got his text and responded with a simple "okay". The conversation with her mother drained her more than she was willing to admit.

Halima also tried to get in touch with Kudirat. The fact that Ekene was coming to pick her up and Kudirat, in her misguided attempt to help, had given a stranger the address to her house was a recipe for disaster. She tried reaching her friend to tell her to abort the mission no one sent her on. That too was for naught. The picture of the guy she sent her wasn't half bad, but she had enough complications in her life right now.

"Ewww, he flirted with you?" Ebele screamed.

"What do you mean by ewww?" Ibiso asked. "Watch it."

Ebele waved her off. "You know I don't mean it like that SoSo—"

"Hmm, then how did you mean it?"

Halima looked between the two women as Damisi shook

her head. They were all close, but Ebele and Ibiso always had these little petty arguments just like their husbands did. Her mother once told her, you slowly become who you marry.

"What's going on?" Halima asked.

"SoSo's other personality is on the rise." Damisi laughed and Ibiso rolled her eyes at her.

"You know she likes to think someone fears her. She was saying how Kammy tried to flirt with her when she met Rasheed, who quickly put a stop to it. I said ewww, not because she's not worth hitting on, but no one wants to hear that their husband had a thing for their sister-in-law." Ebele sucked her teeth and turned her back toward them.

The ladies sat in silence for a moment and Halima waited for Damisi to do her thing. She was the peacemaker of the group. Damisi gave Ibiso a hard glare and leaned her head toward Ebele.

"Ebi, I'm sorry. For the record, your Kam didn't even get close before Rasheed shut him and Jabir down," Ibiso said.

"What do you mean and Jabir?" This time Damisi's voice went up an octave. Ibiso put her head down and Halima wondered how they got here.

"Don't even go there, Dami. You know that man is all about you. Stalking you for six years is no joke. With me, he was just trying to get on Rasheed's nerves." Ibiso waved her off. "Y'all don't know how stone cold that man really was…"

"But you thawed him out, didn't you?" Ebele asked.

They all laughed. Over the next two hours, the ladies enjoyed conversation, laughs and were also treated to finger foods and wine. Leaving the spa, they went to get their dresses fitted and ended up in a restaurant for lunch. They all opted for grilled chicken salads since they would be eating full course meals later. Once the waiter brought out their meals and placed it in front of them, the ladies joined their hands together.

"Lord, make us truly thankful for this and other blessings, in Jesus name," Ebele prayed.

"Amen."

The chatter was light, and the forks clinked against the plates as the women ate. Halima had been itching to talk to them all morning. They were all closer to her age, so they might be able to shed light on her turmoil.

"How did you know your husbands were the ones?" Halima asked.

There was silence as they all turned and looked at her. She rubbed her earlobe before Damisi grabbed her hand to calm her nerves.

"I think for all three of us, our husbands pursued us. They saw what they wanted and went after it," Ibiso offered.

"But how we knew they were the ones? For Kam, it was love at first sight, but it was all kinds of wrong. He was a brat, and could be a bully, but all that was to cover up his hurt. The day I knew for certain was the day he let me see him. The real him. I knew then that despite everything we went through, my life would mean nothing without him in it."

"Awww," they all cooed.

"For me, I had been through so much, following a man across the country with no ring," Ibiso started.

Halima frowned.

"Hali baby, trust me I know. Looking back on it, I don't know what I was thinking as well. However, all that led me to your brother. Do you know how hard it was to get that man to let down the walls he'd built? I knew he was the one, but I wasn't willing to go through what I went through before for any man. So, when he ran to London, I concluded it was a wrap because I wasn't fighting for anyone that didn't want to be fought for." Ibiso chuckled. "But it was cemented when my older brother gave his stamp of approval and helped Rasheed get me back."

Halima shuddered. If only it were that easy for her. That

night, after they talked about the case, Rasheed stayed with her and they had a long talk about Ekene. He expressed his shock, displeasure and less than enthusiastic support. She understood all the points he made, but this was something she needed to figure out on her own. As long as she and Ekene were aware and were in it together, then she would follow her heart. No more playing it safe for her.

"Jabir and I did everything backwards, so don't look to me for advice. We both fell in love when both of us were party goers. There was no part of the campus where there was a party that we weren't there. We partied from dusk to dawn on the weekends. It always irritated me how he could keep up his grades studying medicine and I was struggling in mass communications." Damisi smiled.

"See the way she's cheesing. I don't even want to imagine what you're thinking about." Ibiso smirked.

"Have you seen my husband?"

"No, because I have mine. Now answer Hali's question. Can't you see she's going through things?" Ibiso nudged Damisi's shoulder and both of them laughed. Ebele shook her head and lifted a forkful of lettuce to her mouth.

"Anyway, I became a Christian—"

"Became a Christian? I thought you were already a Christian?" Halima asked.

"Yes, I was but I didn't practice it. Meaning, I didn't try to live holy like Christ instructed. What I should've said is when I became born again—"

"Huh?"

"Let me explain this. Dami will have us here all day," Ebele laughed. "Our religion is Christianity. As you know, that means followers of Christ. But we've all sinned and come short of His glory. Our relationship with God was severed. But He loves us so much He sent His Son Jesus Christ to die for us. With His blood, we are reconciled to God and now have a second chance at that relationship. When we confess with our mouths and believe in our hearts that Jesus is Lord and we are baptized, for us that means we've been born again with the Spirit of God."

"So, after that one time, that's it?" Halima asked.

"Pretty much. Then we strive to live every day up to the expectations He has laid before us in the Bible. The greatest of which is love," Ebele concluded.

"Do we have struggles? Yes… Do our demons disappear? Do we never sin? No, but with Jesus, we can rise above them and cope. His mercy and saving grace are our super weapons," Ibiso said.

Halima contemplated all the information that had just been thrown at her. This was further confirmation that the God of the Bible was a good God and He was love. In her own faith, she felt more scared to do anything wrong, rather than loved despite her mess ups.

"Thank you, Pastors Ebi and SoSo," Damisi snickered. "Anyway, Hali for your brother and I, I had to run. I changed and he decided to remain the same. For my sanity, I had to escape because although I loved him, I loved my soul more. How did I know he was the one—"

"If a man stalked you for six years, he better be the one," Ibiso joked.

All of them shared a boisterous laugh while Damisi and Ibiso gave each other high fives.

"Well, there is your answer," Ebele said.

The noise around them died down and after a few moments, Damisi spoke, "You know you can talk to us. We are sisters, Hali. May not get along all the time but our sisterhood is strong, and nothing means more to us than the wellbeing of this family."

Halima remained silent for a few seconds. "Yes, I know that. I've always been a loner until I met my brothers and they turned around and married you, ladies. Your friendship has been invaluable—"

"Why are you giving a speech like we are your employees?" Ebele asked with a smile.

"Oh lawd, this one is turning into mini Kam, no filter," Ibiso said.

"Anyway, what I mean is, I appreciate you." Halima paused. "I'm just so confused, my faith, my feelings, his feelings?"

"His? What did I miss?" Ebele asked.

"Unless you've been living under a bridge, you should know she's talking about Ekene," Damisi said as she and Ibiso shared an incredulous look.

Halima giggled.

"You and Ekene? When? How? Does Kammy know?" Ebele fired off questions.

"You see if you got out from under Kam and the twins once in a while, you would know," Damisi chided.

"That man is so sweet but when it comes to his "E", he's borderline controlling. I know you like it so I'm not hating, but when you miss out on gist like this don't be surprised," Ibiso said.

"My baby is not controlling. He just loves me…" Ebele defended.

"Hmm, okay. Hali, continue *jare.*"

"Well, I've known for a while I didn't want to marry Danladi anymore. I didn't say anything because frankly, I feared the blowback."

"What changed?" Damisi asked.

"During the DeSab case, I spent a considerable amount of time with Kene and the attraction grew deeper. I shouldn't be feeling these things, but I do. I knew then that even if nothing came out of it with Ekene, I couldn't marry Danladi." She sighed. "I see how my brothers love you and I want that. I deserve that."

"Yes, you do. The attraction for you might have started some months ago, but honey, Kene has had eyes for you for years. Only difference between him and Jabir is he didn't stalk you," Ibiso swished her drink in her mouth and let out a loud pop with her lips.

"You will stop calling my husband a stalker. He was just in the pursuit of love."

Ebele and Halima burst out laughing as Ibiso gawked at Damisi.

"Anyway, that aside. Ever since I got back from Abuja a couple of months ago, I've constantly been bothered by a voice asking if I want to be healed." Halima observed the women looking at her with wide eyes.

"Then I started having dreams. They become more vivid each time I have them. So, I started to attend church, occasionally. I need to prove to myself that Islam is where I'm supposed to be so all my attempts at searching the Bible and attending church is to find holes. But the deeper I seek to prove your Jesus a mere prophet, I see Him as merciful, compassionate, and loving. Someone I want to serve. But at what cost? My mom will disown me. Uncle Musa will drag me through the mud..."

"And we will love you through it all," Ibiso said, holding Halima tight.

This was the first time she was able to get it all out in the open without judgment.

"Hali, you know we love you no matter what you are. Honestly, we want you to know our Christ and confess Him as Lord, but we never pushed because we never wanted you to feel pressured. Salvation is personal. But we did invite you to church and Christian functions and left room for questions in case you had them," Damisi said.

"Sometimes God uses bad situations to help you change the trajectory of your life. Look at your brother, he was all set to play in that huge competition, then he got injured. Him getting injured exposed pieces of him that he had kept hidden for so long," Ebele said.

"I just don't know. Now I'm in a stupid legal battle, my mom hates me, Ekene is probably fed up with my indecisiveness and I'm no closer to a revelation," Halima sighed.

"God uses visions and dreams to speak to us. The revelation would come, but you have to be open to receive. Ask your brother how he got saved." Damisi placed her fork on her now empty plate and leaned back in her chair.

"In the meantime, open your heart to that man and stop giving him the runaround," Ibiso added.

"Yes! Because we know he's already going to have to put up a fight with your brothers, especially your *dan uwa na*." Ebele massaged her temples.

"That's another thing. Kene is my date tonight and I haven't had a chance to tell Jabir and Kamal. Rasheed knows and nearly fought him. And my friend set me up with a blind date for tonight."

"Huh? You went from Miss Modest to Miss I've Got Options." Ibiso snapped her fingers. Halima rolled her eyes and shook her head. She was glad someone thought it was funny.

"SoSo, how did you totally skip over the part where your husband tried to fight his best friend?" Ebele asked.

"Because I expected nothing less. No man is good enough for their baby sister, period. Humph, Ekene better be on his game because he still got Jabir and Lord help him, Kamal, to deal with."

"Hali, don't worry. I'll get Jabir to behave," Damisi reassured her.

"Ha!" Ebele and Ibiso shrieked in unison before laughing.

Ebele placed her hand on Halima's shoulder. "Sis, I'm not going to sell you false dreams. Kamal will show out, but to what degree is something I can help you out with."

Halima took in a breath and exhaled. She took a sip of her drink and motioned for the waiter to bring the check. Her sisters-in-law weren't telling her anything she didn't already know.

Ekene better be ready. She wouldn't let them be unfair to him, but to deal with her he had to deal with them. The waiter arrived with the check moments later. Halima checked the time. They had approximately five hours to be at the venue. She paid, and as they stood up to leave, a fine specimen of the male kind approached them.

"Hi, Ebele! I thought that was you." He leaned in to hug her while Ebele gave him her side. Because of her height, her head landed right under his arm. Halima, like Ibiso and Damisi, had her hands on her hips, waiting for anything to go awry.

"Ladies, this is Victor," Ebele said. Her ever sweet tone was now tight.

"Nice to meet you ladies," Victor said.

They all mumbled their response. Mainly because they knew him as her ex-boyfriend. Halima also knew him as the man Kamal had a run-in with in Ebele's apartment.

"It's been a while," he said.

"Yes, it has. I trust you're doing well."

"Yes, I am. Thanks for asking," Ebele responded.

Halima turned up her nose when she noticed his eyes roam all over Ebele's body. On instinct, she looked around. Kamal had a way of showing up when his wife was being approached by anyone of the opposite gender. It was almost as though he had a tracking device on her. In the event he did show up, Halima wanted to locate the nearest exit.

"I'm so sorry to hear your facility is out of commission. It was the talk of the country when it opened."

The ladies frowned, but it was Ebele who spoke. "Who told you that? I just opened a second location in Asaba."

Victor's brows creased in confusion. "Okay, there must have been a mix up. I saw your husband several months back and asked about it. Two of my dancers had injuries and everyone said you were the best. He said you're no longer in business."

Ibiso, Damisi and Halima all tried to stifle their laughs the minute that explanation left his mouth. Kammy strikes again.

"Oh, he did, did he?" Ebele said.

Halima's gaze traveled to Ebele's hands. They shook, a sign they all knew meant she was furious. Halima toyed with the idea of calling her brother and giving him a heads up on hurricane Ebele that was about to come his way. But then she thought that if he was occupied sucking up to his wife, he wouldn't have time to bother Ekene.

"Yes. Have you opened back up? I need—"

"Actually, she has, but is on mid-year break," Ibiso said, cutting the conversation short and putting her arm around Ebele's shoulders.

Victor smiled. "Okay, I'll look for you next time I'm in Abuja. We can talk business." He winked, nodded his head and sauntered away.

"I'm going to kill him." Ebele shrugged Ibiso's arm off and stormed toward the exit.

"Controlling..." Damisi and Ibiso laughed while Halima shook her head.

"Ebi wait *na*... remember he's papa twins o." Ibiso ran after Ebele.

Damisi looked at Halima as they strolled out of the restaurant. "Should we warn him?"

"Nah," Halima responded.

Chapter 16

kene stood in front of his mirror and fastened the cuff links to his black custom-made suit by Davidson Petit-Frère. He finished his look with an ear stud and a watch on his wrist. It was the night of the Danjuma dinner, and he had only one goal in mind. Get back into Halima's good graces. He knew she was angry. That was evident in the fact that she kept it strictly professional with him. Like sending documents he needed for his case through her assistant, rather than bringing them over herself as she had begun doing over the past several weeks. Also, the one sentence or no response to his texts were now playing with his mind.

Ordinarily, he would've chased her down and made her talk to him. But he did get it. She was overwhelmed, and the fact that he had called Rasheed had annoyed her. Therefore, he gave her space. What also helped was his case load. However, he was going insane without her and time was up. Before he could take them not talking and being in the same space. But he had gotten to know her intimately and that was no longer an option.

He was a lawyer and hadn't lost a case yet. Now that he

had Halima, he was not planning to lose her either. She'd ask that he meet her at the venue. He preferred to pick her up but knowing this was work for her, he agreed. He did plan on making sure that no one would be confused on who her date was.

Ekene turned his head from side to side, brushing his freshly cut hair and beard. He put on what she told him was her favorite cologne and stepped back to give himself another glance over. Satisfied with his look, he grabbed his keys and wallet before making his way out the door. Once in his BMW M850i, he called his dad. Between his professional and super complicated personal life, he'd missed a couple of Sunday lunches.

"*Mgbede Oma* sir," Ekene greeted in Igbo once his dad answered the call.

"Ah! *Ndewo* my son. *Kedu?*"

"*Adi m mma,*" Ekene responded. He wasn't fine, but that wasn't something he wanted to involve his father in.

"Good, good. How is business? I saw you on the news the other day. Your friends' company is in the media again. That his sister keeps getting them in trouble."

Ekene felt his fist clench extra hard around the steering wheel. Halima was off-limits. His dad didn't know that, but he was about to educate him. "Old man, you of all people know that not everything you hear or read in the press is real. Halima isn't the problem here. People who are greedy and want to benefit from where they didn't sow are."

He took in a breath and continued. "Against company policy, that driver took three extra shifts back to back. He already cost them millions of Naira in a breach of contract suit with their customer. I know it's not nice to talk about the dead, but now he's no more and his family wants to capitalize on his death."

Sweat gathered around his forehead, clear evidence of

how heated he was. This case was a total waste of time, but anything to drag others through the mud for personal gain seemed to be the modus operandi.

His father remained silent and Ekene wasn't sure they were still connected. "Dad?"

"Yes, I'm here." His father laughed lowly.

"What's so funny?"

"You. So that young woman has been able to do what I've been praying for."

"What are you talking about?"

"Look, my son, the youth can walk faster, but the elder knows the road."

Ekene remained silent as he took in the meaning of the proverb. His father, probably knowing he needed to process it, remained quiet.

"You don't have to discuss it if you don't want to. I'm glad that you've opened your heart to the possibility. But son, I also want to caution you, love isn't all there is to a relationship."

"Unconditional love is…"

"And to that, I agree, but it is also nice to have some commonalities when you consider a relationship, so that when problems arise – which they will – that unconditional love will hold."

"Are you saying this because she's Hausa?"

"You know me well enough to know that's far from it. At the core, you and her don't believe in the same thing. How will you raise your children? What holidays will you observe? Those kids will be so confused. Is all that worth it?"

"I love her, Dad. I have for years. I don't know how to get my heart to stop. Neither do I want it to."

"Then I'll be praying for you. Remember sugarcane is always sweetest at its joints."

"What does that mean?"

"You'll figure it out. Go and have fun and remember we

leave for the village tomorrow. I expect to see you there some-time next week."

"I'll be there old man. *Ka chi foo.*"

"*Ka chi foo* my son."

For the rest of the drive, "Angel of My Life" by Paul Play, played on the old school radio station he loved, as Ekene mulled over his father's words. He got to the light and quickly Googled the last proverb his father used. It meant good things in life might appear difficult, but will be worth it in the end. Ekene smiled as traffic moved. Instead of dwelling on imaginary weddings and kids, tonight he was going to start with the simple stuff; getting Halima to talk to him again.

———

"WE'VE HAD A VERY SUCCESSFUL YEAR, AND EACH ONE OF YOU should be proud. I want to take this opportunity to thank everyone for all of their efforts throughout the year. The success of our company is built on the hard work of our employees. In this past year, we've enjoyed many successes, as well as losses."

Ekene struggled to pay attention to Rasheed giving his closing remarks to Danjuma Group employees. His eyes and mind were wrapped up in the perfection that was Halima Danjuma. The first thing he noticed when he arrived earlier was her hair. She no longer had on the hijab. It hung in big curls down past her shoulders and framed her beautiful face. He had so many questions, but each time he tried to get to her, she had vendors and employees pulling her left and right. He was determined not to interrupt her work, but the longing for her grew with each moment he couldn't talk to her.

The red flowing gown she wore had a big black flower on the upper left corner and was draped snuggly over her curves. The dress exposed her neck and three quarters of her arms. Her fair skin was spotless and glowed under the lighting.

"I'll hand it over to my COO and sister, Halima Danjuma, to say a few words." Rasheed moved to the side as Halima stepped to the podium.

"I've been reflecting on the things that I'm most grateful for. First among those is the talented and committed group of employees here at DG. As our CEO said, we had some wins and some losses. Unfortunately, a month ago, we lost a valued employee. For that, our heartfelt and deepest condolences go out to his family. Thank you again for the work you've done in helping us provide award winning services to our clients," Halima said.

Ekene watched as her kissable, red lips pursed together. She stretched out her arms and clapped for the employees. Then the whole room exploded in applause.

"That's baby sis. I'm so proud of her," Jabir said.

Ekene was invited to sit at the table where the Danjuma's sat with their wives. He was having a hard time paying attention to the small talk going on as he watched Rasheed assist Halima down from the raised platform.

"I'm proud of her, too. For all this crap that's going on around her, she's really holding her head up," Damisi responded.

"I know, right?" Ebele took her fork and cut into her slice of cake.

"Oh, so you're no longer on mute when it comes to everyone else?" Kamal asked, sulking.

Ekene gave Jabir an inquisitive look, trying to get some insight on what had the couple everyone loved so tight.

"He got her mad yesterday, but he forgot sis is just the one to set him straight." Jabir laughed.

"Stop instigating bro, and E, stop playing with me. You were closed when I saw that dude. So, what's the problem?" Kamal asked.

"For installation, Kam. Installation that took one weekend. Leave me alone," Ebele warned.

"And? The man didn't ask for how long or why." Kamal looked at her like what he'd said made all the sense in the world and she was overreacting.

Ekene didn't know the facts so couldn't judge. He had problems of his own. He and Halima exchanged pleasantries when he arrived about two hours ago, but her attitude toward him almost mirrored Ebele's toward Kamal; thankfully not as harsh.

"Look E, I don't know why you're mad. There was no way I was letting you massage that man," Kamal said.

"I don't massage people. And I have workers," Ebele responded in a hushed whisper. "And did you say let me?"

Kamal waved her off. "You know what I mean."

Ebele cut her eyes at her husband and Ekene chuckled. When he first met Ebele, he knew that any woman who could tame the wildest Danjuma was a superwoman. To watch her in action, especially with their size difference, was nothing short of amazing. Kamal was putty in her hands. The love they shared was wild and deep. That's what he was finally ready to have. Tonight, he was laying all his cards on the table.

"It's not like you need his money," Kamal said.

"It's not about the money. It's about you thinking you can control me," Ebele responded. Jabir laughed and Ekene couldn't help but follow suit at the look of disbelief on Kamal's face. Ekene would've felt sorry for him if he didn't see the smirk behind his eyes. Kamal loved getting a rise out of his wife.

"Control? Come on, babe. You know that's not true. You should be thanking me for saving you."

"Jesus is Lord!" Damisi exclaimed with a chuckle.

Ekene and everyone else turned to Kamal in anticipation of what he was going to say next.

"How? Why?" Ebele asked what they all wanted to know.

"The Bible says to not let other Christians stumble. Therefore, I was trying to save you from stumbling." Kamal shrugged.

Everyone laughed but Ebele. Instead, she had a perplexed, hurt look on her face. That quickly silenced those at the table. Ekene looked around and saw Halima and Rasheed still engaged with employees.

"You don't trust me?" Ebele asked.

"What? No. Of course, I trust you." Kamal pulled her hand to his lips and kissed it. "It's him I don't trust. Do you realize how beautiful you are? Inside and out."

"Flattery won't work," she said.

"It's not flattery. All facts." He kissed the back of her hand again. "Now, when what's-his-name tries to make a pass at you, you'll cuss him out. Then because your heart is so beautiful, you'll feel bad, which will lead to you being sad. I'll then be forced to kick his behind. That would make me stumble—"

Jabir laughed placing his head on his wife's shoulder before looking up again. "Make it make sense, bro. How are you saving her?"

"I'm saving her from being left behind. Supposing the rapture happens right then, she'll be straight left." Kamal looked at Jabir with an expression that wondered how he didn't get that.

He then turned and looked at his wife. "I ain't trying to play with our salvation like that, E. We're strolling in those pearly gates together. But if you cause me to stumble, you might not make it. And then miss out on eternity."

Laughter erupted. Even Ebele's mouth filled with air as she desperately tried to stifle her amusement.

"Really? Kamal Danjuma, you don't get it do you?" Ebele asked.

"Ebele Danjuma, no I don't. But I'm tired of you being mad at me." Kamal nuzzled his nose against her neck as he sang the chorus to Justin Bieber's "Sorry."

"Bro, sis still ain't talking to you?" Rasheed asked, walking up on them.

Ibiso appeared from behind the buffet table. She wrapped her arm around her husband and laid her head on his shoulder. In typical Rasheed fashion, he kissed her forehead and looked at her with admiration.

Ekene looked around for Halima. She was just with her brother a second ago. His temperature rose immediately as he saw her standing in the corner talking to a man. It wasn't so much that they were talking, but the fact that he couldn't get that smile out of her all evening. Ekene had never before felt a pang of jealousy that threatened to overtake his rational thought. With the event winding down, Ekene was ready to clear the air between them. Now there was someone in her face, and he was touching her arm. Something that took him years to do. His attention was drawn back to the table at the next words out of Kamal's mouth.

"Yeah, but I got what she needs at home." Kamal winked at his wife.

Ebele placed her face in her hands in embarrassment. "Lord, save me."

"What I tell you about asking for things that's already yours?" Kamal asked.

Ekene returned his focus to Halima and without being told, his feet began to move. With one hand in his pocket, his stride was confident as he maneuvered through the semi-empty tables. He knew the exact moment she felt him approaching. Halima turned and the look in her eyes dripped with apprehension.

Seconds later, Ekene reached her and stood by her side, as close as he could get. The man she was with stepped back, a move Ekene assumed was from recognition of his protective stance.

Yeah, that's what I thought.

In a flash, Ekene took in his appearance. The designer suit and matching shoes he had on were telltale signs of money.

"Ekene…" Halima acknowledged him, her eyes pleading.

He was almost moved, but her use of his full name and the grin and what he recognized as lust in the eyes of her acquaintance kept him focused on his mission.

"Who do we have here?" Ekene nodded toward the man.

"This is Tanimu, Kudi's cousin. Tanimu, this is Ekene. He's the company lawyer and a very close friend of the family." Halima made the introductions.

Oh, that's how she wants to play it.

He knew Kudirat, her best friend, was an Islamic matchmaker. He'd watched her parlay with Danladi, and now that she was free, this dude came along. There was no way he was letting whatever it was, happen.

"Nice to meet you." The man extended his hand.

With a hardened stare, Ekene looked at Tanimu's hand and back at his face. Ekene knew that he was acting out of character, but he couldn't stop himself. He looked between Halima and the man with a blank expression. He felt the fire Halima emitted from her eyes, but he'd deal with that later.

"I need to speak to you in private," Ekene said to Halima.

"Later."

"Now."

They went back and forth like it was only the two of them in the room. A stare down ensued. Ekene knew that her refusal was because of his behavior, but somehow the tension in his heart made him not care. His eyes moved when he saw Tanimu place his hand on the small of her back and try to whisper something in her ear. At that point, all sensibility left him.

"If you don't want to lose that hand, I suggest you keep it to yourself and step out of her personal space." Ekene seethed.

"Ekene," Halima gasped.

"He's got two seconds." Ekene's eyes darted from her back to the man.

"Actually, I'm her date," Tanimu responded.

"Her what?" Ekene raised his voice higher than usual. Not enough to cause a disruption, but enough to have the Danjuma brothers heading toward them.

"Kene…"

"Oh, I'm Kene now? You're on a date, Halima?"

"Let me explain later," Halima said.

"Oh no, we're about to talk now." Ekene grabbed her hand and turned. Kamal halted him by grabbing his arm.

"Yo player, what's going on?" Kamal asked.

"Not now, Kammy," Ekene responded frustration lacing his voice.

Kamal chuckled. "Stone Cold, come get your friend. He can't be grabbing my sister and telling me not now."

"*Dan uwa na*, I'm okay," Halima reassured Kamal as Jabir looked on with a clenched jaw.

"You guys are going to cause a scene and with all that's going on, we don't need any more press," Rasheed said. He looked down at Halima, "Sis, you okay?"

Halima nodded. Ekene gave his friend a grateful nod and glanced at Halima who rolled her eyes at him. As they were about to move, Jabir spoke up.

"I don't know what's going on, but you see her…" He pointed towards his sister. "You got five minutes, then I want some answers."

"You'll have them." Ekene tossed over his shoulder. With Halima's hand still in his, he gestured for her to lead the way. As they moved in silence, he stole glances at her. He wanted to do so many things, first on that list was run his fingers through her hair. A close second was capturing her lips with his. They were going to get to that, but he needed answers first.

"What was that back there?" Halima snatched her hand away from him.

They were now in a vacant conference room in the hotel where the event was taking place.

"I should be asking you that. You going on dates now? I've been trying to talk to you for days and you either ignore me or give me dry, one-line answers. But you have time to bring dates?" Ekene fumed. "You specifically asked me to meet you here. Was it because of him?"

"Ugh! And you wonder why I'm so upset with you."

"You can be upset all you want, then we talk about it. Not show up with dates."

"He is not dates…he is a date—"

"Now is not the time to be giving me English lessons."

"I did not bring him here. He met me here."

"Why?"

Halima sighed, but remained silent.

"Why?" he repeated.

"Kudi set us up on a blind date," she whispered.

"She what?" Ekene loosened the bowtie that now felt like a noose around his neck.

"It's a long story…"

"You better hurry it up then. Your brothers would soon be here. I'm not letting you go until you talk to me and I won't allow them to interfere either," Ekene growled. "So, we just might be making that scene Rasheed is trying to avoid."

She crossed her arms over her chest. "Some lawyer you are."

"Well, baby right now, I'm not your lawyer…"

"Then who are you?" There was challenge and defiance in her glare.

"Why did Kudi set you up on a date?" Ekene asked, ignoring her question.

In the next couple of minutes, Halima explained to him the events that led up to Tanimu being at the dinner with her.

"Why didn't you tell me?" Ekene asked, his voice much calmer, but his irritation still lingered.

She swallowed. "I was not talking to you."

"And why was that?" His eyes examined her with curiosity.

"See, Ekene, one of the reasons I began to question my Islamic faith was the fact that I began to dislike what it meant for me. The patriarchy lifestyle amongst other things, wasn't one I could live with any more or thought I deserved." Halima paced the small space they occupied. "My brothers can be overprotective. Even though I tell them time and time again that I'm a big girl and can take care of myself." She shrugged. "But then again, they're my brothers and know when I'm serious about them backing off.

"For you, it's different. When you baby me, it makes me feel as though you don't have confidence in me or think I'm some weak woman that can't handle her own. In case none of you noticed, I am the COO of a very successful business. I do my job and I do it well. I can also take care of myself."

Her eyes narrowed at him. "You, calling my brother to hold my hand when you gave me the news made me feel slighted. It took me back to those days when I saw my father make all the decisions for my mother. She lost herself in him. And although I almost went down that path trying to make others happy, now I know better, and I can't do better if the people around me do not give me the room to."

She paused and bent her head. Seconds later she looked him square in his eyes. In them, he saw a resolution he had never seen before. Her next words, however, garnered a chuckle. "So instead of dealing with that, I decided I would just distance myself from it."

Ekene was with her right until the "distance" part. However, the more she spoke, the more he knew that living without her was impossible. It hurt him that he was the source of any pain she was feeling. He vowed to keep her smiling at all costs. He walked over to where she was. As he got closer, she took a step backward until he had her trapped between himself and the table. Her breath hitched and so did his heart.

"You can't distance yourself from me, Princess," he said in a low whisper.

"Wha…why?" she stuttered.

"Because the first day I met you. I knew I had to stay away. And I did a pretty good job until I didn't. Listen to me. I have no idea what the future holds right now, but I love you. I know you feel strongly for me, too. I don't want to pressure you into saying anything. Just let me love you and we'll figure out the rest of it along the way."

"You l…o…v… e me?"

"Come on, you can't be that surprised."

"Yes, I am. We have strong chemistry that I won't deny. My feelings are what I can't unscramble, but I know they are there…"

"So, let them guide you." He paused. "Now about what you were saying. First and foremost, you do not get…no, we do not get to shut the other out again. I thought we established that."

Halima nodded.

"I need the words, baby."

"Agreed," she mumbled.

"I'm not trying to control or make you feel less than the independent woman you are." Ekene cupped the side of her neck with his hand and caressed it lightly with his thumb. His gaze held hers. "When you hurt, I bleed. You mean the world to me and I will always try to protect you. Please do not ask me not to."

"Kene…"

"Listen, I know you can take care of yourself. I wouldn't want a woman who couldn't. Your drive, intelligence, determination, and loyalty are all the things I find sexy about you." He looked down at her body. "Well and this dress of course."

"Be serious," Halima smirked.

"I am. Wait until we clear the air and I'll tell…no show you, how serious I am." He focused back on her face. "I know you don't want me smothering or underestimating you, and I won't. But as the man whose heart you hold, you can't expect me to sit by and let you figure out life alone. I can't do it, Princess."

"Okay, Kene."

"Good." He moved his hand to her silky hair and twirled some tresses. "You took it off?"

"Yes."

"Why?"

"You're full of questions, tonight, aren't you?"

"Yes, so answer me woman."

Halima gave him the same explanation she told him she also gave her mother. He didn't want to be the reason she felt she needed to change anything about herself. That was not his glory to take. It would all be for God, but he was going to love her regardless.

"Okay, I get it. To my next question, the second to last one," he said.

Halima raised her brows in anticipation.

"Who's going to tell that chump to leave? You or me? I'm not sure you want me doing it."

Halima giggled. "I never saw you as the jealous kind."

"Over you? I'll be anything. Besides God is a jealous God and I'm made in His image. I do not like to share."

"I'll tell him." She hesitated, before asking, "What's your last question?"

Ekene zeroed in on her lips, licked his and whispered, "May I?"

He recognized the contemplation in her eyes and wasn't going to pressure her. Then she nodded. He cupped her face in his hands and drew her to him. He captured her lips with his and wrapped his arms tightly around her. The action sent shock waves rippling throughout his body. He was caught up in the euphoria of finally tasting her and feeling her body next to his when he heard the door slam.

"Tell me I didn't just see his lips on my sister," Kamal roared.

Halima slowly removed her hands from around his neck but didn't move from his embrace. He liked that. Making sure she was presentable, and he was well adjusted, he turned and saw three angry Danjuma men staring at him.

Chapter 17

Kamal strode toward the couple. Jabir and Rasheed fell into step immediately. In a flash, the Danjuma brothers stood in front of them with their arms crossed over their chests. Ekene wasn't ready to do this now. All he wanted to do was spend the rest of the evening with his love. He also knew this was necessary because, after this conversation, he wasn't having it again. He shifted Halima behind him.

Jabir sneered at the gesture.

"Y'all see this?" Kamal asked, his brows furrowed. "First, he has his lips all over her, now he's protecting her from us. Us?"

"My brothers—" Halima started.

"It's okay, Princess. I got it," Ekene cut her off. There was no way he was letting her get in the middle of his battle.

"Yeah, he got it, *Princess*," Kamal taunted.

Behind his anger, Ekene saw hurt. He knew how close the two of them were, so if she didn't tell him about what little there was to tell about them, he understood his feelings.

"*Dan uwo—*"

"Nah, don't call me that now. I asked you." Kamal's nostrils flared.

Ekene moved closer to him. "Man, if you gonna come at me, come at me, but leave her out of this."

"Who are you to tell me what I can or cannot do to my sister?" Kamal scoffed.

"The minute I told her I love her—"

"Hold up. You love her?" Jabir asked.

Ekene ignored Jabir and kept his eyes on Kamal. He moved a step closer to him. Kamal was about the same height as he was, but his body mass was bigger being that he was once a professional athlete. However, none of that, including Kamal's reckless mouth, intimidated him when it came to anything concerning Halima.

"The minute I told her I loved her, I became her protector, her covering." He glanced over at Halima who looked defeated. That angered him. "This woman holds my heart and I'll protect her from any and every one that causes her the slightest anguish." He crossed his hands over his chest and the two of them had a standoff. Halima's sigh sliced through his ego. He turned to her and pulled her close.

"Princess, I need to talk to your brothers. Can you give us some privacy?" Ekene asked. He saw the objection she was about to make dancing around in her eyes. He bent and whispered in her ear. "Trust me, this needs to happen." He leaned his forehead against hers, then kissed it.

Halima approached her brothers and kissed each one of them on their cheeks. When she got to Kamal, they stared at each other for a couple of seconds. She raised her hand and caressed his face.

"I love you and I'm sorry."

Kamal stared down at her with softer eyes. Then he pulled her to his chest. "This ain't over, but I love you too."

"Be nice," she said.

"Can't make no promises." Kamal shrugged and Halima strolled out of the room.

"Now gentlemen, we all love that woman and she's going

through a lot. I don't want her being placed in the middle of us. First, I should've come to you guys with what I was feeling considering our relationship and her being your sister. I apologize, but that's all I'm apologizing for. So, whatever you have to say get it off your chest because after this we're not revisiting this conversation," Ekene finished.

"You see, that's where you're wrong. We'll have this conversation however many times we want to because that's our baby sister," Jabir said.

"I'm baffled he doesn't know that," Kamal cosigned. "Stone Cold, you too quiet over there, you knew about this?"

"Let's sit down," Rasheed spoke for the first time.

"You've been silent all this time, letting your brothers come at me," Ekene said to Rasheed once they were all seated.

"What's he supposed to do. Whoop us?" Kamal asked.

"Kammy, calm down," Rasheed said. "Jabir, get your twin."

"*Twin*, get your brother. He knew about this and kept it from us." Kamal growled. "Sis takes off her head thingy and suddenly people coming out the woodworks. First funny looking dude following her around all night like a puppy. Now our own friend." Kammy shook his head.

"You done?" Rasheed asked.

Kamal glared at Rasheed. Ekene watched the exchange between the brothers and hated the fact that his happiness was causing so much strife.

"How did this even happen with you and Hali, man?" Jabir asked.

"I don't know bro. I felt it happening over time. Like I told Stone Cold, I tried to fight it—"

"You didn't try hard enough," Kamal said.

"Look Kam, I don't know what your problem is. A couple of months ago, you were gonna let her marry Danladi, becoming someone's second wife, so what's the deal?" Ekene was fed up with the disrespect.

"First off, that's my sister…period. No man will ever be good enough for her. Two, the way you went about it. Three, that marriage wasn't happening."

They all looked at him with confusion etched on their faces.

Kamal returned the puzzled look. "What?" He shook his head. "Y'all disappoint me. How do you think I was ever gonna let that happen? I don't care what kind of promises our dad made. I had people on standby, ready to kidnap Hali on whatever day Uncle Musa thought that crap was going down."

"You were just gonna kidnap her and not tell anyone?" Jabir asked.

"Heck yeah. I don't know what y'all think this is." He looked at all of them like they were the crazy ones.

All of them burst out in laughter and when it died down, so did the tension between them.

"On the real though, so you were gonna sit back and let her marry dude? You sure you love her as much as you claim?" Kamal asked Ekene.

Ekene's body grew hot with anger, at the insinuation and the way Kamal relaxed back in his chair and looked unbothered after his statement. He would've reacted, but Halima's face came to his mind's eye and he had to remember, she'd be crushed if what they had created a rift between him and her brothers.

"Rasheed, you knew and didn't tell?" Jabir questioned, bringing the conversation back to where it originally was.

Rasheed hunched his shoulders. "It wasn't my story to tell, besides he and I already went at it and he knows where I stand."

"Guys, we've been friends for a long time. My love for Halima is deeper than anyone of you can imagine. I don't want this to ruin our friendship, but I won't deny my happiness or hers to please anybody. It's not my aim to play with your sister or intentionally hurt her," Ekene said.

"Haven't you learned anything from my family? Interfaith marriages are hard to maintain," Jabir said. He seemed to be the only logical one. Rasheed was too quiet for him and Kamal was too loud.

"Why is everyone jumping to marriage? We just started dating."

"Just dating? Oh, heck no, so you just want a sample?" Kamal jumped up.

"Kam, sit yourself down," Rasheed said.

Kammy tapped Jabir on his shoulder. Jabir looked at him. "Check my face bro, did I transform into 'Hance?" Kamal asked referencing Rasheed's son, Yohance before he sat back down.

Rasheed shook his head. "Right now, your reaction mirrors his exactly." He paused. "I have my reservations, but Hali seems happy and we all know that Kene is a good dude."

"I'm not feeling this. I know my sister is grown but I'm not trying to see her hurt," Kamal said. The seriousness in his tone wasn't hidden.

"You don't have to feel it, as long as you respect it, we good. I'll never do anything to hurt her," Ekene said.

"Not intentionally, but this thing y'all doing is scary. I know Halima isn't as rigid as she used to be. Since she got back from the U.S, she's become more curious about Christ and the church. But at the end of the day, she's still Muslim," Jabir said.

"I know man, and I'm gonna help her with that curiosity in love. And hope and pray to God that He does what He does best."

"Okay then bro, do what you gotta do," Jabir said.

"Don't mess this up," Rasheed added.

Ekene looked at Kamal who kept his eyes on him as he

stood. He placed his palms flat on the table and leaned in. Ekene knew Kamal needed this so he let him have it. Somewhere during the conversation, Ekene realized it wasn't personal. That was how Kammy would be with anyone interested in Halima, no matter her age. They were that close. Besides two out of three wasn't bad.

"Mr. Protector, you better start with the courtroom and getting those crazy allegations thrown out," Kamal said.

Ekene nodded.

Then he continued. "See, I'm more like savage Jesus. You know the flip tables over, cursing fig tree Jesus. That cast your burdens unto me stuff, I leave it for these two." He pointed toward his brothers. "If my sister sheds one tear over you, it's straight table flipping, no questions asked."

Ekene stood, so did Jabir and Rasheed. After a few moments, he stretched out his hand to Kamal. Kamal looked at it as a beat passed between them. Kamal took his hand in a firm handshake.

"That's fair."

"Then welcome to the family, bro." Kamal smiled at him.

"I was so glad when you guys all came out of the conference room smiling."

Ekene sat in his home office as he watched Halima come in and out of focus on Facetime. She was packing to go with her family to Enugu the next day.

"You know your brothers; they're very protective and rightfully so. But it's nothing to worry your pretty head about. We're good." Ekene took a sip of the cold kunu she'd made for him some time ago. He'd never tasted the creamy delight made from coconut and tiger nuts until she insisted. Now he couldn't let it go. The cinnamon she added was perfect.

His mind went back to the tense conversation he and her

brothers had some hours prior. He still smirked to himself as he remembered little Kammy bossing up on him because of his sister. He remembered their days in London as kids. Who would have thought?

"So, you still won't tell me what happened?" She folded a piece of clothing in the opened suitcase on her bed.

"Nope." Ekene was putting finishing touches on briefs that needed to be submitted to the court the next day. One for the Tijani case and the other to get the frivolous lawsuit against her and Danjuma Group dropped. He had two more days in Lagos before he joined his own family in Enugu. Another thing he and the Danjuma's had in common was that his village was close to the village their mother was from.

"Have you talked to them?" Ekene asked because she left with her sisters-in-law as soon as he and the guys got out of the room.

"Not really, but I know on the flight tomorrow, they'll have a lot to say," Halima giggled. "But I can handle them."

"That's my superwoman. Are you ready to visit the East?"

"Yes, I'm excited. I've never been. As you know, I lived in Abuja all my life except when I went to school and when I started living in Lagos a few years ago."

"I'll be your personal tour guide."

"I can't wait. I'm worried about the company and all the negative press, but I'm looking forward to leaving it all behind. Even just for a little while." She sat on her bed and rubbed the back of her neck.

That caught Ekene's attention. He closed his laptop and stared at her. "Look at me, Princess."

Their eyes connected.

"You know I'll never let anything happen to you. You're a strong woman, kind and compassionate. People are trying to take that for granted, but it's not happening."

Halima remained silent, but he could see the tension roll off her shoulders. If only a little bit. He wished he could reach out and touch her. He glanced at his watch; it was close to midnight.

"Do you need me, Princess?"

"No, it's late. You have work to do and I'll be fine."

He hated seeing the woman who was so goofy and full of life be weighed down like this. "For you, everything stops. Just say the word."

"No baby, I'll be fine. You can do something for me," she whispered.

He wanted to bask in the pleasure of hearing her call him baby, but the anxiety all over her face wouldn't let him keep his mind on it. It was almost like she was scared to say what was on her mind.

"Anything."

"Teach me how to pray…to your God…through Jesus."

Ekene's heart thumped rapidly as he took in her request. He blinked to make sure he wasn't dreaming. In the moment, there were so many questions he wanted to ask, but he was hesitant to do so he didn't scare her off. But he had to make sure. He knew a little about Islam and knew Jesus was Isa the Prophet to them, but he only prayed through Jesus the Son of the Living God.

"Jesus the prophet or the Son of God?" he asked. Chills washed over him as he awaited her answer.

"I still struggle. How can a man be God? Kammy gave me some kind of explanation, but it goes against everything I know."

"Baby, the things of the spirit aren't for the logical mind to understand, hence faith. Jesus is the manifestation of God on the earth. That doesn't make Him any less a God. I know your faith agrees Moses is the prophet God gave the Torah. Remember God spoke to him. Do you even think it's logical for Moses to understand God's language? Or for his ear drums to be able to withstand the voice of God? No. God limited himself in humility so to get to Moses' level. That shows the true nature of God."

"Okay…but still, it's baffling to believe in three Gods."

"But they are not three Gods, God is three in One."

Halima rubbed the back of her neck again. "That's even worse."

Ekene didn't want to lose this moment. He silently prayed that the Holy Spirit gave him the words to witness to her as a disciple and not her man who desperately wanted God to make her fit him.

"Look at it this way, you and I are the same being, human. But we're totally different people or persons. What we are, is the same, but who we are is different. God is one being but three persons; Father, Son and the Holy Spirit." Ekene paused waiting for her response. When none came, he continued. "The sun, according to scientists, is ninety-three million miles away. We can never go there. For one, we can't travel that far and two, we'll be crisp even before we get anywhere near. The sun comes to us through a limited form, because we can't take it all."

"Through light?" she asked.

"Yep. And with that light which illuminates darkness also comes heat or energy, which I will liken to the Holy Spirit."

"Yeah…"

"So from my analogy, He sends the Light of the World, Jesus. It's still the sun. And with it comes heat energy, the Holy Spirit…still from the sun."

"I get it now, better at least. It's a lot to do a total mind shift, but I'm questioning everything I know."

"I know baby, and God will reveal His truth to you in time. Even those that walked with Jesus, He asked them at one point, "Who do people say I am?" Only Peter got it right, but that's only because it was revealed to him."

Several moments of silence passed between them. This time it was comfortable silence. Ekene knew that God's word never returned without accomplishing that for which it was sent out to do and he could only pray the right word was sent out through him.

"Back to this prayer. You ready?"

"Yes."

"There are no dramatics to prayer. It's simply a conversation with God, where you talk, and you listen for His response. The length of time doesn't guarantee an answered prayer. It's the sincerity, motive, and belief that what you ask for will be done if you ask it through Jesus Christ. However, His Sovereignty reigns supreme," Ekene explained.

"You know you lost me on the last piece."

Ekene grinned. "What should we pray about, Princess?"

"Peace and clarity."

"You wanna talk about it?"

She shrugged. "You know the gist of it. I've told you about the dreams; my mom and my best friend are not talking to me. Uncle Musa is determined to turn the Board against me, and I'm being dragged through the mud by the press."

"Do you have your iPad?"

"Yes, why?"

"I want you to download a Bible app. Let's read a verse before we pray."

"Oh, I didn't tell you..." Halima jumped up from her bed and she went out of focus again. When she came back, she was holding a gift bag. "I bought a Bible. I don't know how to use it, but you'll teach me."

"Of course." Ekene smiled. The emotion he was feeling couldn't be put into words. Halima sat on the bed with her legs under her. She opened the Bible in front of her and stared at him through the phone.

"Before we start, I want to tell you that the Bible is made up of two parts..."

"Yeah, I know, the Old Testament and the New Testament," she said, excitedly.

"Look at you. I see you made good use of the time you spent avoiding me…again."

"That last time you deserved it. Now back to the Bible."

"There'll never be a time either of us deserves the other to run from them."

"Why are you spoiling this moment?"

"I'm not. You just seem hard of hearing, so I'm reiterating the lesson."

Halima rolled her eyes at him. "Never mind, I'll just ask one of my brothers."

Ekene grinned. "Stop being a brat."

"You like it. That's why you keep teasing me."

"Since you're my brat, I love it." He watched her cheeks turn slightly red. Before he got lost in those eyes, he remembered what she asked of him. "There should be a table of contents in the front. Look for James. Check the page number and go there we're looking for the fifth verse of that first chapter."

Ekene waited patiently as Halima did what he told her to do.

"I got it. "*If any of you lack wisdom, let him ask God who give liberally and without reproach and it will be given to him.*"

"Okay, hold that page. Go back to the contents look for Isaiah. Look for the twenty-sixth chapter and then look for verse three."

After a few moments, she lifted her head. "*You will keep in perfect peace those whose minds are steadfast, because they trust in you.*" Halima remained quiet, but he saw her lips move. He waited as she switched back and forth between both books of the Bible. Not wanting to interrupt the revelation God might be giving her, he waited.

Moments later, she looked up at him. Her expression wasn't one of confusion, although he didn't quite know what it was.

"So, if I don't know what to do, I ask God and He gives

willingly? What does the without reproach mean? I know reproach means blame. Does it mean the same thing here?"

"Yes, kinda. To receive wisdom, we simply ask, and He will give it generously without despising the fact that you don't already have it. But you have to ask with faith. Total belief and an open heart to receive what he says."

"How do I know what He says?"

"One thing I've learned in my journey is He uses the smallest and closest things to speak to us. It rarely comes with a loud, light bulb, 'aha' moment." He paused. "Through wisdom, He may want us to eliminate the problem in faith or persevere in it by faith."

"Christians base a lot of stuff on faith."

"Yes, don't you?"

"Yes, but it's somehow different when I hear Christians talk about it."

"Without faith, it's impossible to please God. If you're not going to believe what He says wholeheartedly, why even come to Him? That's kind of the premise. Faith is the substance of things hoped for, but not yet seen."

"I'm ready."

"Father God, in the name of Jesus…" Ekene started. Over the next couple of minutes, he prayed over the turmoil going on in her life and asked that God help her surrender her cares to Him. He also prayed that God would answer the prayer of a general seeker of His truth and wisdom. Finally, they prayed for their families, safe travels and a good vacation.

Ekene opened his eyes and admired the peace he saw in hers. They gazed at each other in silence before Halima laughed, causing them both to chuckle.

"Get some rest, Princess, and I'll see you in a couple of days. Remember, I love you and everything will be all right."

Halima blew him a kiss and they disconnected the call. Ekene relaxed against the headrest of the seat and took a deep breath. The events of the whole evening came flooding back through his mind. He rubbed on his beard while getting lost in the uncertainty of the future until his phone dinged alerting him to an incoming text. He picked up the device and couldn't help the smile that spread across his face.

When I think of you, everything is all right. Halima texted.

He responded, *In you, I've found the missing part of me. I love you, Princess.*

Ekene drummed his fingers on his desk as he waited for the message behind the three dots to surface. There wasn't a message, but a bunch of kissy face emojis. Things were back to normal, he dared to say better between them. He prayed it stayed that way.

Chapter 18

"You thought we were just gonna clap for you and it be over?" Kamal asked.

"Apparently, she did." Jabir tossed an M & M into his mouth.

Halima rolled her eyes at her big brothers and looked over at Rasheed who was in the corner of the Danjuma private jet on a call. Her sisters-in-law had taken an earlier flight straight to Enugu. She and Rasheed had to wrap up some interviews earlier, so Jabir and Kamal decided to wait with them. She should've known it was so they could continue this conversation that she thought was dead.

"You guys didn't have to give him such a hard time," Halima said.

"Says who? If anybody thinks they're going to get close to you, they go through us first," Jabir declared.

"I don't get it. None of you did this with Danladi."

"How many times do I have to say it? I didn't sweat that because that wedding wasn't happening. There was no way on God's green earth you were becoming someone's second wife." Kamal looked at her and Jabir puzzled. "How don't any of you know me by now?"

"Well I thought you were saved," Halima said.

"Being saved doesn't make me a punk." He squeezed his face like she'd just insulted him.

"Bruh, I don't know how many times I gotta tell her that," Jabir said. "Is Kene a punk?"

Halima shook her head.

Kamal sniggered, pulled out his phone and began thumbing through it.

"And I keep telling you guys, I'm—"

"Don't give me that I'm grown speech." Jabir chuckled and Kamal looked up at her. "What does that have to do with the interrogation process?"

"You already knew that was gonna happen. That's why you were creeping." Jabir popped another piece of candy in his mouth.

Halima cut her eyes at him. "Creeping? I can't stand both of you together."

"But you love us though." Kamal winked at her and returned to his phone. Halima assumed he was texting with his wife. The two of them fought all the time, but loved even harder. With his eyebrows creased together, he stood up and proceeded to the back of the plane.

Rasheed walked over and squeezed her shoulder. "If it's any consolation, Kene held his own."

She looked up at the head of the family and smiled. "I knew he would."

"Oh, check you out, having confidence in your man," Jabir joked.

"The same way Damisi has in you." She wiggled her eyebrows at him.

Jabir put the knuckle of his index finger in his mouth and let out a laugh.

"E, who's that boy behind my daughter?" Kamal asked. The three of them turned to see him peering into his phone. From his creased brow, Ebele was now on Facetime.

"Does he know his daughter is not even a full year yet?" Rasheed asked, causing her and Jabir to laugh.

"Nah, E, I ain't playing. Tell him to step back."

"Kam, stop, this boy is only three and his grandmother and Mama are friends. They stopped by," Ebele said, with a giggle.

Halima and her other brothers shook their heads at his antics.

"Where's Nasir? Tell him he ain't doing his job." Kamal said, referring to his twin son.

"Bye, Kam. I love you. See you soon." Ebele hung up.

Kamal looked up at them with a frown on his face. "What?"

"What exactly is Nasir's job?" Rasheed asked.

"He's supposed to protect his sister," Kamal stood and walked back over.

"From three-year-old boys?" Halima chuckled.

The double lines on his forehead deepened. "Boys period. Now back to you."

Halima shook her head. "No *dan uwa na*. We're done with me. So, tell me what I can expect in Enugu."

Kamal sunk his body into the chair. She silently thanked God the interrogation was over.

"Enugu is the state. The plane will land there, but we have like a fifty-minute drive to Agwu which is where Mummy is from and where we'll be staying," Jabir explained. "When my mom started letting us come to Nigeria again, you know, after the dad fiasco, we visited our granddad once in a while until he died."

"My mom comes back often, but we don't," Rasheed said.

"I'm excited." Halima looked out of the window of the plane. In the last couple of months, she had done so many things she wasn't used to. But she was enjoying it all. Suddenly her heart raced and before she could help it, she asked, "How did you know your wives were the ones for you?"

"Are you and Kene already talking marriage?" Kamal asked.

"No, but if we were?"

"All jokes aside. I know I jest a lot, but I'm concerned. I love you sis, and marriage is no simple feat. Interfaith? I don't even know what that will look like. Since I gave my life to Christ, I've been trying to make you give yours to Him to. However, I know it's something you must do for you and no one else. Please don't let your feelings for Kene dictate your actions when it comes to your soul. If you're gonna convert, which I pray to God you do, let it be because Christ revealed Himself to you and you love Him more than anything. Not because you feel that's the way to get with Kene," Kamal said, with his elbows propped on his knees.

Halima had seen him in a serious mood, but this was different. Was that what she was doing? She didn't think so, but a thought immediately struck her. If they loved her so much, why didn't they try harder to introduce her to Jesus? Either they didn't believe their faith, or they didn't care if she went to hell.

"You are my brothers. If you thought that when I died, I'd go to hell if I didn't believe in Jesus, why were you willing to risk it?" Halima's eyes darted at all three of them. "You guys do love me, right?"

"Sis, don't play. Do you remember some months after SoSo and I got married and you came over for dinner? Everything was going so well until SoSo asked if you knew Jesus the Son of God?"

Halima thought for a minute. That was so many years ago. After a few moments, she recalled her behavior and lowered her head.

"Oh snap. I forgot about that. You told us she tried to *Da'wah* your behind. Talking about I know exactly who Jesus is. The most powerful prophet, the Messiah, but not the Son of God." Jabir laughed, mimicking Halima's old declarations.

"Sis, you weren't out there gangsta for Islam like that?" Kamal tried to stifle his laughter.

"Stop it," Rasheed said. "My point is Hali, after that, for a while you stopped coming around us. Do you remember how you didn't even stay for Jabir's birthday celebration or the award ceremony in Detroit?"

"I was traveling…"

"Yes, but you and I know you could've moved it. I just didn't want to call you out." Rasheed crossed one knee over the other. Again, Halima knew exactly why he and Ekene were best friends. They were alike in so many ways —stern, calm and thoughtful, but their point was never lost.

"To answer your question, after you'd sulked for a while, we decided on a different approach. We didn't want you to think that unless you are Christian, we wouldn't love you, so we made a point to show you how Christians are through actions and deeds. And break the foundation on which you've stood," Rasheed said.

"Did we do that?" Jabir asked.

Halima's thoughts went back to those days. Her brothers were right. When Zara, her friend, also mentioned Jesus to her, she gave her the same treatment. Zara, like her brothers, tried a different approach. That singular question by an outsider who had nothing to gain by introducing her to Jesus and observing her brother's actions closely did make her more receptive.

She nodded.

"Good, so back to your initial question. I think for all three of us, when you know, you know, even when you try to fight it. It hurt, at least for me, to think of an existence without Ibiso. Those women helped us to become better versions of ourselves," Rasheed explained.

"Well, all that and they fine, educated, can cook, produced some fine kids—" Kamal started.

"And took no crap from us." Jabir cut him off.

Halima laughed. "Yeah, they sure don't." She took in a breath. "I've heard all your reservations, but I completely trust Kene's direction. I don't know what tomorrow will bring, but I'm enjoying discovering it with him."

"Ok, we'll back off as long as you're happy and aware. Correction though, we're not worried about you per se. I'm particularly worried about him if he messes up," Kamal said.

Just in time, the pilot announced that they should prepare for landing. They all got up from the common area, went back into their respective seats and buckled up. Halima couldn't help the smile on her face. They were infuriating, but she wouldn't exchange her brothers for anything. She took in the burnt orange horizon as the plane made its descent. She was really looking forward to the week ahead. She pulled out her phone and checked her notifications.

Nothing.

Her mother who boarded a plane to South Africa last week still hadn't responded to her call or the text she sent two days ago. With the back of her hand, Halima swatted away the lone tear that escaped her left eye. She powered down her phone and leaned back, anticipating the bump of the wheels signaling the plane had touched down at Akanu Ibiam International Airport.

———

THE CLICK OF HER HEELS ECHOED LOUDER WITH EACH STEP AS she strode into the empty sanctuary. How did she get here? Halima had no clue, but the opened door at the far right corner of the room drew her attention. As she approached, her steps slowed while the beat of her heart picked up its pace. Voices, happy though mumbled, floated through the air. Her concentration was precise as she tried to make them out. Now, they sounded familiar. She moved closer and gained the clarity she sought. It was her brothers, their mother and for some reason, her assistant who was supposed to be in Lagos. Her heartbeat slowed and her shoulders dropped in disappointment. She rolled her eyes in annoyance. *Why are they gathered without me?* She shrugged off her displeasure and decided to join them.

The veil that covered the entrance to the room was a mixture of blue, deep red and purple. At first, she thought it was cotton, but on closer examination, she realized it was linen. She stretched her hand to open it, but a force pushed her back slightly. Her eyes bugged out in shock.

Halima tried to wrap her head around what'd just happened when she heard Ekene's voice, multiplying her confusion. *Did he just join the party*? And if he wasn't with her, who was he with?

Halima's face distorted in anger. She hastened her steps to the curtain, yanked and once again stumbled back. She looked around the church. It was still empty. Seconds later, she saw a couple come through the main door. Halima watched them walk up to the curtain. Right before her eyes, the fabric split without them lifting a finger. She hurried to follow them inside, but the garment patched itself back up.

The sound of thunder woke Halima from her deep sleep. Her body jerked into an upright position. She blinked her eyes a few times in rapid succession to regain her bearings. The bedroom in Big Mummy's house she'd occupied for the past couple of days came into focus. She ran her hands up and down her arms to abate the unusual chill in the room. Lifting her hand, she wiped the perspiration from her forehead and shifted herself to lean against the headboard. Pulling her knees up to her chin, she peered at the drawn curtains, but she was unable to discern a hint of light. Her eyes moved to the clock on her right and it read 2:50 am. She smothered a groan.

"Allah, I've been reading the book of John in the Bible with Kene. It does say that Jesus is God. I'm still struggling with that. It's difficult, so I turned to You in my *dua*, to reveal the truth to me through dreams. You are the One who knows all mysteries," Halima spoke.

She'd been having these types of dreams since she prayed for the revelation of truth with Ekene. The previous evening in her dream, she and her family were on a cruise and the boat capsized. Her brothers were lifted and rescued when they reached out and grabbed the outstretched hand of a mysterious man. She, on the other hand, began drowning as water filled her lungs. Her brothers kept screaming "say it, say it" like there was a secret passcode she wasn't aware of. Then there was another dream where she was waddling down a wide road and her brothers strode down the narrow path. How she got on the wide one, she didn't know, but when she wanted to turn around to where they were, she kept getting stuck, just like in the movie *Groundhog Day*.

Halima ran her hand over her face. The thunder roared again. She hoped it wouldn't rain since she was looking forward to seeing Ekene later. Picking up her phone, Halima put the words "tore", "curtain" and "Jesus" in the Google search engine. It led her to Mathew 27 verse 51. She set her phone aside and picked up the small Bible she now carried around. She went to the book and read the whole 27th chapter.

Minutes later, she knew that the curtain she saw in her dream was called a veil and it had to do with the death of Jesus Christ.

She smiled, feeling better that she knew what her dream was about. But then, questions arose. *How do I know that these dreams are true from Allah? Or is it something I'm forcing myself to believe that's showing up in my subconscious?*

Then that other voice started to speak. *Be Still.*

Halima looked around. "Great, now I'm hearing voices again," she muttered to herself. She'd since stopped hearing the, "Do you want to be healed" question.

Be Still.

Now, this verse she knew because she had heard her sisters-in-law advising each other about this all the time when talking about troubles, whether business or family.

Be Still.

"And know that I am God," Halima finished. Placing her phone and Bible to the side, Halima slid back under the covers. Turning over, she closed her eyes waiting for sleep or the faithful crow of the cockerel.

Chapter 19

"I don't care what kind of money is pushing Jacobs to go ahead with this frivolous case. But make sure you tell him this, he better come at me with all he got and something that sticks. Because I will bury him if he wastes me and my client's time in court, once we're done."

Ekene hung up and braced both of his hands against the kitchen table and bowed his head. He'd been in his village, Inyi, for two days now, but still found it difficult to unwind. He'd hoped that while they were here, he'd be able to give Halima the gift of a dropped case. No such luck.

He wasn't so worried about the case against the Danjuma Group because he knew no judge would ever hold them liable since Eric did everything against the rules. It was the personal case against Halima Eric's family refused to let go of, that bothered him. Not because they had any chance of winning, but the fact that she even had to worry about it until trial was what was grinding his gears.

His thoughts roamed to their conversation the previous evening. She was enjoying the village life and he had so much more to show her later in the day. The impromptu phone call set him back by several minutes, but he still had to keep his morning appointment with the Creator.

Dressed in a pair of dark blue sweat shorts and grey tee, he picked up his juice, put his Bible under his arm and headed to the back of the guest house he occupied in his father's compound. As was customary among many families, his father bought him some land when he was just a child. Ekene bought some additional acres and was now building his own country home a few miles away.

He sat down on the wooden rocking chair and inhaled the fresh morning air. The slightly frigid morning was a result of the guesthouse facing the direction of the Orji River. He set the beverage down and opened the Bible plan he started some days ago.

After listening to Halima talk about all her worries, he started to question how much his presence in her life was causing her strife. He loved her with all his heart, but at the same time, didn't want to be the cause of her pain. If he was going to lead her to victory, he needed a clear vision and God's strength.

Let the words of my mouth and the meditation of my heart be acceptable in your sight O Lord, my strength and my Redeemer.

Ekene meditated on Psalm 19:14. He appealed to God to be his strength and rock of hope. He hoped that in due time, God would reveal Himself to Halima toward a personal relationship. He'd stopped deceiving himself into thinking part of this wasn't about him, but he fought every day that he would decrease so God's will would take precedence. He also got consolation from the fact the Lord would give him the desires of his heart.

For the next several minutes, Ekene poured out his heart in conversation to God. He was never big on the theatrics of prayer. He was honest about his feelings and asked for help and guidance.

He closed the book and looked out to the horizon, waiting

to hear anything from God. Instead, he heard his grandmother.

"Ekenedilichukwu, *e ba ta go?*"

Ekene stood, making his way to the front of the house to let his paternal grandmother in. He unlocked the door and beamed as the frail, but still, beautiful woman came into view. Her hair was white and tied in a scarf that matched her outfit. Her skin was wrinkled but still shone.

"*Nne Uku,*" he hugged her, referring to her as Big Mummy. "*Kedu?*"

A warm smile spread across her face. "*Adi m mma.*"

Ekene took the basket of food she held and led her further into the house. He placed the basket on the kitchen table and sent Halima a quick text apologizing that he'd be delayed again, then pocketed his phone.

When he returned to the living room, his grandmother was seated. He sat next to her and she turned her body to his. Her piercing eyes stared at him. He knew this conversation was coming, but didn't expect it so soon.

"You finally decided to come and spend time with your grandmother for this year's festival. *Ehen?* Ekenedilichukwu. All these years, you've acted like this family is not yours. You sneak in and out to see me and give me money. But when the family comes, you're never with them."

"*Nne Uku* it's not like that..."

"Then what is it like? I've kept quiet, but I'm getting old. I want to see everyone at peace and that is not what I'm seeing,"

"Ah, ah *Nne Uku,* did anyone tell you that we're not at peace?"

"Ekene, Ekene. Ekene...*ugboro ole ka m kporogi?* She drew her earlobe for emphasis asking him how many times she called his name.

Ekene smiled and answered. "Three times."

"Good. Family is all that matters in the end. I know you

have forgiven your father, but embrace your younger ones more. They had no hand in what your father and stepmother did. They're innocent and yearning for you to give them attention. I know you do it, but not to the level that you're capable, in here." She laid her palm over his heart and he covered it with his.

"I'll do better *Nne*. It's just that when I see them, I see the life I was deprived of."

"Your life turned out exactly how it was supposed to, my son. It wasn't easy but it has made you who you are. Supposing you came back with your father then? You wouldn't be my successful grandson I see on TV all the time." She stood and headed for his kitchen. "Now let me show you this fresh abacha I made for you and you can tell me about your new girl."

"New girl?"

"My dear grandson, I played this game in my hay days."

"Oh, come on *Nne*, I don't want to hear that..." Ekene covered his ears.

His grandmother spun around. "How do you think your father came about, and then you?" she asked, setting the plates near the Tupperware containing the African salad referred to as abacha. Once she removed the lid, he took in the aroma and moaned. He lifted his hand to grab the enticing stockfish that poked out at the top of the bowl. That action earned him a smack on his hand.

"Stop that."

He pulled up a seat and she dished him a small serving. She packed up the rest and leaned against the table. He was so engrossed in his meal that he didn't notice she was staring at him. He put his fork down and lifted his eyes to hers.

"What is it now, *Nne*?"

"I'm waiting for you to tell me about this woman."

"What makes you think there's one?"

"You texted someone when you took the food to the

kitchen. You've been looking at your phone every minute, and before you even set your mouth to tell me I'm seeing things, both times you checked, you had a frown on. Then the last time, you were smiling like a cat."

Ekene raised both brows at her, in awe of her accurate observations. "I didn't know you were a detective. But when the time is right, I'll tell you everything you need to know."

———

Hours later, Halima stared back at her reflection in the mirror. She brushed her hair and tied it in a messy bun on top of her head. Her makeup was light, just enough to camouflage the bags under her eyes. The events of the wee hours of the morning still lingered with her. A lot was riding on her differentiating between God's voice and her desires. Before she could process the thought more, there was a knock on the door.

"Hali, food is ready," Ibiso screamed through the door.

"Thanks, SoSo, I'll be right there."

From the corner of her eye, she could see her phone light up with a text. She walked over to the bed and picked it up.

Kene: *Left the house. See you soon.*

Despite all the thunder and lightning of the early morning hours, the rain didn't fall. She smiled, replied her acknowledgment, and sauntered back over to her vanity to finish getting ready. She inspected her attire, a thin-stripped, pink and blue Ankara print which she paired with a light sweater. Her well-manicured feet were comfortable in blue ballerina flats made with the same print material. Satisfied, she picked up her purse and phone and left the room.

Several moments later, Rasheed called the kids by age to the kitchen to get their food. "Ana, Ina, 'Hance…"

Halima smiled and winced as they came barreling down the hallway.

"Careful," Ebele yelled walking behind them.

It was mid-morning and the family was gathered around the massive, mahogany table in the dining room, ready to eat breakfast. Ibiso had prepared a feast of Nigerian and Continental dishes which Jabir was now serving. Big Mummy had left the house earlier.

No matter how long she'd been around her brothers, the things they did, like serve and cater to their wives, still amazed her. These weren't things she'd seen growing up. If there was a prototype for a "Break Every African man stereotype," it would be them and her own man, of course. Thinking of men, she couldn't wait to see Enugu through Ekene's eyes. Her brothers had taken her to some places, but she longed for her man's presence.

"Daddy, Ana's food is bigger than mine," Yohance said.

"That's because Ana is older than you. Now if you finish yours and want more, you can always ask for it," Rasheed responded to his son.

Kamal was close behind, carrying his daughter Nafisah. "ID, my main man. Your plate is almost bigger than you," he joked, referring to Jabir's son, Idris.

Halima smiled when her nephew nodded. Her little man was a healthy eater and she had no doubt everything would be gone soon. Kamal helped settle all seven grandkids. Their contagious laughter filled up the room as he tickled them and placed kisses on their foreheads. At the same time, Jabir was placing food on the bigger table for the adults.

Several moments later, everyone had been served. Kamal said grace and the only sounds that could be heard were the clicking of silverware against plates and children talking at the smaller table on the side.

Soon, everyone finished eating. The kids were in the living room playing games while the adults sat around the table in idle chatter.

"I got some news." Halima lifted her cup to her lips and turned to Rasheed at the head of the table.

"What's up, sis?" Jabir asked.

"Mr. Kumpasa from Nizon has moved our proposal to the last stage of bidding. It's just us and one other company." Halima announced.

Although Rasheed was the CEO of Danjuma Group, he gave her the autonomy to negotiate and close contracts when it came to logistics. Over the years, he had come to trust her judgment, and in return, she always made sure he was never surprised by anything. Especially when he had to meet with the Board.

"That's fantastic. You did it," Rasheed said.

"Not just yet, but soon." Halima tucked a strand of hair behind her ear.

"Good job, sis. Since we're making announcements, I got something to tell y'all. I might have to relocate to Lagos for a little bit." Kamal announced.

"Why? What's up?" Rasheed asked.

"I'm bidding for a contract with the Lagos State government, and I was told it's a sure in."

Everyone offered their congratulations. Halima grinned. She was so proud of her brother. He'd gone from super bratty, international soccer player, to well-known speaker, savvy businessman and to top it off, a great husband and father of two. Although he studied architecture, he never practiced until recently here and there.

"I'm happy for you, bro. Ebi, you're not leaving me in Abuja, right?" Ibiso asked.

Kamal gave her a death stare while everyone else anticipated the exchange.

"I'm trying not to." Ebele turned to her husband and gave him an air kiss.

"Sis, 'ppreciate it. But stop trying to put asunder what

God has put together," Kamal said. "Of course, she's going with me. Her and the kids."

All the while Kamal was talking, Ebele was shaking her head behind him, indicating she wasn't going anywhere. Ibiso nodded in understanding and Kamal looked back at Ebele who now had a blank expression.

"Of course, baby. I'm going to uproot the kids, close down my business and come with you." Ebele rubbed his back.

Rasheed and Jabir roared in laughter when Kamal shrugged Ebele off him. He whispered something in her ear, eliciting a deep blush.

"Ebi, you're blushing. Don't fall for it," Damisi warned.

"As if you could resist it," Jabir teased.

Ibiso laughed and Rasheed pulled her closer to him. "You think it's funny? You couldn't resist it either. We're the Danjumas, baby."

Ebele rolled her eyes. "Oh jeez."

"You can't dispute it if it's true. My brothers are catches," Halima placed her hand over her mouth to hide her smile.

"Hali!" Ibiso, Damisi and Ebele exclaimed in unison.

"We'll remember that the next time you complain of being smothered," Damisi said.

Halima giggled. "Don't be like that. You're my sisters. You know I love you, but hey…" She shrugged.

"That's right, sis. Stand up for your brothers. We won't harass you for the next twenty-four hours. We promise," Kamal said.

Halima shook her head. The doorbell cut short whatever comeback her sisters-in-law had.

"I'll get it." Halima scooted her chair back. *It's for me anyway.*

"Why? Who do you know in Enugu?" Jabir asked, standing up with her.

"Yeah, Hali who do you know?" Ibiso teased.

Halima stuck her tongue out at Ibiso, getting an eye roll in return. Before anyone else could say anything, she safely exited the dining room. Her pulse raced with each step she took at the thought of spending the whole day with Ekene. They'd spent time alone together many times before, but this was new territory for her – his hometown. She peered through the peephole, confirming it was him, and opened the door.

Powerful. Confident. Enigmatic. Those were the first words she thought of when Ekene looked at her. They stared at each other for a few seconds, lost to the world around them. At least she was. His cologne wafted to her nostrils as she admired his appearance. He was dressed in a simple pink polo and jean shorts and black tennis shoes. The pink contrasted so perfectly against his chocolate skin that she couldn't take her eyes away.

"Are you just going to stare at me, Princess?" His deep voice jerked her from her enamored state. The cockiness in his tone coupled with the sensuous curve of his grin made her tilt her head down. The heat she felt in her cheeks told her for certain they were as red as a tomato.

He lifted her head with his finger. "It's okay. I love you checking me out. It lets me know I'm not in this alone."

Ekene lowered his head and Halima parted her lips in anticipation. She closed her eyes as she waited for the pressure against her lips…

"Hali, won't you invite your guest in?"

Kamal's annoying voice came through. Halima rolled her eyes when she heard her sisters-in-law laughing in the background.

"Later," Ekene whispered in her ear. He grabbed her hand and led her into the house.

Chapter 20

The last time he'd been through these tunnels was with his mother during one of their family vacations. Those were memories he cherished and would never let go of. Nothing else had come close to his heart than the day he was currently experiencing. After arriving at the Danjuma house and chilling with the family, well, chilling with the wives and children, but being cajoled by the brothers, he and Halima left.

"So, let me make sure I remember, this is where coal was first found in Nigeria?" Halima asked. The way her eyes lit up anytime he gave her a tidbit about Enugu made his heart warm. Never did she once turn her nose up at a piece of his history; instead she soaked it all in.

"Yes. The name Enugu is derived from two words 'enu' and 'ugwu' this can be translated into 'top of the hill'."

"Got it. Because of its landscape." Halima stretched her neck to peer at the mountain top. "I know we're doing the tunnels today, but the hills look perfect for hiking. Let's do that next time."

"Next time?" Ekene feigned surprise.

She pinched her lips together and rubbed the back of her

neck. She was shy and it showed so much more when she felt embarrassed. He found that so sexy, especially because she only let him see that side of her. It was a huge contrast from who she was in the board room.

"You know what I mean."

"And I like it."

"Hmm. Okay, are we going in?"

"Deviating from the topic?" He grabbed her hand. "Yes, we're going in. I hired a guide and he should be here soon."

He led them to the corner of the entrance and pulled her between his parted legs. "Hiking, are you sure you can keep up?"

"I should be asking you, old man. I'm still in my thirties." She raised her eyebrows.

"Not the old man jokes. I'm younger than your oldest brother."

"By a year. And? That's still old." Her lips fought the smile threatening to come through.

Ekene began to tickle her, securing her against his body with his other arm which was firmly around her waist. She couldn't break free; she wiggled against him. The carefree nature of her laugh and her body against his, did something to him. Heat rose up his neck leaving goosebumps in its wake. He loved this playful side of her and lately, she had too much weighing her down.

"Mr. Odili?"

The voice of a tall, younger man interrupted them. Securing Halima by his side, Ekene nodded in confirmation.

"Yes, that's me. Are you the guide? Ofor?"

"Yes, sir. Are you ready? Madam, good afternoon," the man said.

"It's Halima. Good afternoon."

"I got these boots, Sir. You'll need them because the grounds in the tunnel are wet." Ofor handed them two new pairs of yellow, waterproof boots. Ekene had forgotten that the tunnels were damp. He kneeled to take off Halima's shoes, replacing them with the boots. Once she was good, he put his on. She put both their shoes in her oversized bag before taking his outstretched hand.

The fading daylight bounced off the arching sandstone walls as they entered deeper into the tunnels. The guide beamed his torch into the barely lit passageway.

"Is this your first time under the tunnels, Sir?"

"No, but when I came here, I was very young."

"I didn't know that." Halima looked up at him.

Ekene gave her a faint smile. "Yes, my mother brought me here."

"I'm sorry, babe, didn't mean to dredge up sad memories."

"The memories aren't sad. My mother being gone is. However, we're making new ones." He kissed her temple.

"To new memories," she whispered.

"So, this is not my first time, but it is hers and I want her to enjoy the full experience."

"Yes, sir." They walked in silence. The slow drip of water from the low roof contributed to the dewy gust that filled the air.

"The Udi hills are about hundreds of meters above sea level. In 1915, it became the site of the first coal mine to be opened in Nigeria. Sadly, it was closed just two years later. The British Colonial government replaced it with the Iva Valley mine," Ofor said.

"Where is that?" Halima asked.

"It's still here in Enugu," Ekene responded.

As they walked deeper into the tunnel's arching pathway, taking in the reflection of brownish red hues, Ofor continued. "Yes, it is here in Enugu. When this mine was in full operation, Enugu was the only significant producer of coal in the West African sub-region."

"Wow. How can I live in Nigeria and not know this?" Halima wondered.

"How could you? Not everything is taught in schools. Nigeria is a country with a rich history and a lot of different cultures, each one having something peculiar to it. It'd be tedious to keep up. Hence, each state tries to develop its tourist attractions."

They walked for another couple of feet with Ofor explaining more about Udi Hills. A few minutes later, they were being greeted by sunlight which signified the end of the tour.

"I really enjoyed that. So much history." Halima took her sunglasses from her hair and replaced them over her eyes.

Although he had already paid for the tour, Ekene reached into his wallet to get out some money to tip the guide.

"So, the Iva Valley Mine is it like this one?"

"People don't normally tour there after what happened. It is more like a memorial," Ofor responded.

Ekene felt her gaze on him even before she asked the question.

"Memorial? Why?"

"Princess, the Iva Valley is known not just for coal, but what is called the Enugu Massacre. In 1949, twenty-one miners were shot dead by British policemen while striking." Ekene paid Ofor who thanked him and walked away.

"They killed them for that?"

He ushered Halima over to a nearby rock where he helped her change out of the boots. After changing his shoes, they walked hand in hand the short distance to his Jeep. He tossed the wet boots in the trunk and turned to her. He didn't want to dampen the mood of the day because he had a lot more to show her. However, the inquisitive part of her he admired was out and wouldn't go away until it was satisfied.

"History has it that, in those moments of colonial insanity, the colonizers, murdered twenty-one workers and injured fifty-one. Because the workers dared to go on a stop-working strike which the colonial authorities interpreted as a political move. I guess thinking it was to make them leave the country and let Nigeria join other nations free from colonial misrule and exploitation." Ekene opened the door for her and she got in.

He entered and started the car. He glanced over at her and she was still deep in thought. As they rode to the next destination, Ekene told her that a committee was set up to investigate, but the British blamed the union, claiming the workers wanted to attack the policemen, prompting them to use force – although no evidence of that was found.

"That's just crazy. I was in America last year when something similar was being reported on the news. A white policeman who thought he was going to be attacked by an African American shot him dead," Halima said. "All over a thought."

Ekene took in her words and wondered, when the darkness of one's skin began to equate to inferiority and marginalization. He held her hand and navigated the vehicle in silence to their next stop.

———

HOURS LATER, THE COUPLE WAS WORN OUT. THEY'D BEEN TO A few more tourist spots before they decided to call it a day. They visited the National Museum of Unity, where they got to see relics of history and military artifacts from the Biafran civil war. They stopped over at the Polo Park Mall which had several food courts, supermarkets, and other shopping outlets. After getting something to eat and a few souvenirs for her house and office, they were now at their final destination: Ngwo Caves, Waterfall and Pine forest.

They'd visited the caves which were sculpted in limestone rocks while the waterfall cascaded down from small openings. The real intriguing part was that the waterfall had warm and hot water come out together, from the same source.

Now they were in Pine Forest, seated in the spacious, blanketed trunk of his vehicle with the hood raised. The horizon had changed from bright rays to a reddish orange hue. They were done eating and Halima leaned against his chest as they watched the sun go down. Ekene tucked one of her loose tresses behind her ear. "Did you have fun today?"

She tilted her head. A smile danced around the corners of her eyes in mischief. He narrowed his gaze, daring her to say something smart.

"I did sir, very much."

He chuckled. "You just can't behave, can you?"

"What fun would that be?"

"I guess none."

The silence around them was comfortable and kind of their thing. He absently rubbed her hair with one hand while his other arm went around her midsection, pulling her to him. He hoped he could keep them stuck in time to shield them from the reality of what was laying wait.

"Are you cold?" he asked.

Halima leaned further into him and tilted her head again so that their eyes locked. "No."

Their gazes held on to one another for a few seconds. She lowered her eyelids but before she did, he caught the anxiety hiding behind them. He placed a deep kiss on her inviting lips.

Coming up for air seconds later, he asked. "What troubles you, Princess?"

A shadow passed over her face. Ekene brushed his thumb across her cheek. She opened her mouth to speak when her phone began to ring. He groaned and she brushed her lips against his reaching into her purse. Her mood dropped immediately. Her eyes met his and he peered at her hand.

"My mother."

Chapter 21

"Hello, Mother." Halima's voice shook. Ekene's hand rubbing up and down her arm was the only thing that kept her steady. The relationship between her mother and herself had deteriorated to the point that they barely had anything to say. Having any kind of relevant conversation was like taking a walk in a minefield.

"*Yata.*"

"Are you okay, Mother?"

"I don't know. You tell me."

Halima looked over at Ekene whose brows were scrunched together. She raised her index finger to him and got out of the vehicle.

"What have I done this time?"

"The question would be, what haven't you done?" Her mother sighed, her disappointment evident. "Danladi's people called. They want to ensure we'll be ready in three weeks—"

"Why? What's happening?"

"What do you mean why? Did you forget you're supposed to be marrying him?"

"Not to my knowledge. As I recall, I broke up with him several weeks ago. I told you and Uncle Musa I was no longer interested in being anyone's second wife." Halima put her fingers in her hair and pulled slightly. Their relationship had always been dismissive. Nothing Halima said was ever taken seriously. How did they think they'd pull this off without her consent?

"Your father would have wanted this. He arranged it. I didn't think you were serious. Halima, this is for —"

"Yeah, I know, for my own good. You always say that, but funny how none of it ever is." Halima rubbed her palm against her forehead. "It's just you and me mother. We're all that we have. Why are you against me? Growing up, you've always been indifferent to my needs, but this is too much. I have so much going on in my life and I need my mom."

"Hush child. I did the best I could, but your brothers came and ruined it. Now you don't want to marry the man you've kept waiting all these years. You're now seeking some fantasy of the truth when you've been taught the truth since you could talk," her mother yelled. "I see you're set on mudding your father's name and I refuse to let you."

"Let me? I'm a grown woman. My brothers have changed my life for the better and even yours. I want better for myself."

"I do not hate your brothers; I hate what their presence has done to you. You should be more like—"

"Like you? Mother, you allowed a man who was clearly in love with another woman to walk all over you. You sat in second place while he chose when his conscience should allow him to care for you and when it shouldn't. You should want better for me."

"That is the custom."

"No, it isn't. And even if it is, I choose another option."

"You think you'll find it with your brother's friend?"

"His name is Ekene—"

"I don't wish to know. Where do you think this thing you're doing is leading? Even if he takes you as you are, do you think an interfaith marriage will survive? Look at what happened to your brother's mother. There would always be another me that his family approves of."

Halima sighed. "Mother, me seeking truth in my faith and me not wanting to be a second wife are two exclusive choices."

"You can tell yourself that if you want to. But we both know they're connected. Because your conviction in one is what led to the other. The question you should ask yourself is, are you willing to lose it all?"

"What do you mean by that? Are you saying you'll no longer be in my life if I choose a path that you don't agree with?"

Silence passed between them. With the phone still against her ear, Halima turned around. Ekene was staring at her. She loved him and despite what her mother said, the two were exclusive choices. Was she ready and truly convinced that Jesus was the Way or was her longing for Ekene clouding her judgment? She blinked back her tears. He started to move toward her.

"What I'm saying is, are you ready for the fight that lies ahead? This path you tread is apostasy punishable by death."

The chill in her mother's voice trickled down Halima's spine. She kept eye contact with Ekene until he was standing in front of her. His hands were pushed into his pockets. She was grateful, because his touch would open a flood gate of tears and she had one more point to make.

"That's the point, Mother. We believe things because they've been handed down to us. But I've been studying." Halima let out a labored breath, her fight for the day dwindling. "True, recanting Islam is a sin. But nowhere in the Quran does it talk about worldly punishment. Such a decision lies with God. I'm still a Muslim. I'm just confused."

"Doesn't seem like confusion to me. Rather you've made your decision."

"Mother, I love you."

Halima heard her mother draw a breath, then she responded. "And I'll pray to Allah on your behalf, my child."

Then she heard nothing. Her mother had hung up the phone. Halima stared at the device then buried her head in Ekene's chest. His arms wrapped her close, warmth slowing melted away the chill she experienced moments earlier. The dam broke and tears cascaded down her cheeks. For weeks, she thought she could make it through this journey without losing something. Now she was being faced with the reality of what she had heard a pastor say, she couldn't give her heart to the Lord and it cost her nothing.

Halima stared at the phone on her desk. She'd been back in Lagos for three days and she was now convinced of what she had to do. The guilt weighed on her and she was done postponing the inevitable. Part of earning her respect was solving her own problems without Ekene or her brothers' help. The corners of her mouth curved upward at the thought of Ekene, the man who patiently infiltrated her reservations and took over her heart.

Ever since that disastrous phone call with her mother, he refused to leave her side. She wasn't complaining, but she didn't want him feeling obligated to fix her problems or think they were his fault. She didn't need pity. She looked at the double screens in front of her and the half-eaten *ayamse* at the side. Leaning against the massive leather seat in her office at DG, she dialed. The phone was answered after the third ring.

"Hello, Danladi?"

"You have some nerve to dial this number, Halima." His voice didn't hide the disdain for her.

"Look Danladi, I just called to tell you I'm sorry. When I told you I was calling the engagement off, I thought you took me seriously. Apparently, you didn't."

"Why would I? Ever since I've known you, you always followed the rules or allowed someone to dictate them for you."

He did have a point, but the purpose of this phone call was not to argue with him. Rather, it was to provide closure. He needed it if he still went along with trying to marry her. And she wanted it because the last thing she desired was bad blood between them. His family sat on the board of her company so that meant she'd see him from time to time.

"Be that as it may, I still apologize for the time wasted. I know we can't be friends, but again I'm really sorry and wish you well." She tried again with an even tone.

"You think that's all there is to it." He laughed. "You might think this is over but the repercussions have only just begun," he quipped.

She had said her piece and there was nothing more to add. "Goodbye, Danladi."

"See you soon, Halima." He hung up the call.

Well, that went as expected. She set her phone on her desk. The Nizon Company in Mozambique had called earlier. They asked her to adjust the proposal she submitted, and she had herself a deal. What they wanted wasn't too bad, so she gave in. It was a huge deal and she was super excited. She pulled her keyboard close and got back to work.

"Goodnight, boss lady. How much longer will you be?"

The sound of Chiaka's voice made Halima lift her head. She glanced at the clock. It indicated she'd been hard at work for hours.

"Goodnight. Get home safe."

"Do you need anything? You know it's almost six p.m. I could order you dinner."

"No, I'm fine. I'll be gone in an hour. See you in the morning."

Halima stood and stretched. She hadn't heard from Ekene all day. She picked up her phone to ensure she hadn't missed any calls. After Danladi, she decided to put it on silent. She didn't have any calls, but had texts from Kamal, Damisi, her tailor and Ekene. She cleared all the others and went to Ekene's.

Kene: I miss u

Kene: Running into court. Talk later.

Kene: Why aren't u responding to my text woman?

Kene: Omw to your office.

The last text was about forty-five minutes ago. *He should be here soon.*

She responded to Kamal, informing him she wasn't ignoring him and was fine. She confirmed with Damisi that she'd be accompanying her to visit a shelter she was doing a story on. And finally, she notified her tailor she'd be there the next day to pick up her clothes.

Halima put the phone down and began packing up her things. Moments later, her phone rang. A wave of pleasure washed over her. A soft smile curved her lips as she hit "Accept."

"Hi," she said, pulling her bottom lip between her teeth.

"Her phone works." His strong silky voice came through. Except it wasn't through the phone.

Halima turned and there Ekene stood, leaned against the frame of the door. His shirt was tucked into his dark maroon pants, the sleeves of his grey shirt were folded three quarters of the way. His matching suit jacket was hooked on one finger over his shoulder.

Her smile widened, he still held the phone to his ear and so did she. Her heart turned over. Her feet began to move while her pulse raced with excitement the closer she got to the door. His midnight eyes held hers in an intense stare down.

"It does," she said into the phone.

"Good to know." He took her phone from her hand after he put his in his pocket and swept her up in a deep kiss. The earth seemed to stand still as the absence of gravity had her floating with passion. Moments later, he pulled back, making her mourn the loss of the euphoric feeling.

"Good, then use it."

She puckered her lips to give him another quick kiss before using her thumb to wipe her lipstick off his lips.

He gave her a slow once over. The gleam in his eyes told her he liked what he saw. Being the last workday of the week, she'd decided on something more casual, a multi-print kaftan and jeans.

"How was your day? I need to know you were fighting aliens and that's why I didn't hear from you." Ekene walked over to her desk.

"Kind of." She giggled.

Draping his suit jacket over her shoulders, he picked up her briefcase with one hand and grabbed her hand with the other. "Let's grab a bite to eat."

"Where do you have in mind?"

"You'll see."

An hour later, they were seated at their table on the deck of Sailors Lounge. The view was breathtaking, and Halima loved the place. It was kind of their spot. The sheer ambiance was one of a kind, a huge contrast from the bustle of the city. The cool breeze from the sea ran through her hair as calming music floated in the background.

"How was court?" Halima asked, swaying her body from side to side.

Ekene shrugged. "You know the usual, shooting down alternative facts since 19whatever."

"Can you get any cockier?"

Ekene shrugged. "Don't know no other way to be."

Her eyes widened.

He laughed. "I'm messing with you."

"Hmmm, I like it *sha*, so you're good."

"You like it a lot…" he challenged her.

"I plead the fifth. Do people really say that or only on the court shows on TV?" She pushed her hair away from her eyes.

He grinned. "You watch too many court shows. And the fifth is an American amendment, so no we don't use it here in *Naija*."

"Well, I'll use it with you. I won't be able to contain the swell of your head if I don't." She smirked at him. "Do you wanna know something?"

"From you… always." He was leaned back in his chair with his two index fingers clasped together under his chin.

Halima could get lost in his intimidating confidence. He commanded the room without too much fanfare. He was known to be calm and collected. But there was another side to him. She, unlike others, was privy to his caring, strong but vulnerable side and she loved it.

Gosh, I love this man so much.

"I always wondered how anyone of faith could be a lawyer."

"Say what?" Ekene straightened in his chair.

"Hear me out. I was often privy to my father's conversations with his lawyers and they were always willing to do anything to win." Halima lifted her glass to her lips, took a sip then set it down. "Getting to know you has dispelled that belief."

"Hmmm, you had me going there for a minute." He paused as the waiter arrived with their dinner. He was having grilled catfish while she opted for tiger prawns over rice. The waiter set everything down, including extra napkins and told them he'd be back to check on them soon.

Ekene took her hand and bowed to bless the food. They ate for a few seconds in silence before he continued.

"I see how people can think that, but I don't compromise my morals. Instead of asking 'What would Jesus Do,' I follow what He did. Like with the woman who the villagers wanted to stone for adultery. She was guilty but Jesus defended, then admonished, providing a more redeeming way for all involved. Being a Christian lawyer gives me the opportunity to guard the system, not exploit it or allow it to take advantage of the innocent."

Halima nodded. "That's why I love you."

Ekene stopped his fork mid-way. "It better not be the only reason."

"I never said it was."

"Smart mouth."

"But you like it." She winked at him and he chuckled.

"Bottom line though, I take my career as my calling and I do my best to honor Him and the people He brings my way to serve."

A while later, the waiter came back and cleared their empty dinner plates. Ekene excused himself from the table while she ordered her favorite snack, peppered snails. Halima scrolled through her social media feed while she waited. The fragrance of Calvin Klein Eternity announced her former best friend's presence before she came into view. That'd been her desired scent for as long as Halima could remember.

"Aren't we now the social butterfly?" Kudirat's disapproving gaze washed over her.

"Did you need something?" Halima asked. Their last blow up, after her cousin's date disaster, was still fresh on her mind. The curses Kudirat rained on her cut deep. Halima spent days wondering why what she wanted to do with her life hurt those closest to her most. To the extent, they were willing to cut her off.

"Never thought you'd really go through with it," Kudirat said.

Halima's eyebrows rose. "And by it, you mean…" She had a lot more to say but didn't need a scene. Her name was just leaving the news cycle.

Kudirat shifted her eyes to the phone, keys and half-empty glass on the table indicating another presence.

"Why wouldn't I? It's my life and as I recall, you wanted nothing to do with it. So again, do you need something?"

"It won't last. You know that right?" She sneered.

"You really don't expect me to answer that do you?"

"Why are you being so stubborn? Nothing good will come out of this. You could lose everything. And for what? A Christian who won't marry a Muslim or a faith that goes against all we've been taught?" Her expression was puzzled.

Halima closed her eyes to control her rising temper. She stood. "Not that I owe you an explanation anymore, but if it doesn't work, it'll be my lesson to learn." The evenness of her tone made her proud.

"Just remember I called it. But when the time comes, I'll be a good friend and allow you to cry on my shoulder without saying I told you so," Kudirat said. She adjusted the strap of her purse.

Halima's eyes shifted to meet Ekene's. He was headed back to their table in hasty strides. The last thing she needed was for him to try and fix the situation or see another piece of her life erode due to her choices. She fixed her stare back on Kudirat. "Leave."

Kudirat's gaze followed hers and she gave a deceptive grin. "He's not bad. But somehow, I don't think he's worth it." She turned and walked right past Ekene without giving him another look.

"Wasn't that your best friend?"

"Ex..." Halima mumbled

Ekene looked back. "What did she want?"

The waiter brought her peppered snails, but now, all she wanted was to be between her sheets so she could sulk in peace. She asked him to take it back and package it to go.

"Princess, what happened?"

"Nothing. Can we go?" She didn't meet his eyes. Instead, she placed her phone in her bag and tucked her flying hair behind her ear.

Halima could tell he was studying her for cracks, but she didn't have the energy for what would ensue if he saw any, so she chinned up and met his stare.

"We can do anything you want, but first, I need to know that you're okay."

"Nothing's wrong. Nothing that matters anyway." She shrugged.

"If it has you looking like that and wanting to cut our date short, it does matter. But I'll give you space tonight. Tomorrow is a different story. Deal?"

She couldn't give him the answer he wanted, but from the way he leaned back in his chair and folded his arms across his chest, that wasn't an option.

"Fine. Deal."

Without another word, Ekene stood and helped her out of her seat. He picked up her to go bag and with his hand on her lower back, he led her out of the restaurant.

About an hour and some minutes later, Halima was showered and in her bed. She drew the covers to just below her breasts and stared at the ceiling. Her mind was not focused on anything in particular. Instead, it was running amok and she didn't know how to get it under control. Moments later, she threw back the covers and knelt near her bed. She reached for the Bible that now had a permanent place on her nightstand. Opening it to a random page, she clasped her hands together and bowed her head. In silence, her tears dropped on the thin opaque page.

"Dear Jesus, please reveal Yourself and Your plans to me. I've had so many dreams, but my feelings are mixed up and I can't trust anything. I'm losing people I love, so I really need to know You're real. I mean I know You're real, but I'm talking the Son of God, is the only way to God, real. Show me something concrete. I need courage to continue through these trials. I'm trusting You *o*. Please, I'm putting everything on the line. Assure me that everything will be all right. Amen."

Halima opened her eyes and immediately, felt like the weight was lifted off her shoulders. She got back into the bed, but before she closed her Bible, she looked at the page she had opened. The book was Jeremiah. It was on chapter 33. She closed her eyes and opened it back up as the words from the third verse seemed to be raised from the page. She blinked again to ensure she wasn't seeing things.

She read the words slowly, *"Call to Me, and I will answer you, and show you great and mighty things, which you do not know."* She repeated them several times, smiling. Next, she picked up her phone and constructed a text.

Thank you for allowing me to navigate the storms within me. I love you.

She kept her phone away, not expecting Ekene to be awake. She knew he had a volunteer activity early the next morning, then his pro bono stuff at the office. That was one of the reasons they decided to hang out after work. She knew it couldn't be easy remaining by her side, but he was there. Never wavering. Her phone buzzed and the words set her heart on fire.

Kene: I love you too. Not just for the calm parts but for the no matter whats.

She sent him a couple of heart emojis and settled into a restful sleep. For the night at least.

Chapter 22

One down, one more to go. Days later, Ekene grinned at his accomplishment, as he rode down the highway headed to the courthouse. The frivolousness of naming Halima personally in Eric Okon's wrongful death lawsuit was ludicrous and was rightfully thrown out. It had taken a while, simply because the judge assigned to it had an emergency at the last minute and had to leave the country. Rumor had it that his oldest child had gotten into some trouble in Europe.

As Ekene hoped, the moment he presented his argument in court last week, the case was thrown out. Halima had nothing to do with it and Mr. Jacobs knew it. Now he was on his way to the judge's chambers. Judge Boyega was also assigned to the negligence case against DG and he wanted both attorneys in his office to see what they had before he even thought about proceeding to the courtroom.

Halima.

All he wanted to do was love and protect her. However, all he seemed to do was cause her pain. Some days after their dinner at Sailors Lounge, they were invited to his father's for lunch. Everything was going well. His dad was cautious at first, especially when Ekene told him she was still Muslim. He wasn't so much as worried about Halima, who charmed her way into the older Odili's heart, but he was nervous about the road they were on – that is, if she never converted and they decided to get married.

Ekene understood everyone's reservations, but he knew Halima better than anyone and believed that God was indeed working on her. What he wasn't expecting was that his father's wife had overheard their conversation. She and his sister treated Halima like she was an alien. They weren't nasty or disrespectful. They just kept looking at her as though she would grow an extra pair of eyes on her forehead. And talked to her like she was slow or hard of hearing. Simply because she had a belief different from theirs.

Ekene hadn't been so angry or disappointed in all his life. The worst part was that he knew Halima felt uneasy, but kept up a smile and braved the scrutiny. The ride back to her house was filled with silent tension. He couldn't apologize enough. But with each "it's okay," she whispered, he felt her detaching mentally and he couldn't afford that. His heart couldn't take it.

Five months had gone by since they started dating and despite the initial bumps in the road, he was exactly where he wanted to be. From the moment they woke up until they retired in the evening, they were inseparable through texts, calls, and Facetime. Their bond deepened by the day. They continued their cycling meetups, attended painting classes every Tuesday night, or simply went out to movies and dinner. She discussed her latest deals with him and although he couldn't discuss his work with her, he gave her hypotheticals and was always amazed at her opinion. It often gave him clarity. He tried out a coffee tasting with her. He hated it, but the smile on her face was worth every awful drop.

She had tried her hand on some of his construction pieces. The most memorable time they'd spent together was babysitting Jabir's kids when he and Damisi went on a two-day couple's retreat. To see her maternal nature caused a longing in him he hadn't dared let exist before. Between feeding their minds, they also found time to feed their souls by talking and sharing about Christianity. Something was something holding her back because, although she hadn't voiced it, he knew she'd found what she sought. He was determined not to pressure her, but to be there when the time arrived.

Ekene looked at the gridlock ahead. He had about ten minutes to his destination, but at this point, he knew he'd be several minutes late. He activated his Bluetooth and dialed Judge's Boyega's assistant.

"Madam Joy, how are you today?"

"My future grandson-in-law, I'm fine. When are you coming to pay dowry?"

Ekene laughed. He'd known the older woman for some time now. She had been the assistant to some other judges he worked with over the years. Madam Joy, as he fondly called her, was forever trying to marry off one of her granddaughters to him. He always teased her back, replying soon, but now he had to burst her bubble.

"I'm afraid that might no longer be an option."

"*Chai*, you mean some girl has captured you in her net."

Ekene chuckled. "Not a girl, but a woman and I was the one that did the capturing."

"Hmmm, what can I do for you? This news requires a moment of silence."

Through muffled laughter, Ekene responded. "Can you tell the Judge I'm on my way, but there's a hold up at Lekki-Ikoyi link."

"Okay, but you know if you're later than thirty minutes, he'll have me reschedule."

"I know and I'll get out of my car and walk before I let that happen because it would be another couple of weeks."

Madam Joy snickered. "Okay, I'll let him know. See you soon."

He disconnected the call. As Ekene released the brake to close the gap made by the car ahead, "Before I Let Go" by Frankie Beverly and MAZE came on the radio and he laughed thinking about Halima and her jokes about his outdated taste in music. Ekene looked at the passenger seat and grinned. Later, he was going to surprise her with tickets to Adimu Live. She was a Kenyan Christian performance artist visiting Nigeria for the first time for a concert. Her performance was unique in that she ministered through dance, spoken word, and song. He couldn't wait to swing by Halima's office later.

He wasn't naïve enough to think they'd never come across more challenges, but he was enjoying the bliss they were experiencing together. Until the next storm which he knew they'd be able to conquer. Although for a minute there he wasn't too sure. He saw through the façade she put up and knew there was only so much one person could take. Ekene did everything within his power to be there for her. But he didn't dare pretend he knew what standing in her shoes felt like.

———

"MR. JACOBS, YOUR CLIENT IS SUING FOR COMPENSATION claiming that Danjuma Group was negligent when Mr. Okon, one of its drivers, died from injuries sustained while he was on the job. Your complaint claims Danjuma Group should've known the driver had taken multiple consecutive shifts causing exhaustion which led to him falling asleep at the wheel." Judge Boyega looked up from the rim of his glasses, waiting for confirmation.

Mr. Jacobs nodded. "Yes, Sir."

"For the record. Just to be sure, this is also about to the

wrongful death lawsuit you had against Ms. Halima Danjuma?"

"Yes, Sir, but you threw that case out," Ekene answered.

"Mr. Odili, I'm not senile. I know what I did. Don't interrupt me again."

"Yes, Sir."

The judge turned to Mr. Jacobs and raised his brows.

"Yes, Sir."

"Okay, so your complaint says Danjuma Group's behavior was reckless and willful and as such, they should be punished with the imposition of punitive damages. Am I correct?"

"Yes, Your Honor."

"Mr. Odili, present your argument why this shouldn't go to trial."

"Your Honor," Ekene picked up the papers that he had shared with the prosecuting counsel and handed them to the judge. "This is clear evidence that Mr. Okon knew the rules of Danjuma Group when he decided to take those extra shifts. It's in his hire agreement."

"Your Honor, Danjuma Group can't absolve itself from responsibility of duty. That is, the duty to guide and protect their drivers while on their time. The late Mr. Okon wasn't delivering his own products. He was delivering cement on behalf of the company. Therefore, someone should have known that he'd worked all those shifts prior. Danjuma Group not only failed in their duty, they breached it, thereby causing harm to Mr. Okon and his family since his demise."

"Sir, Mr. Okon signed up under another driver's name," Ekene argued.

For the next hour, both sides went back and forth. Ekene knew the only reason Mr. Jacobs had a semblance of a case was that out of the six unauthorized trips Mr. Okon made, the manager on duty that night could only get him three records. With the remaining three missing, it wasn't an open and shut case. The judge then reviewed what was ahead of him.

"I'll send both parties for mediation. Hopefully, you can come up with an amicable agreement. With what I have in front of me, both of you have an argument, but not strong enough to sway me one way or the other. However, I will not go to trial unless it's the last option."

Minutes later, Ekene grunted again while unlocking his car. This wasn't the outcome he was hoping for, but it gave him some time to go back to the drawing board. Mediation was probably not a bad idea. The judge was right; Danjuma Group didn't have the proper precautionary measures. That mistake had since been rectified, but Ekene wasn't willing to keep Halima, her brothers or Danjuma Group through the news. They'd been there enough in the last several years.

First, when their high-profile father died, and the brothers the public barely knew came home. Then there was the death at the DG Lokoja plant, and Jabir's wife's fall from grace to grass when Kamal was believed to have fathered her unborn children. To Kamal himself and his numerous run-ins with Nigerian and British law enforcement for unruly behavior.

Ekene made up his mind to talk to Halima, then Rasheed about possibly settling. It would require the board's buy-in, but saving the company's reputation would be the way to go because of the sympathy the public would have for two widows who just lost their breadwinner. He turned his car toward the opposite direction; making his way to the person he really wanted to lay his eyes on, Halima.

A short hour later, Ekene neared the doorway to Halima's office. Her assistant's chair was vacant, so he continued back. As he took a step closer, he overheard her talking. She was on speaker, and the misery in her voice couldn't be hidden.

"...you know good things are never easy." He recognized her friend, Zara's voice.

His sensible side knew he shouldn't be listening, but the curious part of him won, gluing his feet in place.

"They've always been for me," Halima said.

"That's because you always went with the flow. Go against the grain and people show you their real colors."

"I miss my mom. But she's so cold towards me." Halima sighed. "As much as I want to be strong, I don't know if I can."

"You can. Lemme tell you how my sis, Ola tells me. On the day of judgment, everyone will answer their own name."

He expected Halima to laugh but she sniffled instead, indicating that she had been crying or was trying to hold back her tears.

"I'm so sorry, Hali. I can't say I know what you're going through. Just know I'll always be here. And that fine man of yours."

Ekene's pulse quickened. He found himself waiting with bated breath for Halima's response. She did know that he would always be there for her right?

Halima responded with a feeble chuckle. "That's just the thing. I've been on this journey for about three years now, but my search intensified after Kene and I became closer. Am I allowing my feelings to lead me? Am I convinced of Jesus or the idea of Him because of the man I love? The pain and mourning at the end of this journey…is it worth this love?"

Ekene's heart plummeted to his stomach at the deep regret in her voice. How could she still be confused? Was he so blinded by his belief in them that he missed the signs of her regret? He knew it was a process, but he hadn't stopped to think about it from her end. She had to be sure of her walk with Christ for herself. He didn't want to cloud her judgment because she'd resent him for the things she had to sacrifice.

There was a pregnant pause.

"Halima Danjuma, you're running scared. Remember you told me to slap you if you did that again. Search within and tell me what you really believe."

Ekene couldn't bear to hear anymore. He turned on his heels and walked out the way he came. Once he was outside, he threw the tickets in the trash. He always told himself, if it came down to her happiness or his heart, he'd sacrifice his heart every time. Letting go would hurt but the tightness he now felt was excruciating. He got back in his car and headed home with a new resolve to distance himself from her. At least for now.

Chapter 23

Halima turned her salad over with her fork and thought about Zara's question.

"I'm waiting," she said.

"Stop rushing me."

"You're stalling and unlike you, I'm sure about my man. So certain, that if I don't hurry up, he'll make up an excuse not to go to the movies tonight."

Halima laughed. Apart from her brothers and their wives, the Willis's were her favorite couple. Whenever they came to Lagos to visit Zara's mother, Halima made sure she got to spend time with them.

"Okay, you're right. I'm terrified." Halima picked up her phone and walked barefoot to the front of her desk. "I let another phone call with my mother throw me off-kilter. I love Ekene with all my heart and I know that he loves me too. But not even he would make me denounce my religion if I didn't truly believe—"

"Did you say didn't?" Zara yelled. "Did you say didn't?"

"Yes didn't…"

"That means now you do?" Zara asked in expectation.

Halima remained silent and smiled.

"Hali, if you don't answer me—"

"Calm down, fighter. I haven't told anyone. Ekene has been in court all day and I wanted to tell him first."

"You see *yasef*? I remember when all you could muster was a blush when you talked about Ekene. Now, I'm the one getting secondhand info."

Halima rolled her eyes as though Zara could see her. "I still love youuuuu."She giggled at her friend's grunt. "Anyway, long story short, recently I asked God to reveal his Son to me..."

"How many—"

"Don't start. Yeah I know, I've had multiple dreams and visions. But I truly couldn't tell if I was just conjuring it up. Anyway, remember I told you I bumped into Kudi. That night, I was at my wits' end and desperate. Her words cut deep. Since that prayer, I've been extra vigilant, so I don't miss the sign. Today, I drove out for lunch—"

"Baby Danjuma, you mean your driver took you to get lunch," Zara teased.

"You should talk, between Terrance and your brother, you can barely do anything either. So, stop interrupting me."

"Okay, go ahead. Uh, wait hold on. Trey, babe, Halima finally found Jesus *o*. We can skip the movies."

Halima's mouth hung open. "Are you for real, Zara?"

"He didn't want to go anyway. But hold on, he's here. I'm about to put the phone on speaker." After a few seconds of muffled noises, Zara spoke. "Okay, we're listening."

"Hi, Terrance."

"Hello, Halima. This is fantastic. What finally did it?"

They weren't who she'd wanted to tell first but considering their history, they deserved to share this with her.

"I went to get lunch today, and the place I normally go to was closed. My driver recommended another place and we drove there. It turns out the owners are Christians. There were Scripture passages and artifacts scattered around the quaint store." Halima paused. Chills took over as she remembered what took place. "I placed my order and walked up to a picture of Jesus—"

"White Jesus or the real Jesus?" Zara asked.

"It doesn't matter," Terrance quipped.

"As I was staring at it, a lady walks up and stands by me. She took my hand. First, I wanted to ask why she was touching me. But it was like something kept my mouth shut. Then she spoke, 'He is real. His name is Jesus of Nazareth, the Lamb that was slain for our sins. He's the only way to the Father'." Halima would never forget those words. She rubbed her hands across her arms as the familiar chill set in.

"I don't understand. Why was this different?" Zara asked.

"Because I was in some sort of trance, I promise you. When the shock wore off, the lady wasn't by my side. My order was ready by then, so I went to pay and asked of the woman. Get this, they said I was the only customer they had in the last hour."

"Wow!"

"Praise God!"

Zara and her husband spoke in unison.

"The people looked at me as though I was crazy. But I know what I felt and saw. I asked specifically for Him to reveal Himself and He did," Halima said.

She'd been too scared to tell anyone. She wanted to marinate in the revelation. She'd returned to her office and soon after, her mother called, and they got into another argument. Halima wanted to scream and, as though Zara knew something was wrong, she called. That had to be the hand of God.

"I'm so happy for you," Zara spoke through light sniffles.

"Are you crying, Z? Gangsters don't cry." Halima joked.

"I guess she hasn't told you the news," Terrance said.

"No, what's wrong?" Halima's heart raced.

"We're pregnant. That's what I called to tell you when I heard your voice and you sounded bad," Zara cried.

"Oh my God, Z! I'm so happy for you." For the next couple of moments, the friends rejoiced.

"Halima, now that Jesus has been revealed to you, what's your next move?" Terrance asked.

"I don't know. I'm just taking it all in. I'll go and see the pastor of the church I go to, then I'll tell my family of my decision."

"Okay great. If you don't mind, I'd like to pray for you," he said.

"I'd like that. Thank you."

"Father God in the name of Jesus, we thank you for answering our prayer. Dear Jesus, You left the ninety-nine and went after the one. One of the ones has finally come home. We just want to say thank you, Father. Glory be to Your name. Forever and ever. Amen."

"Amen."

"I'm proud of you, Hali."

Zara's encouragement inflated her heart. Having someone outside of her family be there for her, especially at this time, wasn't something she'd always gotten. After a few more minutes on the phone, she packed up for the day. As her driver drove her to Mt. Zion church, she called Ekene several times but was met with his voicemail each time. She knew he'd been in court most of the day, but he'd never been unreachable for this length of time.

They came to a halt in front of the church and the white Altima she had become accustomed to seeing was out front. She turned off her phone, got out of the car and headed inside.

———

Halima climbed the short stairs. What she had come to admire about the church since she'd been coming here was its modesty. It was smaller than her brother's home church or Ekene's, but the sense of family was rich. She walked down the familiar passage to the office she was told she had an open invitation to. She'd done this walk several times over the past months but now seemed different. Halima's heart thumped with every step. Once she got to the door; she lifted her hand to knock. Her hand felt heavier, but she subconsciously willed through.

"Come in," Pastor Kalu called out.

When she peered her face through the half-open door, he raised his hands. "Ah Halima, how are you? Come in. Come in."

"Good evening, Pastor. I know I didn't call but—"

"I see for once you took me up on my 'come at any time' invitation," he teased.

Halima lowered her eyelids then took deliberate steps toward the chair she always sat in, in front of his coffee table.

He stood from behind his desk and sat opposite her as he always did. "Do you want anything to drink? The staff has gone, and I was about heading out myself, but something kept pulling me to stay. And now you are here, so I'm glad I obeyed."

"No Pastor. I'm fine."

"Tell me, what has you troubled?"

Halima hesitated for a second or two, then lifted her head. She looked the pastor straight in the eyes and said. "Jesus Christ revealed Himself to me."

The look of surprise she'd expected in his eyes or unbelief was absent. He didn't look at her like she was crazy. Instead with eagerness.

"Tell me more," he said.

"You don't seem surprised."

"I'm not because I know Who I serve. He's the God of

impossibilities and nothing is too hard for Him." The twinkle and conviction in his eyes were glaring. "Don't keep an old man waiting. Tell me more."

Halima drew her strength from his certainty and told him the story. From how she asked God in desperation to reveal Himself, to the Bible verse, then concluding with the old lady earlier.

"Glory to God."

"I'm ready, Pastor. I don't know what lies ahead. My battles may have just begun but I'm convinced Jesus Christ died, rose on the third day for my sins and He is the true Living Son of God."

"I won't paint a picture of roses. However, I'll assure you that He'll always be with you. All you must do is call on Him and trust Him." He stared at her and she nodded. "Let me have your hands while I say the sinner's prayer with you."

Halima put her hand in his and bowed her head.

"You'll repeat after me. It is key to understand that this prayer does not save. The repentance and faith behind the prayer holds salvation. Understood?"

"Yes," she whispered.

"Lord Jesus, for too long I've kept you out of my life. I know that I am a sinner and that I cannot save myself. No longer will I close the door when I hear You knocking. By faith, I gratefully receive your gift of salvation. I am ready to trust you as my Lord and Savior. Thank you, Lord Jesus, for coming to earth. I believe You are the Son of God who died on the cross for my sins and rose from the dead on the third day. Thank You for bearing my sins and giving me the gift of eternal life. I believe Your words are true. Come into my heart, Lord Jesus, and be my Savior. Amen."

Halima repeated the prayer as directed. When she said the final "amen," she opened her eyes and blinked. "I don't feel anything, Pastor."

"Were you supposed to?"

"This may be ignorant of me, but I thought that I'd be floating on air or something," Halima giggled.

The pastor chuckled. "Nope. No floating, but I want to caution you about human feelings when it comes to your new-found faith." He waited for a response from her.

She had none, so he continued. "Feelings are often fleeting and will change from one moment to the next. God never changes. His love and presence remain constant." He shrugged. "Compare it to how some days, you feel excited about going to work and some days when you see the things you have to do, you don't feel so excited. It doesn't change the fact that your employment is a done deal. You have a job and can handle your financial needs. Same thing applies when it comes to your salvation. Jesus has paid the price; you're now a daughter of the Kingdom."

"Okay, I just thought I'll feel different."

"The feeling will take some time as you become more active in church, read your Scriptures, pray and surround yourselves with those who are no longer babies in the walk. I believe your family isn't. But again, you are born new. No longer a sinner, but a forgiven saint and that should give you the giddiness you seek." He smiled. "It's a good feeling to know that the wrong things you've done have been forgiven and forgotten."

"Yes, that does feel good."

Halima and the pastor discussed for a few more minutes. He gave her Scriptures and pamphlet readings and told her he expected to see her on Sunday. She got back into the car and headed home. She turned on her phone to dial Ekene again when a text came through.

Kene: Caught the last flight to Ghana. The case I was working on as a consultant got moved up. I'll call when I land with an update on how long I'll be gone.

Halima frowned. That case wasn't supposed to be for

another week, and he told her that he could consult over the phone. Something wasn't right. The irony of where she just left and this wasn't lost on her. It was her first test, and she was up for the challenge. She closed her eyes to enjoy the ride just as the melody of "Excess Love" by Mercy Chinwo came through the speakers. She allowed the lyrics to build root in her soul as she basked in the newness of this kind of peace.

Chapter 24

Three whole weeks.

Halima walked to the spice rack in her kitchen with a dish towel draped over her shoulder. She'd just placed her carrot cake in the oven and was now in the mood for brunch. Her food of choice was oven-baked, spinach eggs.

Several minutes after getting out of bed, her nerves were all over the place, hence baking the cake before breakfast. It had been three weeks since she gave her life to Christ and the one person she desperately wanted to share the news with had gone Houdini. Yes, she could've done it over the phone, but she wanted to see his expression. Her family was going to kill her when they found out. It was silly, but she wanted to do things her way and wasn't apologetic about it. This was a decision she now regretted.

Chopping up the spinach and tomatoes with more force than intended, she glanced at her phone. Her finger itched to dial, but she willed herself not to. Since Ekene had been in Accra, she'd initiated all communication. He only texted and those were short and far in between. She had no time for games, so she wasn't intentionally keeping score, but after a while, it began to bother her. Something wasn't right and she was angry that he wasn't telling her what. She didn't want to ask Rasheed, because any hint that they were having issues he'd turn into her dad. Her brothers were all respectful and giving them space and she wanted it to stay that way.

She whipped a couple of eggs, added salt, pepper and the chopped spinach and tomatoes. Next, she greased the cupcake pan and filled it with the mixture. Placing the pan in the top oven, she walked over to the island and began cleaning up. Minutes later, she decided it was time to call her family. She picked up her iPad and called Kamal on WhatsApp video. He answered after the second ring.

"*Dan uwa na.*"

"Nope. Don't do that. Where have you been? Is that man telling you that you don't need your brothers?"

"Kam leave Hali alone," Ebi yelled.

Halima giggled. "I love him too and never pay him any attention."

"Is that Hali?" Ibiso yelled.

Great, that probably means that Rasheed is close by.

"Yes, it's her," Kamal responded.

"Madam, didn't you see my missed call?' Ibiso asked, coming into view.

"Hey, sis," Halima said.

Ibiso narrowed her brows and whispered. "Don't hey me. You asked for my carrot cake recipe, so I know you're stressing. What is it? I hope it's not that case *o*."

Halima ignored her question. "Hold on. Don't drop." She walked to the living room, picked up her cell phone and dialed Damisi.

"Hello, Hali, are you okay? Your senior wife was just complaining barely an hour ago that she was trying to call you," Damisi said, not giving her a chance to speak.

"Yeah, she's on WhatsApp now. By the way, that's *your* senior wife. She's my wife since my brother is married to her," Halima teased.

"What do you want smart mouth?" Damisi asked.

Halima laughed as she walked back to the kitchen. "Is my brother there?"

"You don't have his number?"

"I do, but you're more likely to answer your phone, so there."

"Whatever."

"You know I love you. Call him, *abeg*." Halima placed her cell phone on speaker next to her iPad and hurriedly removed the cake and her eggs from the oven.

"Ana, Ana, call your daddy. Tell him Aunty Hali is on the phone."

Seconds later, Jabir joined. "Hey, sis."

"Hey, you," Halima greeted looking into her iPad. "SoSo is big bros there?"

"I'm here, Halima. What's going on? Are you okay?" Rasheed asked.

Halima inhaled and exhaled. "Okay now that I have all of you on...three weeks ago, I converted to Christianity," she blurted out.

A beat of silence passed, and no one responded to her announcement. She looked at her iPad screen and thought the bad connection had the screen frozen. As the silence prolonged, fear took over. Her heart beat widely against her ribcage. "Hello?"

Suddenly, that same heart leaped as her ears threatened to bleed with the screams and roars that came through the line. It continued for several minutes. Halima laughed, then started to cry. Her tears of joy couldn't be contained. Her family was her everything and with a little luck, they didn't hear her say three weeks ago.

"Wait, three weeks ago! Halima, three weeks."

No such luck as Kamal stayed true to who he was. Everyone else followed suit and Halima allowed them to express their surprise and disappointment.

"I'm sorry. You all are right. But I wanted this for me. Selfishly, I wanted to preserve it for a while. Not that I don't love you guys, but this has been a tumultuous journey for me. It's not like anything you've experienced. You were raised, Christian. I wasn't. I had to mourn the loss of what I knew and embrace the unknown with a certainty required for my salvation."

After a few moments, Jabir spoke. "We understand sis, and we're so happy for you. We should celebrate."

"And we will in due time. I still have to tell my mom and with this case, now isn't a time to be throwing Danjuma parties," Halima said.

"True," Rasheed agreed. "Does Ekene know? And I have to ask, I hope you didn't do this for him."

Halima was almost offended but knew that he cared deeply for her and was only looking out.

"Big bro, no he doesn't. I want to tell him in person. And no amount of love for a man would make me give up my religion if I didn't believe. I know you love me, but trust me to know what's right."

"Okay, I apologize but I wouldn't be your big brother if I didn't ask."

"And I love you for it."

"Aww, look at two of them bonding," Ebele cooed. "Bros Rasheed all in his feelings."

"Sis, don't do my man. Nobody told Kam to be aggressive all the time," Ibiso said.

"How did I get in it? Okay, I'll remember that next time you need me to go smile in some people's face as Kam, the soccer player, so you can get the contract closed."

"Hmm," Ebele cosigned.

The others laughed while Ibiso pleaded with Kamal, but was still going at it with Ebele. Halima shook her head. Ibiso should know by now that unless Ebele said it, Kamal wasn't doing it. So, she was pleading with the wrong person. The family joked together for a while before Halima hung up.

She plated her still warm eggs, made two pieces of toast and a cup of tea. Minutes later, she settled herself on the couch and picked up the remote. Turning to DSTV, she flipped through the channels until she came across a movie called *Muna*.

Early afternoon, two days after his return from Accra, Ekene paced in front of the large windows of his office. With a large manila envelope in one hand, he used the other to wipe the nonexistent perspiration from his forehead. It was his first day back at the office and what would've otherwise been an astonishing view of the Lekki skyline was presently a blur among his jumbled thoughts.

He tried convincing himself he didn't have regrets or wasn't disappointed at the turn of events between Halima and himself. But that would be self-deceit. He'd spent the last three weeks trying to figure out what he could've done better. But fell short each time. At first, his only goal was to give her some space, then he chided himself for not talking to her. Instead of retracing his steps, he allowed time to pass and suddenly found himself in self-preservation mode. He knew his heart couldn't take her confirming what he had heard. He did owe her a conversation and after three weeks away, he planned to give it to her. However, this morning other pressing issues arose. Chief among them was the contents of the envelope he was holding.

Judge Boyega had indeed sent them to mediation, and Ekene wasn't a fan of the mediator that had been assigned to the case. Although Ekene was all in favor of them reaching an agreement to avoid the media attention, he still knew, now more than before, that it would be a tedious process, especially when it came time to go to the board to get the negotiated amount approved. He had a feeling in the pit of his stomach that warned that the coming weeks or month ahead were not going to be easy to navigate. As he walked back to his desk, he made a mental note to stop by Halima's office later in the afternoon and give Rasheed a call immediately after.

Hours later, a soft knock on the door brought Ekene's head up. He'd spent the morning reading over briefs, making notes for his assistant of things that needed to be done and for his paralegal of cases he needed researched.

"Come in." He interlocked his fingers and stretched his arms while moving his head around to ease the tension.

"Mr. Odili, it's one-thirty. I came to remind you about your lunch meeting with the Dysons," his secretary said. "The reservations are booked under the firm's name."

"Shoot, that's today?"

The older woman smiled and nodded.

"Thanks, Eunice."

She turned and walked out the door and he groaned. If he'd remembered, he would've had the appointment moved. Not only was he going to have to deal with two-plus hours of endless idle chatter, but it was at his and Halima's favorite restaurant.

The Dysons were sent to him by his dad. The brother and sister duo were spoiled and entitled, in his opinion. But there was nothing in his code of ethics that said anything about not seeking justice for bratty, rich kids. The partners of the firm their late parents had fought so hard to build were now challenging the will of the deceased in an effort to take the mantle of leadership from the kids.

Granted, the oldest heir was barely twenty-five years old and had no business experience, but their rights and not their experience were at stake. He glanced at the time. He had exactly half an hour to get to the Sailors Lounge.

His chest tightened. That was he and Halima's spot and despite the state of their present relationship, it would remain sacred to him and hold a lot of memories. Now was too soon to be visiting it with them at odds.

Ekene stood, put his navy suit jacket back on and exited his office. In a little over twenty minutes, he was strolling behind a waitress to the table where his party was already seated. He gave a satisfied nod when the ambiance of the daytime had no resemblance to the ambience he and Halima experienced.

As he reached the table, Chris Dyson stood. He stretched out one hand and gestured to his sister with the other, reintroducing her. Ekene shook hands with Chris and acknowledged the young lady, Erica, completely ignoring the lustful stare she had whenever she was in his presence. Besides being more than twenty years his junior, she was his half-sister's friend.

Several minutes and some small talk later, their food arrived. Ekene wasn't hungry, so he settled on an appetizer. After a few bites of his gizzard and plantains, Ekene picked up the napkin and dabbed the corners of his mouth.

"So, here's the deal. I've reviewed the papers filed, looking for grounds and justification that the other partners would have for contesting your leadership. I found none. However, your past could have a damaging effect on your competence with the investors."

"I wasn't looking to run my father's company anytime soon, so I was sowing my wild oats," Chris said with a smug grin plastered on his face. "That doesn't mean that I'm going to allow that greedy Mr. Kendem to take what's rightfully mine."

"Ours," Erica corrected.

"Uhmm… Yeah, ours." Chris waved her off, hesitated, then turned to look at her. "You know I own the majority of daddy's shares?"

His question was met with an eye roll. Ekene lifted his finger to his temple. He wanted to knock the younger man out, but then he remembered his dad and his agreement to represent them. He knew what he had signed up for. But to satisfy his curiosity, he asked, "What are you going to do if the company is under your control?"

"*When* I win…My pops always raved about you when he was alive. So, I know we'll win, right?"

Ekene gave a faint smile, not wanting to directly answer his question. He watched as the young man contemplated a little more. A few beats passed between them; the silence ensued.

Finally, he said. "Truthfully, I don't know. But it's the principle of the whole thing."

"While I do agree. And I'm in no way a pastor to preach, but you must think about the huge responsibility on your shoulders, young man. The things your parents sacrificed to build that business. It would be nice to have a plan so that when we do appear before the judge to ask for a stay of the vote and potential takeover, you'll be able to paint a good picture."

Chris deadpanned him while tearing his crab into two with his hands. "Yeah, I understand."

Ekene wasn't sure he did, but then again, he had given his best advice. When Chris spoke again, Ekene was certain he didn't understand.

"Or I could just get Tracy to come up with something."

"Who is Tracy?" Ekene asked.

"Our father's trusted assistant," Erica responded.

It was at that moment that Ekene knew the company was doomed, and thousands would lose their jobs as a result. For the first time in a long time, he wasn't getting justice for the right person.

———

SOMETIME LATER, EKENE ADJUSTED HIMSELF IN HIS SEAT. HE'D mentally checked out about an hour after the lunch started. It was a struggle to get to the end of the time he had allotted to them, but finally, it was over. A heavy silence settled over the table, the uneasy tension, a contrast to the atmosphere around them, as he and Erica waited on Chris to return from the restroom. He felt her stare burning through his temple as he checked his email.

In the few minutes they'd been alone, she'd done everything to get a reaction out of him. Swinging her legs sideways, uncrossing and crossing them, deliberately driving her skirt up, and batting her eyelashes at him when she asked him to repeat something about the case that he had already discussed in detail.

His irritation grew and he knew he would lose his temper with her antics. He was tempted to scold her like he would his younger sister, but he needed to conserve his energy. He mentally prepped for a conversation with the love of his life. Her office was his next destination.

Just in time, the waiter arrived with the dessert he had ordered for Halima in a Styrofoam box. The check had been paid and he was ready to leave.

"Let me go powder my nose and use the little girl's room. It's a long drive back to the Mainland." Erica stood and so did Ekene.

She stumbled into him and his reflexes took over grabbing her around the waist. He helped her sit back down and frowned at the monstrosity on her feet.

"Are you okay?"

He squatted near her to ensure her ankle was not twisted. What made him do that, since she had been on his nerves all afternoon, he had no idea. Except it was something he would've done for his sister. The second he decided to be kind, he regretted the gesture immediately. Erica's hand gently landed on his shoulder while she let out an exaggerated groan. At that moment, the hair on the back of his neck stood. Ekene's gaze followed the direction of the invisible tug. His eye narrowed, searching for the source of the familiar pull. He locked eyes with Halima through the railing to the lower level of the restaurant. The reason behind Erica's groan dawned on him when he noticed she saw Halima too.

His heartbeat accelerated. The look on Halima's face went from hurt to disgust to blazing anger, all in a matter of seconds. He wanted to move, but somehow the memo didn't travel to his brain fast enough. When it did, he shrugged off Erica's hand and stood. Picking up his jacket from where it hung across the back of his chair, he bumped into Chris.

"Easy man, what's the rush?" Chris tried to steady him.

"I'll be in touch through my assistant. I have to go." Ekene turned to look at where Halima was seated, and the space was now empty.

Hurriedly he ran down the steps and got outside just as her white SUV was pulling off. Handing the valet his ticket, he waited for his car. He wanted to call Halima, but he wasn't sure if she drove herself or a driver did. If it was the former, he didn't want her any more upset than she was while driving. As his car made its way around the corner, his phone buzzed in his hand. He looked at the screen and it was his father's wife.

"Hello," he answered fastening his seat belt.

"Ekene... err how are you? Ummm, your dad collapsed, and we're at Redstar Hospital."

Ekene didn't ask any further questions. "I'm on my way." With a groan, he said a quick prayer and turned his car in the opposite direction. His conversation with Halima would have to wait till later tonight. Right now, his only surviving parent needed him.

Chapter 25

Men are scum. Her father was her first teacher.

Later that evening, seated in the back of her car, Halima rested against the leather headrest as her driver navigated through Lagos traffic. Somehow, she'd made it through the day without betraying her emotions. She forced herself to laugh at jokes she barely heard, interacted with her staff and carried on as if her heart hadn't just been shattered.

The meetings she had scheduled couldn't be postponed just so she could process her feelings. But now, she let them run free. Her skin prickled and heated up in rage, and if she were honest, disappointment. How could someone so sweet, protective and loving turn into a jerk overnight?

The Ekene she thought she knew would've been in her office or at least called her on his return, but nothing. She was so used to shutting down when the rug was ripped from under her, but her new quest for respect and coming into her own demanded she confront things head-on. That was exactly what she tried doing by calling him a couple of hours after she left the restaurant, but the phone went straight to voicemail. After the initial attempt, she was done. No level of women empowerment would make her chase a man or try and keep him where he didn't want to be.

"Madam Halima, do you still want to stop at Shoprite?"

Halima opened her eyes and lifted her head. She looked out the window to get her bearings.

"Yes, thank you."

Minutes later, she was wheeling her cart around the aisles, picking up a few household items. All that was left was her favorite brand of chin-chin. She spotted it and wheeled the cart in that direction. At that same moment her phone dinged, and she reached into her bag for the device when another cart collided with hers.

"Oh excuse —"

"You're excused." The woman hissed at her.

Halima stared into the face of Eric Okon's second wife. The woman gave her a once over which Halima returned. Granted she'd lost her husband, but none of it was Halima's fault and she and the company had done more than enough to help the family out. Halima wondered where the woman's disdain for her came from. It felt personal. Was this really because of her husband or was it about the money? Halima lacked the will to engage, so moved her cart around. The next words she heard, halted her steps.

"I see the fact that the judge has us going to mediation has humbled you," she said. "You thought the judge would throw the case out like he did the last one. Not this time. You rich people will pay." Her voice dripped with disgust.

The iciness of her tone caused Halima to again question her motives. If it was money, she felt pity for her as it only led to more problems. But that wasn't Halima's focus. The fact that they were going to mediation was news to her. Halima kept her expression blank, straightened her back, picked up a pack of chin-chin and proceeded to check out. Once in the car, she retrieved her ringing phone. It was Rasheed. Just the person she needed to talk to.

Answering the phone, she skipped the pleasantries. "Did Ekene tell you we were going to mediation?"

He muttered under his breath. "Halima is everything—"

His tone told her everything she needed to know. He was trying to handle her. She hated when he did that.

"Brother, I'm fine. Please just answer me." Her voice shook. For the second time that night, as she listened to her brother, Halima questioned how she could've pegged Ekene so wrong.

"Ekene. Ekene."

Ekene sat up, opened his eyes and stretched his neck. His father's wife, Nkiru came into focus, standing next to his father's bed.

"Good morning," he growled.

"Good morning. How is he? Thank you for staying." She placed her hand on his father's cheek. The man was now resting peacefully after a rough night.

Ekene stood, peered at his dad and glanced at his watch. It was a little past seven a.m.

"It's not a problem. He's also my responsibility." He picked up his keys and phone. "I hope you had a good night's rest?"

Nkiru nodded. Her eyes misted and for the first time in years, he saw her love for the man, something he was blind to because of their huge age difference.

"Don't worry. He'll be fine. The doctor should be by later." Ekene walked to the door of the private room he made sure his dad was moved to. "When he wakes up, tell him I'll be back soon. Call me if you need anything before then."

"Thank you."

Ekene strode to the nurse's station, said his goodbyes and

told them to take care of his father and lastly, call him if anything came up.

Moments later, he sped down the highway in the rental that he was now kicking himself for getting. His own car needed to be serviced so he needed it, but the timing couldn't have been worse. His phone was dead and there wasn't a charging dock in this vehicle. He looked at his phone for the umpteenth time that morning, mentally willing it to obtain power and work.

His thoughts were running wild. There was no telling the stories Halima had told herself about him in the last several hours. He knew he couldn't blame her as his behavior over the last couple of weeks, joined with what she saw yesterday, provided her with varying damaging plot lines. He just hoped he could unravel the damage. No matter what he'd heard her say a while ago, he loved her and couldn't exist in this world being on her hit list.

Soon after, he slowed down and turned onto the road leading to his Ikeja neighborhood. He'd spent the last twelve plus hours with his dad and they were the longest of his life. His dad had suffered a mild stroke.

Ekene lifted his hand to his chest, remembering how his heart pumped rapidly before he set eyes on the older man. It took some persuasion, but hours after he'd arrived and his father was stable, Ekene convinced Nkiru to go home and get some rest since he was going to stay. When she left, he made sure his father was comfortable, then settled in the large chair by his bedside. He thanked God for sparing his father once again.

Then like a flood, the events of earlier popped back into his mind. He'd pulled out his Smartphone to call Halima, but realized its battery was on its last leg. He dialed several times, but the phone wouldn't connect until a nurse told him that there wasn't reliable phone service in the hospital.

All his attempts to change positions and dial before that

information finally killed the battery. Worst of all, he didn't have her number memorized since she was saved in his phone as **Princess**. Accepting defeat, he'd settled in for the night. Ekene asked that God help him fix the mess he'd created. After that, he'd leaned back and shut his eyes.

Walking into his home, Ekene headed straight to his room. He connected his phone to its charger and entered the bathroom. Minutes later, with a towel wrapped around his waist, he emerged tired, hungry and still agitated. He sat on his bed and laid back. Without his permission, his heavy eyelids closed. *Just a few seconds*

Those seconds turned into hours as he succumbed to sleep's call.

———

LATER THE SAME DAY, EKENE PACED UP AND DOWN HIS OFFICE floor with his earbuds in his ear. He rubbed his fingers across his forehead as he waited for the person on the other end to answer the call. It was almost noon, and this wasn't how he had envisioned the day going. When he woke up, his first want was to call Halima, but a monstrous headache and a growling stomach reminded him of his immediate needs. He hadn't had anything to eat since lunch the previous day. At that moment, the need to regain his energy preceded anything else. After that, he'd called her several times but couldn't get in contact with her.

"Hey man, where have you been?" Rasheed said, once he answered the phone.

"You don't even want to know. I've had the worst twenty-four hours ever."

Rasheed grunted. "Worse than the time you had to walk around school the whole day with pants torn at the seam because you wanted to impress Sandra with the flip?"

"Don't even play about that, but yes." Ekene spent the

next several minutes explaining what happened, careful to leave out anything that concerned him and Halima.

"Wow. Sorry to hear that. Where is Popsie now?"

"He's still in the hospital, but should be discharged tomorrow or the day after."

"Okay good. We'll be praying for you and God's complete healing."

"Thanks, man." Ekene paused. "So, did you think about what I told you yesterday?"

"Yeah, I did but what I don't understand is why you didn't tell Halima."

Ekene let out a sigh. "I didn't have the time. And I've been trying to call her, and she hasn't answered me." He was so frustrated and knew it showed.

"This is what I was afraid of with the two of you—"

"Leave it alone, 'Sheed…"

"How? When my sister seems so miserable and thinks that I'm not observant enough to notice."

"Imma fix it."

"I hope you can because Hurricane Halima is on a warpath."

Apprehension swept through him. "Why do you say that?"

"Because we had a very strained conversation last night. I had to pull out the 'I'm your big brother' card."

"Explain.".

"I thought you wanted me to stay out of it?"

"'Sheed, man…"

Rasheed chuckled and Ekene plopped down and twirled his chair as his friend told him what had occurred. Ekene ran his fingers across his hair. This was worse than he thought.

"Okay man, thanks for the heads up. Back to business though. Were you able to call an emergency meeting with the board so they could approve the amount I think we might need?"

"Yes, I did, but there was some hesitancy. Almost like they were hiding something."

Ekene twirled his pen like a baton between his fingers. "That's because they are."

"What? How do you know?" Rasheed fired off.

"My retainer costs a pretty buck, so I keep my ears to the ground to protect my clients' interest. I'm not only your company lawyer, but I also represent the family."

"Stop stalling. Tell me what you know."

Ekene let out an exaggerated breath and told his friend what had him pacing a few minutes ago. Just as he tried dialing Halima one more time, his private investigator called and informed him that a couple of board members held a secret meeting earlier in the morning. The consensus was to hold a vote to force Halima to resign. They were citing her contributions to the bad press, increased settlement payments, and dwindling public trust.

"That's what I was calling to tell you," Ekene said.

"We'll never allow that to happen. The controlling shares are in my family," Rasheed seethed.

"Halima has to be ready to —"

"Ready to do what?"

The voice that would've soothed his soul now sounded like it wanted to take it. Ekene turned and the look in her eyes matched her tone. Her stony stare, scrunched eyebrows and hands on her hips took nothing away from her beauty. Her pouted lips did nothing to help his deep need to kiss her.

"Ermm…'Sheed man, let me call you back. The hurricane has landed," Ekene mumbled.

Chapter 26

"Ready for what?"

Ekene's eyes held Halima's glare. He removed the buds from his ears and strode towards her. Silence between them had never been awkward. However, so much had happened that he didn't know what to address first. He settled on an ordinary greeting.

"Hi, Halima."

Grateful that she had shut the door behind her, he waited for her response.

"Hi, Halima? Is that all you could come up with? Hi? Really?" she snapped. With an eyebrow raised, she propped her body weight on her right hip in challenge.

"Princess—"

"Don't! Just tell me what I should get ready for. Everyone seems to know but me."

"You know that wasn't my intention—"

"Forgive me, but I have no idea what your intentions are anymore. But I'm done worrying about them."

Her words stabbed him in the gut. At the moment, he regretted how he had handled things with her before he left for Ghana. What seemed like a wise decision was now anything but that.

"Can we sit?"

Halima glanced over to his sitting area then returned her gaze to him. Relief washed over him the moment he saw the hesitation in her eyes disappear. She walked over to the area and he followed with calculated steps. Halima put her bag on the coffee table and crossed her legs at her ankles. Although this was the wrong time, but his body immediately reacted to the shift of her skirt. It took all the willpower he could muster to remained focused on the seriousness of the matter at hand. Staying away from her might not have been his best decision, but now he was reminded of why he made it.

"Are you going to get on with it or keep staring at me?" The irritation in her tone brought him out of his trance.

He sighed. "I have so much to tell you. First about yesterday…"

"No, we are not doing this. Just tell me what I should be prepared for. I already know about the mediation from my brother. What else is there?"

"Halima…"

"No, Ekene. You don't get to explain anything to me now. What? You want to talk about how you left for Accra for three weeks? Or the fact that you barely communicated with me? Or let me guess, the reason why I didn't know you were back in the country until I saw you with someone else having lunch." She stood.

Ekene looked up at her. Now that she said it out loud, he cringed at how cowardly his behavior was, but she owed him the chance to explain. She didn't get to dismiss him so easily. He stood and stepped closer to her. As suspected, she didn't back down from him.

He shoved his hands into his pockets and leaned into her. "Princess, you don't get to dismiss me. No matter what's going on I love you and we're going to talk like two adults."

Halima let out a dry chuckle. "It's not fun when the shoe is on the other foot, is it?" She sighed. "For the last time will you tell me what's going on with the Danjuma Group case or do I have to call Rasheed?"

Ekene decided on a different approach. He'd give her what she wanted. He told her about the judge's ruling to send them to mediation. Then he narrated what he told Rasheed earlier about the board. A few beats passed and she hadn't yet said anything. She moved to the front of his desk and leaned against it with her eyes lowered. He turned to face her but didn't move from his spot. Her eyes finally met his.

"I thought you saw what I was about. Believed in the woman I'm fighting so hard to become. One that owns her voice, deserves respect and can make independent decisions. I've been under the shadow of men all my life. My dad, Uncle Musa, Danladi…" She paused. "I've lost friends, my mom barely speaks to me but I'm okay with that because I refuse to live my life led by others anymore. I thought you knew that."

"I do know that…"

"No, you don't. If you did, you wouldn't try to handle me all the time. I'm not a dog that needs a handler to show it the way. I want to fight my battles and not have you consult my brother trying to soften the blow. I'm not a problem to be fixed or a delicate flower to protect."

Ekene walked toward her. "I know that. Your strength—"

She shook her head. "I thought we were headed somewhere with a relationship, but now I see that you'll probably never give me the respect I deserve."

"What?! How can you even think that?"

"The real question is how did I convince myself not to."

"I told you that you can't stop me from trying to protect you," Ekene snapped.

"Protect me from what?" she yelled. "I want someone who'll see me as a team player, not someone that he can control…"

"Wait. Hold on just a minute here. Fine, I didn't tell you

about the mediation when I first knew it was a possibility. I couldn't tell you when I wasn't certain that it was going to happen. The board situation just happened this morning." Ekene seethed.

"We were in a relationship. I should've been your first call. Before Rasheed. I know he's the CEO, but this affects me. Me!!"

"Like you've been so forthcoming."

"What's that supposed to mean? I'm not the one who ran away…"

"Ran?! Believe me, after what I heard you say on the phone, that was the best I could do for both of us." He scoffed.

Halima furrowed her eyebrows.

Ekene took in a breath and exhaled. "I heard you tell Zara on the phone how much pain you're in and if our love was worth it."

Halima's jaw dropped. However, she quickly recovered, and her cheeks took on a deeper red shade. She was livid. He wondered why when she did say that, and he heard her.

"Let me get this straight. You heard that and decided to travel out of the country to spare my feelings?"

"Halima…"

She raised her hand to silence him and walked to the coffee table to pick up her bag. She placed the strap on her shoulder and without a word she walked toward the door.

"Halima!"

"You've just proven my point once again." Her tone was resigned. "If you had waited to hear the full conversation, you would've heard me say although I was confused, I love you deeply and trusted you'd never leave my side. But instead, you decided to *handle* it."

Ekene's heart thumped. "Halima. Princess, wait give me a chance to—"

"Deep down inside, I've always feared that our relationship was doomed. The challenges were many, but I had a glimmer of hope that we'd fight those trials together. It's time for me to stop dreaming."

Ekene scowled. "What's that supposed to mean?"

"It means that all information regarding the case should be passed through my assistant. I'll get with my brother to find out what I need to do for the board."

"What about us?" His tone mingled with desperation and anger. His ego couldn't handle her dismissive reaction.

"*Us* doesn't exist. I'm back to being just your client."

The finality in her voice sent him over the edge. "Halima, don't—"

"See you soon. Goodbye, Ekene."

His heart ripped in half as he watched her walk away. He'd coached himself to believe that this was what was best, but now he was faced with the pain of how wrong he had been and hadn't the slightest clue how to undo the damage.

———

MONDAY MORNING, TWO WEEKS LATER, HALIMA GOT OFF HER knees and proceeded to the bathroom. She'd been up for the past couple of hours worshiping and praising God. A lot had happened over the last couple of weeks leading up to the board meeting that would take place in about three hours. After talking to Rasheed, they both decided to skip a long mediation and offer a settlement instead. It was accepted and finalized within a week.

Just as Ekene had warned, right after the settlement was announced, the Board sent a letter formally summoning her to a meeting. The letter stated their concerns about her competency but gave her the option to address the Board before a vote was held.

Halima undressed, wrapped herself in her robe and made another call to her mother. She picked up her toothbrush as the phone rang. She almost gave up when her mother answered.

"Hello."

"*Barka da safe*, Mother. *Ina kwana?*"

"Halima, *lahiya lau. Kina lahiya?*

She stared at the phone, still in disbelief at how strained their relationship had become. She sounded so disinterested. How could she be so blasé when she was facing the biggest battle of her career?

"I'm okay, Mother. I called last night to—"

"Your brother already told me what's going on."

Halima had tried numerous times to reach her mother over the last several days, but she refused to answer or return her calls. Rasheed had done all he could getting the buy-in of the board members he was good with. Uncle Musa and Danladi's family had shares and seats on the board. However, not enough to vote her out.

"And?"

"You see this was what I was trying to warn you about. Allah's wrath."

"Mother, what are you talking about?"

"None of this happened until you started going against His ways. First, you break off your engagement, take off your hijab, convert to a person of the Book. Only to be faced with the possibility of losing your birthright and still no husband."

Halima rolled her eyes. She regretted the decision to call her mother. She should've allowed Rasheed to handle her as offered. Deciding to ignore her mother's comments, Halima asked.

"So, are you flying down with him?"

At this point, with the way Rasheed predicted the voting might go, her mother's shares would be the tiebreaker.

"I plan to."

"You plan to? Is that a yes or a no?" Halima was becoming frustrated with her mother's attitude.

"Show some respect, Halima. I didn't put you in this mess. Your rebelliousness did. I just said I plan to. Now let me go get ready." Her mother hung up without even giving her a chance to respond.

Halima stared at the phone and cupped her face with her hands. "Dear God, help me to not be afraid. To trust that You will not let me be put to shame. In Jesus' name. Amen." She went to YouTube and typed in "Good Good Father" by Chris Tomlin and proceeded with her morning routine as the melody began to play.

Several minutes later, Halima walked into her kitchen to prepare a light breakfast. She buttered two slices of bread and toasted them while she made herself a cup of wild raspberry tea. In the time it took her to put on her navy-blue pantsuit, she'd taken calls from all her sisters-in-law, Big Mummy and Zara. She adjusted the sleeves of her light pink linen blouse and shifted the pants that were tapered at the end, so they rested on her nude stilettos.

Looking at her reflection through the side of the toaster, she tucked a loose tendril of her hair into the low ponytail. Her eyes roamed to the miniature bicycle Ekene won for her during a cycling competition some months ago and the familiar ache she'd come accustomed to returned. Despite her heartbreak, she'd maintained a strictly professional relationship with him. Not for his lack of trying to resume the conversation several times. She had shut him down on every attempt. It hurt too much to revisit and their failed relationship wasn't in the top spot of her worries.

Moments later, she sat on the barstool to eat while she looked over her notes. Soon after, her doorbell rang. Halima dabbed the corners of her lips with a napkin and strolled to the door. She peeked through the peephole and smiled. Opening the door, she stared at the handsome men she was proud to call family, Rasheed, Jabir, and Kamal. They had on different colors, black, brown and navy blue, in what seemed to be the same suit style.

"You ready, sis?" Jabir asked.

"Yes, and you guys look great." She left them at the door and walked back to the kitchen to get her stuff.

"And so do you. I see you still trying to be like me." Kamal said. "What did you do? Call E to ask what I'm wearing?"

Halima giggled. "*Dan uwa na.* Leave me alone." Then she paused as it dawned on her. Someone was absent. She turned to Rasheed. "Where's my mother?"

Her brothers dropped their heads and remained silent.

"Rasheed…"

"Hali, she didn't fly in with us. Kam and I went to get her, but she wasn't there and didn't answer my calls. I couldn't be late," he said.

Halima staggered as the weight of his words sunk in, the devastation made her stomach hurt. She braced herself against the sectional and hung her head. Seconds later she felt a hand on her shoulder.

"Hali," Kamal whispered.

She turned and the three of them stood before her.

"Your mom might not be here, but we are, and the family is praying. Remember, her vote would be the deciding vote only if there is a tie and we don't expect there to be," Rasheed said.

"Let's pray," Jabir said.

They linked hands and bowed their heads and Jabir led them in a prayer of thanksgiving.

"And let the Danjumas say…"Kamal urged.

"Amen!" They said in unison.

Rasheed turned to the door. "Let's get this over with."

Chapter 27

*T*hree men and a Princess.

That would've been the name he'd give this movie if it weren't such a serious matter. Ekene had been at the Danjuma Group headquarters for a while. Rasheed texted him informing him they were on their way, but nothing prepared him for the sight of her. With deliberate strides, the Danjuma brothers made their way down the hallway with their sister in front of them. They were like a human defense. He took a deep breath, expanding his chest as his eyes roamed over her, taking her in. When her eyes met his they were void of any emotion and that sent a pang through his already injured heart.

Rasheed's eyes met his and he gave him a knowing look. His friend knew a little of the strain between him and his sister.

"All right, bro. Now is not the time," Rasheed cautioned him, patting his shoulder, before walking to the conference room. They had about forty minutes before the meeting.

Ekene cleared his throat. "Don't you guys look like some fake men in black." His remark earned him a giggle from Halima while her brothers took turns clowning him back.

"I see you got jokes." Kamal shifted his gaze to Halima and landed them back on Ekene. He furrowed his brow. "Hmmm, I'm more interested in why you ain't trying to suck on my sister's face." Kamal kept his eyes on Ekene.

Ekene didn't give him what he was looking for and neither did Halima.

"What's going on?"

"Nothing," Halima answered. "Kammy, please behave."

"Kam…" Jabir started.

Kammy raised his hands in surrender. "A'ight. But let me find out…"

"Man, get on with those empty threats." Ekene waved Kamal off. He wasn't a pushover but now was not the time or the place. He moved closer to Halima. With his hand on her elbow, he ushered her away from her brothers.

"How are you?" he whispered in her ear. This was the closest he'd gotten to her in two weeks. The fragrance of her perfumed sent tiny tremors up his spine.

"Fine." Her lips barely moved.

"Princess—"

"Don't."

"I miss you. Just let me be there for you," he pleaded.

"You are here, aren't you?"

"Oh, come on. I said I was sorry."

"So…"

Ekene narrowed his eyes and bit down on the back of his teeth. He didn't want to rattle her anymore, so he backed off. He used his index finger to raise her head.

"It's going to be okay. I believe in you." His voice was slightly above a whisper.

"Thank you." She responded and for the first time, she met his eyes. He smiled and she returned the gesture, although he knew it was forced. They'd have plenty of time to get back to them. If she thought he was letting her go, she was sorely mistaken.

———

"THE FACT IS, OUR INVESTORS ARE STARTING TO GET ANTSY about the rocky nature of our reputation," Alhaji Nuru said.

"And when did that happen?" Rasheed asked. "The last I heard, we were doing fine,"

"You would say that because the person bringing the unwanted attention to the company is your sister," another board member chimed in.

"She has a name. Address her by it." Kamal seethed.

Halima shifted in her seat. The meeting had commenced about thirty minutes ago and as expected, her brothers and some other board members were in a back and forth debate with Uncle Musa's loyalists. Strangely, however, he wasn't present. Neither was Danladi. Jabir and Kamal sat on the board, even though they didn't have active roles in the company.

"Gentlemen, we are not getting anywhere with this," Dr. Pearson said. "Granted, people like their investments to be stable – a controlled environment with predictable people at the head of affairs. Someone they can trust—"

"Trust? Are you kidding me? Not only have I and Ms. Danjuma made Danjuma Group a multi-million dollar, not Naira, dollar success. We have made our investors a lot of money. How dare you question our trustworthiness over something that was out of our control?" Rasheed's tone was sharp, and it conveyed his growing impatience with this game the board was playing.

"If you had let me finish Mr. Danjuma, I was going to acknowledge you and Ms. Danjuma's accomplishments over the last few years in the areas of expansion and community development in all our cement plants," Dr. Pearson concluded.

"That's all good, but Ms. Danjuma's name has been tied

to, not one, but two deaths. We can't overlook that fact," Mrs. Nkurma, another board member, said.

Halima cringed. Her past had come back to haunt her. Uncle Musa had lured her into a deceptive plot, six years ago that led to a young man's death at the Lokoja plant and was also the person behind her present predicament. Without Uncle Musa's enticement, this meeting wouldn't even be taking place. However, she was an adult when she agreed to his plan back then and she was one now, so she took full responsibility.

"What company do you know has existed without being sued?" Jabir asked.

"Being sued is one thing, deaths and subsequent large Naira settlements are another. I know we agreed to the settlement on advice from Mr. Odili to get the company out of the spotlight. But we never should've been there in the first place," another one of Uncle Musa's henchmen said.

"Two deaths that were proved not to be the fault of Ms. Danjuma. The autopsy was done for the young man years ago and his death was unrelated. And this recent driver broke company rules," Rasheed defended.

Halima stood and cleared her throat. She'd had enough. This was a preposterous witch hunt and she wasn't going to stand for it anymore.

"Ladies and Gentlemen of the board, we've been here for a little under an hour going back and forth. I may be a lot of things, but a murderer I'm not. I would never deliberately cause harm to anyone. The fact that this board now thinks I'm so dangerous and a possible threat to our stock value is laughable."

She took a deep breath as her eyes connected with each one of her detractors who, incidentally, were seated opposite her. "I've given my life to this company. It's all I know, and I would never do anything to hurt it. Those deaths were unfortunate. However, let me say, I do believe that someone was paying the media to keep my name and the companies' name in the news.

"I will leave the room now for you to vote and I'll take whatever decision that's made." Halima headed to the door of the conference room. The bad feeling she had when she didn't see her mother with Rasheed earlier, resurfaced when the door opened and a smiling Uncle Musa and his sidekick Danladi entered the room.

"Hello, everyone. Apologies for being late but I see we're right on time for the important part," her uncle said.

Danladi winked at her and Halima left the room headed to her office.

Several moments later, Halima was still stretched out on the couch in her office on the sixth floor, two floors above where the meeting was still being held. Except for a few catering staff downstairs, the office was closed today, so she was relishing the much-needed silence.

Kene: *How is it going? On my way back.*

Halima read the text that appeared when she powered on her phone. He left right when the meeting was about to start. He couldn't sit in on the proceedings and had an appointment that couldn't be moved. She began to respond when there was a knock on her door. She placed the phone to her side and sat up.

"Come in."

The door opened and her brothers entered. Their expressions were blank. Dread took over and her temples pounded.

"Is it over? What happened?"

"Let's sit down, Hali," Kamal said.

"No, tell me. I'm fine," she insisted.

They looked at one another. Jabir was about to speak when Ekene came rushing in.

"I came back as fast as I could. What happened? Is it over?" He fired off questions, coming to stand by her.

Although she was still upset with him, the hand he placed on the small of her back provided her with some comfort.

"Sis, they voted you out," Rasheed said.

"How? I don't understand. From my own father's company? I thought you said—" Halima stumbled back. The weight of the news knocked the wind out of her. Ekene steadied her.

"And I stand by what I said. It would have worked," Rasheed continued. "But…"

"But what? What happened? Why are you not telling me?" Halima's eyes darted from one brother to the next. None of them agreed to meet her eyes. She turned to Ekene whose furrowed brow expressed his own confusion. Then it hit her.

"My mother?" she whispered, almost afraid to ask.

"Sis, she didn't come but signed a proxy for Danladi to use her vote. That vote was the determining vote."

Halima froze in shock. The realization that her own mother had pulled the rug from under her world was unbearable. All emotion left her. She couldn't even cry if she wanted to. She felt their eyes on her as she walked back to the couch and put her phone in her bag. She looked around her office and walked up to her brothers.

"Please take me home."

Chapter 28

"Halima!"

Ekene raised his hand and knocked, more like banged, on the door. It had been a couple of days since she was voted out, and no one had seen her. Her brothers had tried. She refused to see them but did return their texts.

Ekene neither saw her nor got a response to the multitude of texts he'd sent. This had been his routine. He'd close from work, bring dinner over, and he would bang on the door. She wouldn't open it, and he'd leave. Well, with the day he just had, that wasn't going to fly this time.

"Halima! I know you're in there and I am not leaving until you open the door." He leaned his tired frame against the door and prayed. He prayed for God to touch her and let her allow someone to help her. That was another thing they hadn't talked about – faith. In their estrangement, he didn't want to ask her because that would give her more leverage to block him out if she felt that he needed her to be what she was not. He made a vow never to ask her brothers things about her again, so that was out.

Minutes later, the locks turned, but the door didn't open. Ekene turned the knob to open the door. He followed the sound of the soft music and saw her sitting on the couch with her legs drawn up to her chest. He took her in.

Her face was red, eyes swollen, her hair covered in a scarf. She wore a pair of faded lounge pants and an oversized tee-shirt. She looked worn out, but she was still the most beautiful woman on the planet in his eyes. Another thing he noticed was the vibrancy in her eyes was gone. The look she gave him was distant, devoid of depth.

"Princess."

"Why are you here?"

"I came to see how you're doing…"

"Well, I'm doing great. You can leave."

Ekene understood she was hurting and trying to push him away so she could resume her pity party, but he wasn't going to let her. "When was your last meal?" he asked, ignoring her aggression.

She rolled her eyes at him but gave no response. He took the bag of food to the kitchen. He had gotten her favorite meal and dessert.

"Halima…"

She entered the kitchen and frowned at him. "What, Ekene? Why are you here? In what capacity? Do you make house calls for all your clients? Will this visit be billed to DG? You do know I no longer work there," she snapped.

"You need to eat."

"Is this you, handling me again?"

"No, this is me caring about you, but from the look of things, you need to be handled." Ekene regretted the words the moment they left his lips. "I didn't mean that. I'm here because I care."

"I don't need your care. You can leave." She opened the refrigerator door.

"I've told you before, you don't get to dismiss me."

"And you don't tell me what I can or cannot do." She took out a bottle of water.

"You're being a brat."

"Says the man who left me all alone because his feelings were hurt." Halima banged the fridge shut.

They had so many unresolved issues and her recent setback only added to it. "If only you'd let me explain. I've been trying to for weeks now."

"Why? To ease your conscience? Guess what? Your comfort is not at the center of my universe." Halima folded her arms across her chest.

He raised his hand to his forehead. "Halima, would you shut up and listen to me."

"No, I won't let you explain. You should've talked to me before you left," she yelled.

"Our tempers are running wild. Can we discuss this like adults? Or tell me what to do to make it right?" Ekene pleaded.

"I'm sorry. I can't do that…"

"Why?" he barked.

"Because I don't know!" she screamed back. She took a deep breath and whispered, "I need time."

They engaged in a stare-off, neither one willing to back down. Ekene sighed and broke eye contact. This wasn't going as planned. All he wanted was to see how she was doing and feed her. But it was like the more he pushed, the harder she pushed back. This wasn't just about him. It was bigger than him and he owed her the space to figure it out. Ekene walked over to her, kissed her forehead and headed to the front door. He opened it and looked back.

"I love you, Halima. Don't forget that. I'll give you time, but I'm not letting you go."

With those parting words, he walked out the door. He didn't go to his car until he heard the locks turn.

———

"Yesterday we cried and sulked. Today is a new day, so what are we doing?" Ibiso asked.

Halima moved her scrambled eggs around with her fork. She saw a tiny eggshell in them and tried to remove it with her fingers.

"Mama SoSo always trying to take charge. Doesn't it get exhausting?" Ebele asked.

Halima looked up from her plate. She loved her sisters but could do without the bickering between these two. Ibiso and Ebele had arrived the day after she and Ekene had their spat. The same time as he normally did every evening, there was banging on her door. She was ready to tell him off, furious that once again, he wasn't respecting her wishes. However, when she opened the door it was Ibiso, Damisi, and Ebele. They'd been smothering her ever since. That was two days ago.

"Yeah, it does but someone has to do it," Ibiso sassed.

They were all in her kitchen dressed in matching pajama sets –Damisi's idea of slumber party attire.

"Tell me again where my nieces and nephews are since you girls are here?" Halima asked.

"Don't start, Hali. You'll not push us away like you did your brothers and Ekene. We're family. We mourn, rejoice, be happy, sad, fight and lose together," Damisi said.

"The kids are with your brothers while we came here to get you together."

Halima rolled her eyes. "I'm not a broken toy, you know."

"Nobody said you are. Stop playing the victim. Everyone needs someone else to lean on from time to time. And here we are." Ibiso's eyes conveyed the sincerity of her statement.

Halima looked over at Damisi and Ebele. They were nodding their heads in agreement. She lowered her head briefly, then looked up again. Damisi sat with a half-eaten bowl of yam porridge in front of her. Ebele was working on boiled yam and egg sauce while she and Ibiso had fried yam chips with scrambled eggs.

"DG was my life. I spent so many days in those offices as a little girl. Even then, I was invisible to my dad as he worked, but I needed him to be proud of me, so I hung around even in adulthood. When I went to college, I did business management in the hopes of running the company one day. I knew of my brothers, but didn't know them. Except that they hated our father because I would hear dad lamenting to my mom. So, I took it upon myself to make up for that. Unlike many of my friends, when I was done with college abroad, I came back home. DG is all I know.

"I'm still new at this trusting Jesus thing, but I'm doing my best to believe there's something else I can do, but not knowing what it is, is crippling. Especially for someone like me who started working there at seventeen." Halima finished.

"You do know that God's ways are not our ways. But the good, bad and the ugly all work out for the good of those who love Him," Ebele said.

"You do love Him right?" Damisi asked.

Halima laughed. "Of course, I do. Just because I'm having a hard time doesn't mean He's not real and alive. And I know He loves me."

"Okay, just checking…" Damisi said and the three of them grinned.

Ebele held a piece of yam to her mouth. "You know when you go through trials, God is preparing you for something. Listen so that you'll hear Him. You'll have a testimony from this, it always comes from your pain." She put the food in her mouth.

"Hmmm…of the heart or mind?" Halima muttered.

"Phew! honey, I'm so glad you brought that up." Ibiso dropped her fork and rested her chin in her palm. "So, what's up with Ekene?"

Ebele and Damisi giggled.

"Keep laughing as if you didn't want to know." Ibiso rolled her eyes at the pair, then returned her stare to Halima. "You know your brothers are suspicious of him breaking your heart."

"He did. But that stays with the four of us. Tell your husbands and watch them go to jail for assaulting someone at your own risk." Halima said.

"What happened, Hali? You guys were so good together."

Halima contemplated for a few minutes and then told them the story. From Accra, to him coming back and not telling her; him barely communicating with her, the woman at their restaurant and finally, the way he handled the Okon case.

A few beats passed and none of the ladies responded.

"Say something," Halima urged.

"I'm still trying to digest it. But all I'll ask is, are you ready to see him love another? Is not letting him explain and you guys getting to the bottom of it worth the pain?" Ebele asked.

"Ebi, I hear you, but I know exactly what Halima is feeling." Ibiso sipped her tea. "Your brother did the same thing to me. At the first sign of trouble, he ran back to London and left me to deal with everything by myself."

"Jabir didn't leave me, but I know what it's like to have your whole world turned upside down and the one person you thought you could lean on is not what you thought them to be. Your brother had a whole wife he hid from me," Damisi said.

"You girls always talk about my Kamal, but he knew what he wanted from the beginning," Ebele smirked. "I was the one like Halima. After I found out who my half-sister was and her relationship with my man, I needed time. But my friend Nse asked me the same question I just asked you." Ebele shook her head. "Up until the day we were supposed to leave for the wedding, I was still confused. When I realized my mistake, see me running to the airport—"

"We know!" Ibiso, Damisi, and Halima shouted in unison.

"Kam teases you with that story every family gathering," Ibiso said. "I agree with Ebi though—"

"Agree? Oh my God, please check if the rapture has left us behind," Damisi exclaimed.

"Something is wrong with you," Ebele laughed at her.

"What? SoSo agreed with you on something and *fear no dey catch you?*"

Halima chuckled.

Ibiso waved her off. "Dami, whatever. What I'm trying to say is, give him a chance to explain his side."

Halima agreed, just to end the conversation. They spent the rest of the day between the front of the television and the kitchen. The ladies were leaving in the morning and she would miss them tremendously. But they were right. It was time to get back to the business of living.

———

THE NEXT MORNING, HALIMA WOKE UP AT DAWN AND JUST AS Ekene taught her, she talked to God. "Good morning, Father. Thank you for a peaceful night's rest. Thank You for the strength and renewed mercies of today. Thank you for my family and grant my sisters journey mercies back to their homes. Your hope doesn't disappoint. Thank You for showing me that verse last night. You will restore all that the locust has eaten. Thank you for that promise. I still have four weeks before I'm out of DG for good. Please show me what I'm supposed to do after that. In Jesus' name. Amen."

Halima walked into her closet and pulled out a Chanel traveling bag. She'd had a lot to mull over during the night and one of them was finishing what she started in Mozambique. Right before they settled the Okon case, she got a letter of the awarded contract. It had been a couple of weeks and she needed to close the deal. They required her to be present to sign the final agreement. The previous night, she decided there was no time like the present. So, as her sisters left, she was leaving too.

An hour later, she was done packing and ready. She took her bags downstairs where she heard the ladies cooking break-fast in the kitchen.

"Good morning, fam!" Halima greeted, walking over to the coffee pot.

The three women stared at her, mumbling greetings in return.

"Why are you looking at me like that? You wanted me to feel better *abi*? Now I'm better. Not great, but better." She sat next to Damisi.

Ibiso stood and dished her a bowl of custard and a plate of akara. Setting it before her, she said, "Okay. We'll take it."

"We're happy you're feeling better. Great will come with time.

"Halima, are you running away?" Ebele asked.

If she didn't have genuine panic on her face, Halima would have laughed at her. "Huh?'

"Why are your bags packed? Where are you going? Yesterday you were in sweats, today you're in skinny jeans, "Ebele explained.

Halima shrugged. "The Lord works in mysterious ways."

Damisi and Ibiso laughed while Ebele waved her off.

"Ebi, I love you, but you really have to check if my brother is injecting you with his serum while you sleep. I hear him anytime you speak," Halima said.

"Let her tell it, it's love. But seriously *sha*, where are you going?" Damisi asked.

"Before I was fired, I was working on one of the biggest deals Danjuma Group had ever seen. My resignation doesn't take effect until the end of the month. I talked to Rasheed before, and I have his blessing to close the deal. They can fire me, but I'll make sure they never forget my impact."

"So, you're on your way to Mozambique?" Ebele asked.

"Yep. After I close the deal, I'll take a little vacation." Halima took a bite of her akara.

"What about Ekene?" Damisi asked.

"I'll see him when I get back. If he can love someone else in two weeks, then he never loved me at all."

"You go, girl!" Ibiso yelled. "*Pepper dem.*"

"I'm a Danjuma. We know no other way." Halima winked.

Chapter 29

The melody of "Talk" by Falz filled the background as Ekene made his way down the stairs. It was a typical Sunday, and after church and a nap, he was ready to get something to eat and relax. As he had done for the past couple of weeks, he worked himself so hard during the week including Saturday, that the only day his mind caught up with his reality was Sunday.

He entered the kitchen and glanced at the bowl that sat in the middle of the island. It contained the marinated fish he placed there earlier. Walking into his pantry, he picked up a few ingredients to make a quick lunch. He washed his hands and began cutting up the onions as his mind did what it always did when it was idle. Think of Halima.

He couldn't get the look on her face the last time he saw her out of his head. The disappointment and the anger that danced in her eyes made his heart constrict. He wanted to reach out and tell her the reason behind his actions, but he figured he'd done enough already. He didn't want to add to her crisis any more than he knew he'd already done.

I don't know if it's worth it.

Those words he overheard her speak, despite her explanation, replayed in his mind like a broken record. Ekene reached in the pockets of his grey shorts and retrieved his vibrating phone.

Jabir: Hey Kene? You home?

Ekene's brows came together as he read the strange text from Jabir. Ever since Halima appeared before the board a few weeks ago, he kept his relationship with the Danjuma's strictly professional. He knew it was a terrible thing to do, but he wasn't in the mood to explain anything to them about his relationship with their sister. If things didn't get better, he knew he'd have to one day, but now wasn't the time.

Yes.

Jabir: Be there in a few.

Okay.

Ekene sighed. It seemed like today would be the day.

Several minutes later, Ekene put up the last dish, wiped his hands with a paper towel, trashed it and exited the kitchen. Picking up the remote, he sat back on the leather couch and began surfing for something to distract him. He found a game show just as his doorbell rang. Seconds later, he was staring at the middle Danjuma brother in eyes that were less than friendly.

"*How far?*" Ekene asked.

"*I dey*. Can I come in?" Jabir had both hands in his pockets.

As he asked the question, Ekene already knew it wasn't really a "yes or no" request. Ekene moved to the side as Jabir made his way in.

"Would you like something to drink?" Ekene asked, walking Jabir to the living room.

"No, thank you. I don't intend on staying long."

Both men sat in uncomfortable silence for a few moments before Ekene decided he might as well get this over with. "Look, man—"

"Didn't I tell you not to hurt my sister?" Jabir asked cutting his explanation off.

"I didn't set out to hurt her…"

"Then what did you set out to do? Because from where I'm sitting, it's not looking good."

"I love that woman. You have no idea what I'm going through. But this is best for now."

"Leaving her? Didn't we warn you not to start what you can't finish?" He paused. "And whatever you're going through is self-inflicted."

"Be that as it may, it still hurts. How is she?"

"If you wanted to know, you would. I only came here to look you in the face and get your side." Jabir shook his head. "I told Kammy and Rasheed, I'd kick your behind if I need to on their behalf."

"That bad?"

"Heck, yeah. They were ready to go straight past talking. I don't want them beating you up, then you'll have to defend them in court against… you."

Ekene ran his hand over his face. "That doesn't even make sense."

"This is Hali we're talking about. It doesn't have to make sense."

"I saw her pain. I felt her internal turmoil. What the relationship with her mom was turning into. I didn't want that for her, so I decided to back off."

"Do you know how Dami and I got together?"

"Yeah, you stalked her for six years." Ekene laughed.

Jabir chuckled. "Very funny. She lost everything because of me. It was both our faults, but it fell solely on me. I had to deal with the effects of her guilt, shame and mood swings. And like you, I was tempted to give up. But I didn't for two reasons. One, I couldn't exist without her and two, Rasheed talked some sense into me over the phone one night when I called him to complain."

"I was trying to be selfless."

Jabir waved him off. "Man, that stuff doesn't work with the one who holds your heart. I agree with Kam. The savage in me comes out when my family is concerned."

"To be the one that was in school the longest, you're saying a lot of stuff that makes no sense." Ekene chuckled.

"Okay, let's hope you're still laughing when my brothers and I start negotiating bride price with the other dude."

Ekene jerked to his feet. "Dude? Who? We've only been apart two months. What are you talking about? You're joking right?"

"What happened to being selfless? Now you're ready to tear Lagos up?"

Jabir stood and walked closer to Ekene. With each step he made, Ekene ached at the insinuation that Halima had moved on that quickly. What he was trying to achieve giving her space was no longer relevant. The thought of what Jabir just said being a possibility caused his temperature to rise with rage. He trained his eyes on Jabir, looking for any sign of a joke. He found none.

"Where is she?"

Jabir shrugged. "I didn't lose her..." He walked toward the foyer.

Ekene expected him to stop so didn't follow him.

Jabir did and looked back at him. "You did, so find her." He turned back around and walked out without a backward glance.

The click of the door caused Ekene's feet to move. Within seconds, he was in the kitchen looking for his phone. He dialed Halima many times and there was no response. His call went straight to voicemail. Whether her phone was off, or she had him blocked, he couldn't tell.

Between the other two brothers, the one that might be willing to give him a shot was Rasheed. Ekene knew the conversation with his friend wouldn't be pretty, but he dialed him anyway.

"Yeah?" Rasheed answered on the third ring. His voice was laced with ice.

"I'll fix it," Ekene said, skipping the pleasantries that probably wouldn't be welcome anyway.

"Oh, I had no doubt. Just that, with each passing day, the duration of your beat down was getting longer."

"Huh?"

"I gave you a grace period of two weeks. After that, with each extra day, the time I'll spend kicking your behind increased by a minute."

Ekene chuckled. "I'd like to see you try."

"I'd like to see you not go get my sister."

"You know me, I never meant to hurt her…"

"But she was hurt anyway." Rasheed paused. "However, considering I ran from the love of my life too, I'll cut you some slack."

"I guess you already know Jabir just left."

Rasheed remained silent.

"Will, you at least tell me where she is?"

"Nope. You lost her, you find her. Goodnight, Kene."

Before he could say another word, Rasheed hung up. Ekene wasn't even going to try Kamal. Instead, he decided to meet Halima in her office in the morning. He wanted to look into her eyes, make her listen to his explanation and apologize again. He was going to fight to get her back. Whatever they had to face, they'd be doing it together. He wasn't proud that it took the mention of another man to make him see the light, but he saw it bright and clear. No way was he leaving her uncovered.

———

THE NEXT MORNING, EKENE WALKED INTO THE OFFICES OF THE Danjuma Group. He had a court briefing in an hour, but his personal life could no longer wait. He waited for the elevator to open and rode it to the sixth floor. Once the doors opened, he made his way down the hall to Halima's office.

"Chiaka, how are you?" he asked.

She stood to her feet and smoothed down her skirt. She let out a nervous chuckle. That was a first. She was usually comfortable with him. She glanced at Halima's closed door and that made his antenna rise.

"Is Halima in?"

"Erm… no sir."

"When will she be back?"

"She went to Mozambique some days ago, to see our new client."

Ekene clenched his fists. He could punch himself in the face right now. "Do you know when she'll be back?"

"No sir, I don't know."

Ekene sighed. He wanted to ask Chiaka where Halima was staying, but he didn't want to alert Halima to his plans and have her put up her defenses. He thanked Chiaka instead and walked towards the elevators. His mind told him that the sane thing to do was to wait until Halima returned, but he'd done what his mind told him to do these past several weeks and it had brought him nothing but agony. Which was why he was on his way to his office to pull up the file for Nizon. He knew when she started negotiating that deal and had a contract ready to go when they needed it. All he had to do now was call them up and ask where she was staying. Then, he had a flight to catch.

Chapter 30

"Okay, gentlemen. It was nice doing business with you. I will tell our lawyer to modify the contract. Once I get to Nigeria, I'll sign and send it over for your signature and then we're all set."

Halima stood and the representatives of Nizon stood as well. Mr. Kumpasa offered his hand and she took it in a firm handshake. She picked up her purse while Umaru picked up her briefcase and they walked out of the room. Umaru still went with her on business travels, but more in the capacity of a bodyguard rather than a *mahram*.

As she stepped out of the building, she was greeted by the warm rays of sunshine. Her hotel was not far from the building, so she decided to walk.

"Umaru, I'll just walk to the hotel. I'll meet you there." They were staying in the Radisson Blu Hotel & Residence and she had yet to enjoy the feeling of simply walking in the city of Maputo.

He stood frozen with his mouth open and eyes wide. Halima laughed at his shock. "It's okay. I promise."

"How about I put your things in the car, tell the driver to meet us there and walk with you," Umaru countered.

There was no use arguing with him, Kamal had him scared. She shrugged and waited for the car to arrive from the underground parking lot. Once the car pulled up, Umaru hurried over, put her things in and gave the driver instructions. She moved to the back of the car, changed her heels to flats and took off her blazer, and placed it on the seat.

The car pulled off and Halima began to walk with Umaru a safe distance behind her. For the first time in a long time, she felt a sense of peace. Before she had thought about peace all wrong. Recently, from hearing Pastor Kalu speak, reading and learning more, she understood it wasn't the absence of a storm, but being calm in it, so she could make it through her trials. Her heart still ached at the demise of her relationship with Ekene. She didn't think it would stop any time soon, but the anguish she had felt internally for almost three years was gone. No longer was she searching for the truth; she had found it. Earlier in the morning, she read a passage where Jesus said His yoke was light. On further research, she learned that being bound to Him meant she could hand her burdens over and rest.

Halima stopped at a kiosk by the roadside where fresh fruit was being sold. The mangos looked fresh without any blemish. She motioned for the seller. After inspecting them and paying for two, she continued her walk. Mangoes were Kudirat's favorite. She still wasn't answering her phone calls or texts. Halima missed her friend and prayed one day she'd come around. Zara was by her side, but it wasn't the same. Kudirat had been with her since childhood.

Her mother, on the other hand, had called her once. There was no remorse whatsoever for what she did, and the bad part now was that Halima had to forgive her. That was something she was still working on and knew it wouldn't be anytime soon. She had no idea where this new journey would lead, but she was ready to find out.

A few minutes after, Halima strolled into the hotel and

immediately spotted a couple in the corner, whispering sweet nothings in each other's ears. Halima cut her eyes away before her own tears could form. She had just closed a huge deal and she was determined to enjoy that without sad memories.

No more crying over Ekene.

He probably was in her life for a time and a reason; the extra nudge to Jesus. For that she was happy. What would become of them in the future wasn't clear. But she wasn't going to ponder on it now.

Hours later, Halima had showered, changed into loungewear and was making her way down to the pool with her sliced mangoes. She hated swimming, but the Infinity pool of the hotel ran right into the Indian ocean. It was truly a sight to behold. Her room had a balcony that faced the Maputo beach. In the mornings, she looked at the scenic views and was further convinced that God loved humanity.

It was now late afternoon and she was excited that for the first time since she got here, she'd be able to see the sunset. For the last week, her late nights and early mornings consisted of prayer, touring the Nizon facility, handling conference calls back home, watching a movie or reading a book to unwind, then prayer, sleep, repeat.

Halima leaned the lounge chair back enough to relax and enjoy the view. She set her plate down and put her headphones on. The melody of "My Everything" by Joe Mettle played, and she bobbed her head and took in the lyrics. Damisi had told her not to look at Christianity as a task, but as a relationship, so she tried to use songs to say what she wasn't proficient in saying yet. She bit into her fruit and closed her eyes. The wind had her hair all over her face and it felt good. A grin spread across her face.

Moments later, she felt a tap on her shoulder. The touch sent shock waves up her spine, but it couldn't be. She kept her eyes closed for a few more seconds before she peered them open. Her heart skipped a beat.

Ekene? How is he here?

They were lost in each other's gaze until she noticed his mouth was moving. She took her headphones off.

"Mind if I join you?" Ekene asked.

Halima blinked several times. No possible scenario for how he was standing before her registered. Unless someone was hurt. Her brows contoured, and she sat up straight. "Is everyone okay?" She searched for her phone to see if she had any missed calls from home.

"Everybody is fine. Why?"

She shrugged. "I don't know. Why are you here?"

"Ouch, that hurt." He grabbed his chest in feigned pain. "So, I can no longer be around you just for me?" Ekene took a seat at the foot of the lounge chair.

Halima raised her brows.

"The past month's experience has taught me that I can't exist without you. My life, my accomplishments, the cases I win are meaningless without you to share them with. I've lived with a void for years and I refuse to do that again."

Halima felt the pain in his voice. It mirrored the pain that clamped her heart like a vice. But she said, "Sounds like a personal problem."

"Come on, Princess, we deserve another try. I insist you give me another chance to make us right. You're everything to me. I acted like a moron and I'm sorry."

"Why?"

"I thought I was doing what was best."

"How? By doing the one thing I asked you not to?"

"Yes. Well, I mean no. But after I overheard you telling Zara about all the heartache and feeling the internal crisis you were going through, I thought it best if we took some time apart."

"And the best way to do that was to abandon me?"

Ekene lowered his eyes, then lifted them again. "I only intended to give you space."

"Men…the conversation wasn't solely about you. Granted, I did tell Zara that, but if you would've waited for the conclusion of the conversation, you'd have had the context. It had little to do with you, but everything to do with my faith." She poked him in his chest. "I loved you, but even you—"

"Loved? As in past tense?"

His expression was puzzling and voice an octave lower. The look in his eyes mirrored the anxiety dripping from his words. But she made up her mind not to put him at ease…not yet.

"As I was saying, even you wouldn't be the reason I committed apostasy."

"And I get that." Ekene rubbed the back of his neck. "Loved?"

"What do you want me to say?"

"Princess, you're killing me."

Halima let a small smile break through her expression and Ekene released a labored breath. "It wasn't easy, but I tried very hard to be intentional about keeping my feelings for you and my quest for the truth separate. This didn't start with you or my brothers. It started three years ago when I visited Detroit and met Zara. I told you that."

"Princess, you said loved…"

She smirked. *This man just ignored everything I said.* "And?"

"You're killing me."

"Again, what do you want me to say?"

"Selfish as it may seem, I want you to tell me you still love me. Tell me you forgive me. Tell me you'll let me be by your side once you do decide to follow Christ…" He held her hands in his. His stare ignited her skin and goosebumps appeared.

"Number one, of course I do. Number two, I'll think about it. Number three, you're too late."

"What? What does that mean? I'm too late. Halima, please don't let me…"

"Calm down before you burst a vein. I mean, I've already accepted Christ."

"You what? When? Why didn't you tell me?"

"That's what I was coming to tell you that day when I overheard you and Rasheed discussing me about being ready. I was so furious at you trying to handle me again that it completely escaped my mind."

Ekene pulled her into an embrace. "Oh my God. Princess, I'm so sorry. I wanted to be there. Who was there with you?"

"No one. Pastor Kalu just said the prayer for me and I confessed. I didn't know it would be that simple. I haven't been baptized yet. There's so much I want to know first. I'll do that when the time is right."

"I'm so sorry. I'll never forgive myself for that. But if you forgive me, you'll never have to go through any of it alone."

"I'll think about it. In the meantime, you're blocking my view. I want to watch the sunset." She smirked.

Ekene chuckled and looked back at the open sea and then turned to look at her. "Can I watch it with you?"

"Sure."

Ekene smiled, stood and walked to the head of the lounge chair. He tapped her shoulder and she scooted down as he slid in behind her. She adjusted herself so that she could lean into his chest. He wrapped his hands around her and the only thing that could be heard was the synchronized beating of their hearts and the gentleness of the waves. The view was magnificent. The horizon was colored in dues of purple, violet, and orange.

"I love you, my Princess," Ekene whispered against her hair.

Halima tilted her head up to him and gazed into his eyes. "I love you Ekene, *e don tey*." She grinned.

Ekene bent his head and his lips captured hers in a kiss that expressed the depth of their love.

Chapter 31

"Are you ready?" Pastor Kalu asked, with a comforting hand on her shoulder.

Halima looked at the man who, for the past six months, had helped her navigate and deepen her faith walk. In the last three years, she had gone from curiosity to the truth being revealed, to loss of the familiar and now peace.

Her relationships with Kudirat and Uncle Musa were no longer existent. After numerous attempts, Halima gave up trying. It hurt not to have her best friend in her life. But for her and Uncle Musa, it was all their way or nothing at all.

Her mother was still standoffish and disappointed. Halima could hear the raw emotion in her voice anytime they talked, or she visited. She wanted to believe that her mother kept in contact with her because she was her only child and loved her regardless, but she wasn't so sure, because it felt more like an obligation. Halima couldn't lose her mother totally, so she took whatever she got, still believing God could fix any situation. The price she had to pay in such little time cut deep, but she'd do it all over again. Hence this moment here.

"It wasn't an easy decision, as most times I think I have a

long way to go. Nevertheless, I'm ready to be fully committed to Jesus Christ the Son of the Living God."

"This is not an easy road, but Jesus never promised us easy. He promised to always be with us."

Halima nodded her head, as once again, the Spirit of Christ overwhelmed her. She thought about her brothers, their families and the love of her life, Ekene. They were on the other side of the room. And if she knew nothing else, she was certain she'd always have their support and love.

"Okay, I'll meet you on the other side." A reassuring smile spread across the pastor's face. He opened the door and walked out.

Halima looked down and rubbed her palms against the white cotton fabric she had on.

"Father God, in the name of Jesus, the only thing I know for sure is I love You and want to follow Your ways. I thank You for showing Yourself to me and for this gift. Amen."

She strode out of the room and looked at her loved ones in the sanctuary. Her family sat with wide smiles spread across their faces. Her eyes locked with the one who her soul had, undercover, been connected to for many years. Ekene stood and walked to the front of the church. He reached her, placed a kiss on her forehead and stood by her side.

"My dear brothers and sisters, today is a great day. It is always a great day when another one of His sheep decides to join the flock." The pastor gave a dramatic pause.

"There was a little boy who created his ideal action figure. He took all the resources available to him and made it to his liking. Somewhere along the way, after a full day of playing with his friends, the toy went missing. He searched high and low, but couldn't find it. Sometime later, he was on his way to school when he saw it in the local toy shop. He ran across the street, zipped in the store and told the clerk that was his toy. The clerk dismissed the boy and told him that if he wanted it, he had to pay for it. Of course, the boy didn't have any money, so started doing extra chores around the neighborhood until he came up with the money and bought the toy back.

"That, my brethren, is similar to how our relationship is with Jesus. We're God's creation, but we strayed into sin and were lost. But He never forgot us. He left His throne in heaven to come to earth to find us. He paid the ultimate price; His death to redeem us."

"Amen."

"Thank You, Jesus."

"Glory."

Her sisters-in-law belted out in unison. Her brothers and Ekene shared the same somber expression. The Pastor wiped his forehead with a handkerchief and continued.

"Ladies and gentlemen, Jesus offers us redemption through love. He's our Redeemer. Today, our sister here who has accepted this love is ready to pick up her cross and follow Him." The pastor stretched out his hand to her.

Halima took it while Ekene's hand rubbed her lower back in assurance, giving his support without words. The three of them walked to the corner of the church. Halima lifted her leg and stepped into the huge, tank-like tub filled with water. She shivered as the coolness of the water ran up her spine. The lower half of her garment stuck to her body.

"Halima, Apostle Paul said in 2nd Corinthians 5 verse 17, *therefore, if anyone is in Christ, he is a new creature; old things have passed away behold all things have become new.* Do you repent your sins and acknowledge your need for a Savior?"

"Yes," she said.

"Do you believe in your heart and confess with your mouth that Jesus Christ is Lord?"

Halima paused, looked over to Ekene and then her family. "Yes."

Kamal rose to his feet. He placed one arm across his chest as the other hand covered his mouth. This was the most pensive she'd ever seen him. His eyes glistened and she smiled.

"Do you believe that Jesus died for our sins and resurrected on the third day?"

"Yes."

"Because of your repentance of sin and faith in Jesus, today we acknowledge your old self is buried and you've been raised to new life in Christ," Pastor Kalu declared.

Her other brothers and their wives joined Kamal and stood. The atmosphere was thick with nervous anticipation. Her heart thumped. The pastor placed his hands on her back and stomach. She pinched her nose together. Fear rose from her feet while a calming spirit crushed it from the crown of her head. She felt the collision in her heart as peace took over.

"In the name of Jesus, I now baptize you in the name of the Father and the Son and the Holy Spirit." The pastor immersed her in the water.

When she resurfaced, the thunderous applause and cheers unclogged her ears. The pastor held up her hand. "The multiplying of the redeemed is the magnifying of the Redeemer. Glory to God."

The applause continued as Ekene helped her out of the tub and a church usher approached her with a large towel. The woman wrapped it around Halima's shoulders and escorted her to the back.

EKENE'S HEART CONSTRICTED. HIS THROAT ACHED WITH RAW emotion as his eyes followed Halima until she disappeared to the back. He shook the pastor's hand and they both walked down the three steps to the sanctuary floor to meet the Danjuma family. Sniffles were heard from the wives while their husbands rocked them in their arms. The mood was ecstatic. It was an overwhelming moment for everyone. The past several months had been trying for the family and Halima's baptism was the rainbow in the cloud.

Ekene wiped a tear from the corner of his eye, the emotions flowing through him were surreal and so much more he couldn't put into words.

"You ready man?" Rasheed was the first one to speak.

Ekene put his hand in his pocket and nodded. "Yep."

Jabir smiled. "Congrats, man."

"Yeah, congrats man. Don't mess up. Remember one tear and I'm at your front door," Kamal said, narrowing his eyes at him.

Ekene chuckled instead of responding to his threat. He strolled over to the pastor who was engaged in conversation with the Danjuma women.

"We all set?" Ekene asked.

"I admire your confidence," Ebele said.

"It's hope, sis. Hope." Ekene smiled.

"It's more than hope. But we like the humility," Damisi said.

"Yes, we are ready *o*. All you gotta do is work your magic," Ibiso said. "Starting now." She raised her chin up gesturing behind him.

Ekene turned and temporarily, forgot to breathe. The adjectives that came to mind fell short in describing her. Halima walked toward them with a smile on her face. Her auburn waves were still damp. She wore a darker shade of jeans with a white tee shirt that was inscribed with the words *Jesus Owned* in red ink and a pair of white sneakers on her feet.

He winked at her and stepped back to let her family have the first shot at extending their congratulations. While they crowded her, he removed the velvet box from his pocket and got down on one knee. He opened the box and within seconds, the family parted, exposing him.

Ekene heard the gasp leave her lips and her hand shot up

to cover her mouth. Taking calculated steps toward him, her eyes filled with tears.

"Princess, the first time I saw you I knew I was in trouble. For years, my heart and my mind battled, and in the end, the heart won. You're the sunshine in my day and your smile dictates the rhythm of my heart. I am complete in Christ, but you're the overflow of my cup. You're my miracle and blessing, beyond my highest expectation. Will you go on this journey called life with me? Marry me, baby, and let's go from the dried ink of pages past to the memories that await." His gaze held on to hers.

She nodded her head in rapid succession.

"Princess—"

"The man needs the words, Hali," Kamal said.

Ekene cut his eyes at him. The family laughed while Ebele nudged her husband, who pulled her closer to him.

Ekene returned his eyes to Halima. "As much as it pains me to admit, Kammy is right."

"Yes, Baby, I'll marry you."

Ekene slipped the ring on her finger. He stood and cupped her face with both hands before pressing his lips to hers. The earth stood still as they snatched each other's souls through the connection. Ekene pulled back moments later. Halima looked at her ring and back at him.

"Ok, let's do it." He kissed the back of her hand and stepped back. "Ladies…" He smiled at her perplexed state as her brother's wives made their way towards her.

"Wait. What? Now?" Halima asked. "I want to tell my mother…"

"Yes, now. I waited many years. I'm not waiting another second. Do you trust me?"

"With all my heart."

"Good. I'll see you soon."

Chapter 32

The stroke of the beautician's brush tickled Halima's cheek as it glided across her delicate skin. Halima closed her eyes as the melody of Ed Sheeran's "Perfect" played in the background. Her mind traveled in flashes as she recalled the small moments that led to this big one. She was becoming Mrs. Odili.

Earlier, her sisters-in-laws had whisked her away to another back room of the church where the most beautiful wedding gown she'd seen in her life laid in wait. There was a hairstylist, manicurist, and cosmetologist all standing there, waiting for their marching orders. On the dress was a note from her husband to be.

You have captured my heart, my treasure, my bride. You hold it hostage with one glance of your eyes, with a single jewel of your necklace ~ Songs of Solomon 4:9.

I can't wait for you to be mine.

Love,

Kene

Three hours later, she was transformed into a real-life Princess. She opened her eyes to see Damisi and Ebele standing behind her. Their eyes locked with hers in the mirror of the vanity. They both wore flowing dresses in her favorite colors, gold and grey, with a high front and a plunging back.

"Oh my gosh, Hali. You're so beautiful," Ebele said.

"Stunning. Are you ready?" Damisi asked.

"Thank you, so do you. And I'm as ready as I'll ever be." Halima looked down at her dress before she met their eyes again. "I still can't believe you all put this together without me knowing."

Damisi waved her off. "The credit goes to your husband to be. That man loves you like crazy. The minute you guys got back from Mozambique, he started asking us to set things in place and be on standby."

"And it's nothing. We're all so happy for you," Ebele added.

Halima blushed. Over the last six months since their return from Mozambique, the connection she and Ekene shared was indescribable and even deeper than before. He helped her adjust from losing her job, and when she was ready to open her own NGO, My Sister's Keeper, he handled all the legal paperwork. Her organization's aim was to provide welfare, educational and vocational training to women who wanted an escape from the traditions they no longer agreed with. Halima never wanted any one of them to feel as alone as she would have without her family.

She loved him with every part of her being, but now they were connected in soul. Even when they weren't around each other, she could sense when he was happy, sad or frustrated. And he could do the same for her. When she needed to talk to him, his phone calls came right on time or he showed up. He sensed her need for him.

"Where's Ibiso?" Halima asked.

"Where the food is, of course. You know she's not going to let anything go wrong. Especially now that she's also branched into event planning," Ebele said.

There was a knock on the door. Halima stood, and Damisi

walked to the door while Ebele handed her the bouquet. Damisi placed her hand on the knob and turned back to them. Halima took in a deep breath and nodded.

Rasheed stepped through the door and halted. "You look amazing, sis. Are you sure you're ready to do this? If not, I can send him home." He teased and feigned an attempt to walk out the door.

"Send who home?" Ibiso asked, walking up on them. "Oh, my Lord, Hali, that dress fits you so well." She snaked her arm around her husband's waist. He pulled her closer and kissed her lips.

"Thanks, sis. Don't mind big bro here. He's trying to play with my emotions," Halima said.

Ibiso lifted her eyes to her husband and he gave her another kiss, silencing her.

Rasheed walked closer to Halima and kissed her on her forehead. "I love you, sis."

"I love you, too. All of you. The day you walked in on daddy's will reading, I knew my life would never be the same. And it hasn't, but in a good way. I couldn't have imagined the last several years without all of you." Halima took turns connecting with each pair of eyes in the room.

"Okay, okay, this is not a therapy session. It's a happy moment. Bros Rasheed, please, *oya*, escort her out," Ebele said.

"I keep saying it. Sometimes I can't tell you and your husband apart." Damisi chuckled.

Rasheed hooked his arm and Halima placed hers in it. Ibiso opened the doors and they walked out. The instrumental of Timi Dakolo's "The Vow" began to play as Halima and Rasheed strode down the aisle to her man. Her heart skipped a beat as she took him in. He had on a charcoal grey, one button slim fit tuxedo.

Moments later, Rasheed placed her hand in Ekene's waiting one. The couple walked up the three steps together and stood in front of the pastor. Halima briefly shifted her eyes to take in the small, but intimate crowd.

Big Mummy, her nieces and nephews were now present, everyone dressed to impress. Some members of her staff, Zara and Terrance, and some members of the board were also there. Ekene's family, Jide and a few people she had seen in his office were also in attendance.

Her eyes widened when she saw her mother in the back. Although Halima would have loved her full support, her presence alone was a start. Her eyes misted with tears she refused to let go of. She turned her head back to Ekene who lifted his hand and lightly caressed her cheek.

"Thank you," she whispered.

He put his right palm over the left side of his upper chest and gave her a slight nod. "Your heart's content is my life's mission."

The pastor spoke, "Today, ladies and gentlemen, we're gathered here to join this couple in Holy Matrimony. The groom specifically asked for a short ceremony." The crowd laughed.

Ekene wore a smug expression. Halima read the deeper meaning behind it and agreed with him. She looked at the pastor who cleared his throat and got back to the order of the day.

He said a few words about Christ and the church and the reason for marriage. Halima listened to the analogy and silently prayed that God gave her the strength to show people Him through her marriage. Her thoughts were interrupted when the pastor asked them to say their vows.

Jide handed Ekene her ring. He lifted her hand. The heat of his stare made her blink.

"Halima, the day 'Sheed asked me to drop him at your house all those years ago, was the day my life changed. The minute I set my eyes on you, my heart began to beat at a different frequency. Our journey has been far from easy, but I can't imagine not doing it again. Same mistakes, same lessons if it will lead me back to this moment with you. You're the light of my life and comfort to my soul. I promise to protect, provide, adore, submit and cherish you all the days of my life, so help me God." He slipped the ring onto her finger.

Halima fanned herself then looked at her finger. "*Haba!* How do I follow that?"

The crowd laughed.

After a few moments, she took his ring from Damisi and lifted Ekene's hand. "Unconditional love never fails any test. It can struggle, but the bond cannot be broken. You make my ordinary moments special and if my heart could talk, it would scream your name. I'm so happy that all my lasts get to be with you. I promise to honor, submit, love and protect you now and forever." She slipped the ring onto his finger.

There was applause from the crowd that was quickly interrupted by the pastor saying, "Without wasting any more time. I now pronounce you…"

The pastor's words were cut off when Ekene pulled her close and his lips came crashing down on hers. Whatever was being spoken was lost in the fireworks that ran through her body as she locked her arms loosely around her husband's neck.

God is Love and He'd given her the second greatest expression of it she could ask for.

THE END

Glossary

<u>Muslim/Islamic Terms</u>

Mahram

a family member who is forbidden to marry a woman. Includes brother, father, son, uncles, nephew, father-in-law (stepfather), son-in-law (stepson). Marriage to them would be considered a haram. They are usually used as travel companions for the single Muslim woman.

Nikah

The Muslim wedding ceremony

Assalamu Alaikum

Greeting which means; Peace upon you

Dua:

The term is derived from an Arabic word meaning to 'call out' or to 'summon', and Muslims regard this as a profound act of worship.

Deen

the word refers to the way of life Muslims must adopt to comply with divine law, encompassing beliefs, character and deeds

Da'wah

serves to invite all people, both Muslims and non-Muslims, to understand how the worship of Allah

Jumu'ah

Also known as Friday Prayer or Congregational Prayer

Hausa/Igbo Translations

DA GASKE? SERIOUSLY?

ban yi imani da wannan : I don't believe this

yi imani da shi : believe it

ba za ku yi magana ba : You will not speak?

Wannan abin ba'a ne : This is ridiculous

Yata, me ke gudana: My daughter, what's going on

Suna d'auke ku daga gare ni: They are taking you away from me

mahaifinka ya san abin da ya fi kyau : Your father knows what is best

Ina son ka uwa: I love you mom

Ina son ku ma: I love you too

Yi hakuri: sorry

Ina tsoro : I'm afraid

Ina son ku: I love you

Yata: My daughter

Mgbede Oma : Good evening

Ndewo: Hello

Kedu? How are you

Adi m mma: I'm fine

Ka chifoo: Let daybreak (Goodnight)

e ba ta go: you have come in?

ugboro ole ka m kporogi: how many times did I call you

Barka da safe: Good morning

Ina kwana: How did you sleep (Good morning)

Lahiya lau : In health

Kina lahiya: How are you (said to a female)

Final Note

Wow! That was a journey, right? Thank you for reading Halima & Ekene's story. As I said in the author's note, (beginning of the book) this my friend really is the end of the Danjumas story. They might make cameos in other books (wink). If you haven't read any other books in the series, you should start with A Scoop Of Love, here.

If you liked this story, I trust you might like some of my other titles. But before we get to those, never miss sales, new releases or freebies. You can ensure that by joining my mailing list http://bit.ly/UNUpdates I'd love to stay connected.

Also please consider leaving me a review. I greatly appreciate honest feedback, even if it's one or two lines. They really go a long way.

Also by Unoma Nwankwor

Stand Alone Books

An Unexpected Blessing

He Changed My Name

When You Let Go

The Ultimatum Series

The Christmas Ultimatum

The Final Ultimatum

Sons of Ishmael Series

A Scoop of Love

Anchored by Love

Mended with Love

Redeemed Through Love

Mixed Tidings

The Invisible Shackles Series

To Live Again,

To Breathe Again

The DuBois-Arazi Family Novels

A Promise Fulfilled

Destiny Fulfilled

The Billionaire Pact

Vegas Nights

Second Shot

Pretend Bae

Away To Africa

New Year's Kiss (Prequel)

Rent-A-Bae

His Makeshift Fiancée

A Suitable Wife